LUCKY THING

Also by Tom Baragwanath

Lorraine Henry Thrillers
Paper Cage

LUCKY THING

TOM BARAGWANATH

BASKERVILLE

An imprint of JOHN MURRAY

First published in Australia in 2025 by The Text Publishing Company
First published in Great Britain in 2025 by Baskerville
An imprint of John Murray (Publishers)

1

A CIP catalogue record for this title is available from the British Library

Hardback ISBN 9781399808156
ebook ISBN 9781399808170

Typeset in Bembo MT Pro

Printed and bound in Great Britain by Clays Ltd, Elcograf S.p.A.

John Murray policy is to use papers that are natural, renewable and
recyclable products and made from wood grown in sustainable forests.
The logging and manufacturing processes are expected to conform
to the environmental regulations of the country of origin.

Carmelite House
50 Victoria Embankment
London EC4Y 0DZ

www.johnmurraypress.co.uk

John Murray Press, part of Hodder & Stoughton Limited
An Hachette UK company

The authorised representative in the EEA is Hachette Ireland,
8 Castlecourt Centre, Dublin 15, D15 XTP3, Ireland (email: info@hbgi.ie)

For Alma

IT'S NEARLY DUSK by the time I get Bum-Bum saddled. The air around the stables is still warm from the hours of sun, the day giving itself over to the dark. I should've been here an hour ago: Dion took bloody ages with the statement from the timber-plant bloke. A forklift stolen and ditched down by the bridge, laid out across the railway tracks. It makes me smile, thinking of the 4:55 from Wellington waiting for someone to clear the line, windows full of office workers staring out like jowly cattle. Kids, no doubt. The foreman reckons he'll put up a camera facing the road, but who knows when he'll get around to that. Anyway, a place like Masterton, there are worse things than a forklift joyride.

As everyone knows.

'Easy, now.' I set a hand to Bum-Bum's stout grey neck as we come past a couple of mares huddled together over the fence. They'll be having a laugh at his expense, I'd say. Either his name or his rider. 'Easy.'

He had the name when I got him, obviously. He was a lawn decoration for some lifestyle-block types out near the boarding school at Langsford. Their little girl got fed up with him not going fast enough and tried jumping him in front of some mates. He threw her, breaking both her wrists. The parents were damn near giving him away. I've tried calling him Bertie, or even Bump, but he doesn't come to it. So Bum-Bum it is.

They've been helping, these rides. A long afternoon in the police station file room, hemmed in by those leaning stacks of paper, and an hour in the saddle is quite the salve. The steady movement, the feeling of the animal under me. I'd never have managed it before last year, but my niece Sheena nagged at me to get the hip done, and I finally gave in at Christmas. The old ball joint's still in the freezer, the poor suffering thing. It looks like a golf ball dragged under a car.

At the far edge of the hayshed, Roxy waves as she climbs into her ute, pointing to the bag of grain she's left for me. She's done with her lessons for the day, all the gear put away, every last private school riding student shuttled home by Mummy. The ute coughs to life, her headlights sweeping low over the grass bitten to stubble by the ponies. She's giving me quite the deal, Roxy: half the usual grazing fees, and the grain for free. It's because Bum-Bum's a good influence on the others, she says. Calming. Not to mention Roxy's Dion's aunt. I've been keeping up my end of the bargain correcting the spelling mistakes in his statements.

We take another lap to finish, the horse ambling slow and gentle, and stop at the stile by the shed. I could climb down without it, but it's best not to risk it. Jesus, sixty-five; the Chief's threatened to buy a cake for the station. Bum-Bum stays good and still as I climb down, snorting at me to hurry up with his feed.

'All right, young fella.' I unclip the saddle, giving him a scratch where the straps have been rubbing. 'Must be your bedtime, eh?'

Behind us, the road holds the usual trickle of cars and trucks, a steady stream of headlights golden through the sleepy grey. It's only fifteen minutes' walk from here to Rickett's Circle; I'll be home in time for the *MasterChef* special Friday challenges.

Then a wail of sirens cuts through the evening, low at first, building to a rude swirl of red light through the blue dark. An ambulance coming from my side of town, fast, gunning it for the hospital with a cruiser in tow—the Chief's car. The old feeling moves through me for a moment, a shard of ice breaking away and falling through my chest. When they're gone, I hear my phone buzzing from where my poncho's slung over the fence. It's a text from Sheena.

U about aunty? The bubble bounces onscreen. *Tuck was asking if we seen his niece.*

My fingers tap across the white glowing square. I've just hit send when Dion calls.

'Another forklift?' I chuckle. 'You get all the important calls, don't you?'

'Chief said to call you,' says Dion. 'He's on his way to...'

'The hospital. Yep.' I look towards the road. 'Just saw him.'

There's a stab of static in my ear, then: 'They found a girl.' He's dropped an octave, his voice hushed and low. 'Some tourists. Up in the Tararuas, near Holdsworth. A teenager, the Chief said.'

More ice slides through me. 'Is she...? She's not...'

'Nah, nah. But not far off it, they reckon.' I hear his cruiser spurt to life in the background. 'He said to get there sharpish. You're over at Roxy's, yeah? I'll come by.'

Across the fence, there's the soft glow of the lights from the new hospital. 'Faster to walk from here.'

'Righto.'

The line clicks over, the white light dimming to black. I zip up my poncho and cut sideways through the gatepost and up the rise, fingers working the latch automatically, heart swelling like a sponge.

They found a girl.

If the Chief's driving was anything to go by, it's serious. In the distance, the outline of the old hospital hangs in the air like a tall black door. I've rushed towards that shape a few times: when my sister Debbie was early with Sheena, and when dad's heart finally went. Tonight, it's the new hospital I'm heading for, the low white building with windows staring through the warm dark. Behind me, Bum-Bum stamps at the earth, snorting in outrage. He'll have to wait for his grain, but

4

my gut is telling me there are bigger things on the way. The air pulls close around me, a plastic bag drawn tight over everything. My horse gives a shriek and the sound follows me as I walk.

CHIEF AMBROSE IS in the hallway when I arrive, phone pasted to his ear. I see him through the wired glass, his head shining in the bright overhead lights. The nurse at the front desk nods and waves me through, keeping his eye on a thin stick of a woman muttering in the waiting area: a muddled soup of vowels as she leans forward with her head in her knees. It's been this way these last few years, budget cuts and all. The emergency rooms are having to deal with headcases of all stripes.

'Germans, I think.' Ambrose holds a finger up for me as I approach. 'Or Dutch? Sod if I know. Yep, yep. I'll call you.' He slides the phone into his pocket. 'Dion reach you?'

I nod. 'I was just across the paddock.'

He looks me up and down, frowning. 'Ah, the horsies.'

Through the door to the intensive unit, I see bustling forms in green and white, reaching past each other and shunting machines about. Strange, the way television prepares you.

'She's in there?'

'Yep.' He shakes his head, his eyes clouding. 'Cracked skull, the paramedics said. But the exposure's the main thing.' He pulls out his phone again. 'Some trampers found her about an hour ago, near Atiwhakatū stream, coming down from Jumbo. Dutch, I think.'

'Or German. Not an accident, then?'

'That far out, with no gear?' His mouth pulls tight in a buried yawn and he thumbs the phone open. 'Wouldn't say so. Look.'

I'm not ready for it. A long, slender shape, ginger-haired, wearing stubbies and an eggshell-blue hoodie. She's in a hollow, spread out across the leaves, the thick trunks of matai and beech beyond her. It was still light when the photo was taken, but you can tell the day was leaking away.

'They took these before they moved her. Bloody smart, really.' He swipes again, letting me see the girl's face: her pale skin, the cheeks slack and red under the eyes. I grab the phone from his hand as he thumbs ahead to the next one.

'Wait.' I try to zoom in but it takes a while; my hand feels like a tuber. 'That's...that's Jessie. Jessica Mowbrie.' I squint. 'My niece was just saying something about Tuck coming by. He was...'

'Tuck Mowbrie?' A thin stream of air comes through Ambrose's teeth, his eyebrows lifting. 'He's her dad?'

'Uncle.' I look to the ICU door again, but get only disembodied glimpses through the doctors and nurses. Long white fingers, strands of bright hair stuck against a forehead. 'She's not far from Sheena's. Pretty much just around the corner. Moko, Sheena's man, he and Tuck used to…'

'I know.' His expression hardens. 'I know about that lot, Lorraine.'

When his eyes go to the window again, I see a new shade of worry in them, mixing with relief. Worry at the name I've given him; relief at the side of town the name is from. He might have to juggle a few hot tempers, but he won't be getting any calls from the papers.

That lot.

A place like Masterton, it's easy to slot someone away, categorised and neat. Trouble, or no trouble at all. Worth keeping an eye on, or not worth the worry.

'Moko's well out of it now, Rick. Been straight this whole last year, pretty much.'

'It's the Mongrels, Lo.' Ambrose shakes his head, his hands resting at his hips. 'You think the patch comes off just like that?'

My skin feels hot; the lights in the hallway are too bright, all of a sudden. 'Why don't we just stick to the task at hand, eh? Leave my bloody niece out of it, for once?'

He looks down into me, making himself taller, but then some of the vinegar seems to drain out of him. 'I suppose you'll want to give Tuck a bell, then.' He nods through the glass. 'Or…Jessica, you said? That's the girl's name? Maybe you should be the one to call her mum.'

'Me?'

'They're already asking Sheena about it, aren't they?' He nods, congratulating himself on the logic. 'Probably easiest, I reckon. Rather than getting it from a stranger.'

'You reckon, do you?'

My arms come across my chest. Mine has been quite the fluid job description lately. Fetching the biscuits for the staffroom, piecing together Dion's spidery pages of notes into something the prosecutor's office can read, covering the Chief's updates to Head Office while he's at Bunnings. Light child-recovery duties. And now, apparently, calls to next of kin.

Past the Chief's uniformed shoulder, a doctor shuffles to the side, and I see the hospital bed in full.

Jessie.

It's her, definitely. Mushroom-pale, her eyes red and swollen, and all that lovely long hair tucked down behind her, tamed. I've never seen her this small. She's always looked so tall, coming past Sheena's with her cousin, Michaela, the two girls moving in a single unit of giggles and screams, arms already reaching up and around, flailing in their shared story, always singing, always yelling. Those two, Sheena calls them.

Those two.

Then the doctor reaches sideways again, and my view through the glass becomes the same blur of shifting shapes. Green and white, the silver shine of tools and machines, the clear tubes ferrying liquids and draining others. An urgent dance, a sense of keeping something at bay. Some patient animal thing, a beast that could wait forever.

'How long was she there, do you think?' I speak to Ambrose

with my eyes on the glass. 'How long, in those trees?'

He's quiet for a while. Then he clears his throat. 'Paramedics reckon the night at least.' His hand goes to my shoulder, his fingers pressing just enough to let me know he's there. It's new since last year, this whole physical contact thing. The Wellington version of the Chief I've known, a new thread of empathy in him. It takes me by surprise sometimes. 'The nights aren't too cold yet, lucky thing. A few more weeks into March and we'd be having a different conversation.'

Lucky thing.

I breathe deep in my chest. My phone slides from my pocket; through wet eyes I see another text from Sheena. 'I'll ask my niece for Bea's number. That's her mum. Beatrice Mowbrie.' There are voices mixing low in the hallway behind us. 'You'll want Dion here too, before they arrive.'

'The mother too?' Ambrose frowns again. 'She a handful, like Tuck?'

'Look at the state of her kid.' I nod through the glass. 'Anyone would be, mate.'

~

In the end, Sheena does my job for me. As soon as I tell her what's happened, I hear her footsteps down the hallway, heavy even through the phone, and the confused voice of her boy Bradley—my great-nephew—asking what's going on. Then the front door slams and the call cuts out. Bea and Jessie are only a stone's throw; it's not long before Sheena texts to say they're on their way.

Tuck too? I text back, nodding to Dion as he pushes through the doors to the ward.

Micks. She was at Beas place. More bouncing dots. *Tuck off on a late run up Napier ways. Seemed a little tense when I got there.*

A little tense. Sheen's been getting a taste for understatement lately.

All right, I write. *Thanks love.*

I pass the word to Dion and Ambrose. As soon as they learn Tuck's not on the way—not immediately, anyway—their shoulders relax.

'Simplifies things,' says Dion. 'Right, Chief?'

Ambrose nods, looking to me. 'What else did your niece say?'

'You'll want to sort a room out, I'd say.' I nod down the hall. 'I'm not sure this is the best spot to be chatting and all.'

They stare at me just long enough to establish that they're not being told what to do.

'Just my two cents, Rick.' I stare at the linoleum. 'Up to you.'

After another pause, Ambrose nods Dion into action then pulls out his phone and starts flicking through the day's headlines. I could tell myself he's checking to see if any of the papers have picked up anything about the call, but I'm not feeling charitable.

'Listen.' I move closer, my voice held low. 'Before the others get here, were there any signs of…ah…any signs anyone might have…'

'None that they could see.' The Chief gives a tight nod,

breaking away from his screen for a second. 'I called in the rape unit from over the hill just in case. If the mum gives us the go-ahead we can make sure.'

'Okay.' There's a slackening in my chest. Strange, the relief that comes through me. A young woman, a girl, thrown down into those trees like an old log, given over to the birds and the mossy dark. But still, it's something.

'Don't worry, Lorraine,' he nods. 'I'll be here when they arrive.'

'You'll be here?' My cheeks are boiling. 'Of course you'll bloody well *be* here, Rick. You're the one running things.'

His jaw trembles, but before he can find anywhere to put his anger his eyes lift over my head to the door at the end of the hall, his expression widening. It's Bea Mowbrie, in a tidy pair of jeans and a good fleece. Michaela's not far behind. They're both as pale as the paint around them.

'Lorraine.' Bea grabs my hand, falling forward into me; it's all I can do to keep her upright. 'Where is she? Where's my…' Then she looks past my shoulder, through the glass to that many-limbed medical anemone at work on her daughter, her tall and lovely thing made into an object on that bed, all those lights and machines at work beside the sleek watching surfaces of screens. She leans into me and a sob shakes from her, small at first. Then she lets herself fall, and I catch her. I have to.

'It's okay, Bea.' Her forehead pressed into my shoulder pushes against the pins keeping my collarbone whole. There's smoke on her, and worry, a sour smell like washing left in the machine. 'They're taking care of her.'

Ambrose backs away from us, leaving Michaela on her own, mouth open and slack, eyes pinned to the glass square. Micks. She's shorter than her cousin but she still looms over me. I can see the full whites around her pupils, an expression in her I can't quite place. Shock, but also the look of a question being answered, a suspicion confirmed.

Then Dion appears in the hallway behind her, catching my eye and mouthing with as much discretion as he can manage, 'Room four.' He gestures over his shoulder, keeping himself at a distance.

'Come on.' I move my hand across Bea's quaking back. Unlike her girl in the room behind us, Bea is about my height: her head slots neatly into me. 'We've got a room for you.'

'We can chat,' says Ambrose. 'It'll be easier in there, for all of us.' He takes a tentative step forward, arms open, palms held out like he's selling something. 'This way, Miss Mowbrie.'

'Who's this?' Bea looks to me with red eyes, dragging a wrist under her nose. 'What do you mean, chat?'

The Chief's mouth pulls tight; he looks to me like I'm throwing out life jackets.

'We should let them do what they need to do in there, eh?' I take Michaela by the hand. Her skin is hot. 'Come on, now. We won't be far.'

We move slowly away, leaving Jessica behind the glass with so many other bodies around her, so many strangers making her their project. Maybe it's safer that way. Maybe strangers are what she needs.

~

13

There's a couch, at least. We get Bea and Micks settled and I perch next to them within reaching distance as Ambrose gives them what we know.

'I'll go see about some coffees, eh?' Dion hovers at the open door. 'Any sugars?'

I catch his eye and he makes himself scarce. Next to the couch, Ambrose stands with his arms folded, looking like a bullock in the only dry corner of a flooded paddock.

'I hadn't heard from her all day,' Bea sniffs. 'Not since... not since yesterday arvo. You neither, right?' She looks to Michaela, who drops her gaze to her knees and nods into her chest. I might not be a mum myself, but I've been an aunty long enough to tell there's more in this girl that needs to come out. 'She's got the regionals next week, the debating and that.' Bea scratches at her cheek, her manicured fingernails leaving a row of red marks. 'She was going to do a practice run with me. With us.' She looks to her niece again; Michaela steals a glance to the door. Ambrose gives me a nod. He's picking up on it too, inattentive as he might be.

'There are a few other things I need to run past you, Beatrice.' He pulls a chair closer to the couch and flicks me a glance.

'Run past me?' Bea sniffs. 'What do you mean?'

'Come on, girl.' I pat Michaela's shoulder. 'Let's see where that useless sod's got to with the coffees, eh? He'll need a hand, knowing him.'

Her lost eyes go to mine. When I nudge her again, she stands.

'Don't go far, girl,' says Bea. 'She'll want you close by when she comes to.'

The Chief gives me another quick glance, and I duck outside with the girl, pulling the door gently closed behind us. In the hallway light, I can see bits of horsehair hanging through the air where I've been.

'Here, girl.' My arm goes around her as we walk, keeping her close. There are bathroom smells on her, apricot scrub and sweet vanilla, but it's not enough to mask something deeper: the acrid waft of old booze. A big night wearing long on her—no wonder she keeps looking at the floor. 'I know it must be tough, seeing your cousin like that.'

She takes a big sniff, unsteady on her feet, and rubs a sleeve under her nose; it must be a Mowbrie thing. For a moment she looks ready to speak, and I wait but she stays quiet. I steer us past the muffled shrieks of the maternity ward, then to the chapel. I sat in here half the night with Sheena after Dad went. Mum was still in the room with him, stayed there all night until the funeral place bloke came in to sort him out. It's even quieter in here than I remembered. It must be the heavy doors.

'How about some water, love?' She shakes her head. A good thing, too; I don't know what they do to the holy supply behind the altar. I point us to the last row of pews, and we sit.

'Here,' I dig around in my poncho for a tissue, finding one left under my last toffee. 'Sounds likes it's been a rough day.'

She takes it without looking at me, blowing her nose with

a surprisingly avian honk, the sound swallowed by the thick carpet under us. 'Sorry,' she mutters.

'You're fine, girl.'

With the spent tissue clasped tight in her hand, her shoulders slump forward. I listen to her breathing, certain there's something on the way, some information tucked just under her tongue. In all this quiet, all I need to do is wait. I stare at the wooden cross hung behind the altar, its deep colours muted and serene in this quiet light.

'Where, uh...' There it is. Steady, now. Steady. 'Where did you say you found her?'

'Not me.' I squeeze her shoulder. 'Some tourists were tramping the Jumbo loop, coming down past Atiwhakatū. You know the spot?'

Her eyes stay wide. Then she nods. 'Dad took us up there, once.' Another loud sniff. 'The stream and that. We cooked sausages in the hut.'

'Yeah?' I picture Tuck, his barrel-chested shape stomping along the path with the two girls in tow. Good on him; not many kids get time out of phone reception these days. 'Well, it wasn't far from there. Paramedics reckon she'd been there most of the night.' I let the information sink into her like rain into parched earth. 'Thank god she had her hoodie on.' My gaze stays on her face. 'I think I've seen you wearing it, haven't I? The blue one?'

She gives a small nod. 'It's mine. She borrows it.'

Her hand opens, and she turns the tissue over, looking for a dry spot, but it's too far gone. I look around the chapel.

There's a dark folded cloth draped over the altar; I walk up and grab it, handing it to Michaela.

'Go on.'

'You're sure it's not, uh…holy or something?'

'Everything's holy in here, Micks.' I shrug. 'But they're a forgiving bunch.'

She gives me the tiniest smile, then blows her nose into the cloth. 'Thanks.' Her fingers wipe across her cheeks again.

'Look.' I sit back down, turning myself sideways as best I can. 'Your cousin's going to pull through, I'm sure of it.' I hear the confidence in my voice, the wall of words so smooth and steady, and I wonder where it comes from. 'But to really help her, we need to know where she'd been. Then we can figure out what's happened.'

She holds my gaze for a moment, then looks to her knees. 'I…I don't…' She sniffs, lifting the cloth to her nose again. It's already wet through; they'll need something heavy duty to get it clean. 'I'm not sure I can…I…'

'Your aunty mentioned something about her coming over to your place after school.' Slowly, now. 'Said she took her bag with her and all.' I watch her pupils dance. 'Is that true?'

She blows her nose again. 'Uh huh.'

'All right.' I rub her back. 'So, practice finishes up at what, five-thirty? Six? Then what? It's not so far to your place. River Road, down past Mākoura?' Her chin quivers. 'Did you walk home? I know your dad's been driving the late shift, or else he'd have picked you up, eh?'

When she looks to me again, her eyes are glassy, and wider

than before. 'You can't tell her, okay?' A shard of darker colour moves through her face: a decision, a gamble. 'She'll only get mad.'

'Who? Your aunty?' I squeeze her shoulder. 'She'll be all right, girl. If it helps us put together what happened, she'll understand.'

She takes a long breath, looking over her shoulder to the door. There are footsteps in the hallway. I hold my breath, and they head away from us. I hold myself still, waiting for her to speak. My stomach gives a long indignant gurgle. I sound like my bloody horse. 'Sorry,' I smile. 'Past my teatime.'

'The teachers had a planning day,' Michaela whispers. 'Today, I mean. We were just going to hang out at home for the night, make some clips or something. But Jess got invited to a party.' She pauses, looking around as if the word itself will summon her aunt. 'A woolshed party, out in Longbush.'

'Longbush?' There's the old skip inside me. A cat's paw in a hallway, an orange falling to the ground.

'You know it?' She squints.

'A bit, yeah.' I nod, trying to look unbothered. 'We farmed out there, yonks ago. Near the coast, almost. Steep country.' I feel moisture coming into my eyes; now isn't the time. 'Whose place was it?'

There's a long pause. 'The Kelsons,' she says. 'Stu Kelson.'

My heart skips again, longer this time. 'The Kelsons, eh? Patrick and that?'

'I dunno.' She shrugs. 'Is that Stu's dad?' I take an educated guess and nod, making my face into something gentle. 'He'd been doing the debating with Jess. The interschool team and that,' she sniffs. 'It's mostly boys from Langsford and a few Aquinas girls, but Jess got in this year. The top team, too. Aunty won't stop going on about it.' She shakes her head again, and the tiniest scowl pulls at the corner of her mouth. 'Anyway, Stu and his mates were having some drinks, and he invited Jess. She told him she wouldn't go unless it was both of us.'

I nod, listening closely to what's between these syllables. It isn't so long since Sheena was this age, making me sift through her tales of classroom drama and half-heard gossip for the hard true nucleus of whatever was really on her mind, the real obstacle she needed me to help shunt out of her way.

'So, Longbush, eh?' I nod. 'The Kelson place is quite a way out. Someone would have picked you up, I'm guessing?'

Michaela takes another long breath. 'A mate of Stu's, yep. Tama. He...'

A voice sounds out in the hallway behind us, loud through the closed doors, making her pause.

'Take it easy, mate.' It's Dion. 'She's probably just...'

With a loud rush of air, the chapel doors fly open, and the harsh hallway lights leap over us like a thrown net. A stout, stocky figure steps inside, boots heavy on the carpet. I feel Michaela go rigid in the pew next to me.

'Dad.' A loud sob leaves her.

'Lorraine?' Tuck squints, his eyes bright and hard under the edge of his beanie. Behind him, Dion balances two paper cups, his arms held aloft, towering over the shorter man. 'What the fuck's going on?'

IT'S EASIER ONCE we get Tuck outside. In the chapel he was something cornered with nowhere to go. I lead us out the front with Dion hovering closer than I'd recommend, at least with his uniform on. Then, in the carpark, the cool air comes over us, and for a second I can breathe. There's only the sleepy sound of traffic coming past the hospital, and a baby crying somewhere. Colic, probably. Sheena was the same.

I keep myself at a distance from the two of them. Michaela and Tuck: father and daughter, coming through a scare. They speak low to each other, her head pressed to his chest, his stocky arms wrapping her thin frame. I get close enough to hear them.

'I'm okay, Dad,' she sobs. 'Really.'

His hands are balled into fists at her back, fleshy stones ready to be thrown. He kisses the side of her head, eyes wet with feeling. 'Our Jess,' he mumbles. 'What the bloody hell happened?'

With that, he turns to me, his gaze clear and waiting. It's my question, I realise. I was out riding, I want to say. An hour ago, my biggest drama was making it home for the *MasterChef* challenges. A handful of ice cubes in my rosé and a cat purring in my lap. I stay silent long enough that Dion starts feeling useful, moving closer. I catch his eye and shake my head, but it seems he's not in the mood to listen.

'We had a call from some tourists.' He's still holding the coffees. 'Up near...'

Tuck spins and smacks the cups from Dion's hands fast enough that I hear the splash on the pavement before I register his movement.

'You'll know when I'm talking to you.' Tuck spits the words past his daughter's head, barely turning to face him.

'Fucking hell, mate.' Dion wipes a hand across his cheek, his free hand moving to the cuffs at his belt. Seeing the movement, Tuck squares up again, pushing Dion back against the wall of the ambulance bay.

'Hey!' I step past a confused Michaela and push myself between the two men. Feeling me next to him, Tuck stops in place, breathing hard through his teeth. 'We're all fine, here.'

'Bugger that, Lorraine.' Dion shakes his head, looking over his shoulder and through the main doors. At the front desk, the bearded nurse from before is standing up and pointing to the ward where Ambrose is chatting to Bea. I shake my head and hold up a palm for no.

'Those coffees could've bloody scalded me.'

'But they didn't, Dion.' I gesture to the brown stain on his shirt, trying to catch his eye. 'A bit of laundry, that's all.' Breathe, big fella. Just breathe. 'I reckon Rick could probably do with a hand in there, eh?'

'What?' His nostrils flare wider, his gaze going from me back to Tuck.

'We're all sorted, mate.' I nod for him to head inside, giving him my most imploring expression. This will take some massaging later, but Dion reluctantly takes the hint. He moves inside, his shoulders stiff and wide, checking his shirt as he walks.

'Away you go then, Lorraine.' Tuck moves back to Michaela, gathering her to his side again. 'You lot got a call, and then what?'

With a long breath, and fighting to keep my voice steady, I hold my arms across my chest and give him what we know. Everything until the woolshed party at the Kelson place: his girl can fill him in on that.

'Atiwhakatū?' Tuck blinks away moisture, frowning. 'How'd she get out there? Someone just fuckin' left her there? Our Jess?'

I take a step closer. 'She's got the right people with her, Trevor. She'll pull through.'

That smooth wall of language I find myself building—but what else is there? What else can a person say?

'They weren't bloody acting like it in there, were they? The doctors and that?' He shakes his head. 'Looking at them, you'd think our girl was on the fuckin' ropes.'

'It's all right, Tuck. They...'

He waves me away, grabbing Michaela tight again, his stocky shape pinning her in place. There's a patch of raised skin on her cheek from his stubble. She squeaks in protest and he lets go. 'Sorry, love.'

'Listen.' I move closer, letting him see me. 'We need to put everything on the table here.' Under the hem of his beanie, his expression is softer than I expected. It pays to watch yourself around Tuck Mowbrie, but here, now; I've never seen him like this. There's something crumbling in him, some larger edifice. A niece in trouble. It could have been Michaela; it could have been anyone's kid. 'Go on, girl.' I nod in encouragement, as gentle as I can manage. 'Tell your dad what you told me.'

Tuck leans away from her, looking into her face, a line strung tight between them. It takes her a while, but after a few false starts the details come out: Longbush, Stu Kelson, the woolshed. I watch his expression as she speaks, noting the exact moments his eyes widen, the flaring of the nostrils, and which details make the cords in his neck pull tightest. A woolshed party isn't too much cause for drama on its own, it would seem. But the Kelsons, and Longbush: those words send a wave of scarlet creeping all the way up Tuck's neck.

'The Kelson place? Tārehu?' He looks sideways; he knows I'm watching, sliding things into a drawer for later. Then he glances through the doors and into the guts of the hospital, just for a second. It's quick, but I've seen it.

His sister. Bea.

'I know, Dad. I know it was dumb.' Michaela sniffs, dropping her chin. We left the altar cloth stuffed in the back of a pew for the chaplain to find, so she has to use her jumper. 'We never meant to do anything. You left that chicken in the fridge, the stir fry and that. We were only going to hang out and get the washing in like you asked, then watch some...'

'Steady on, Micks.' His voice is flat, but he opens his arms for her again anyway. It's a feeling I remember myself: Dad split between disappointment and reassurance, distant enough to make a point, but still ready with a hug. For me, and for Debs. For a second I'm there again, inside that steady reliable place, that sanctuary. And yes, it was a cage too.

'You've been out that way a bit, have you?' I get Tuck's attention. 'Tārehu?'

I see his adjustment, the practised way he makes his eyes blank, mouth expressionless. 'A few loads here and there, back when I drove stock.' Calm and measured. 'Not for a while now.' There it is again. His gaze flickers past my shoulder and inside.

'You mentioned someone picking you up, Michaela. Tama, right?' I step closer, my eyes still on Tuck. I should know better than to mention names this early, especially around a man like this, but we're short on time. Jessie's only in the ward because of some trampers with good eyesight, and we can't risk another kid getting dumped up in those trees. 'He's another Langsford boy, is he?'

She clears her throat, looking down and wiping at her eyes again.

24

'We should be in there, Lo.' Tuck nods through the doors, keeping an arm around his daughter. 'We can chat later.' A long pause. 'When our girl's back on solid ground.'

I stare between them. Michaela still looks as though she's about to speak, but Tuck keeps his arm tight to her, his fingers resting on her shoulder like hammers in their brackets, ready and waiting. His expression stays flat and unreadable; I get the feeling he's going to manage this himself.

'Righto,' I say. 'When she's on solid ground.'

They move back inside, the girl's thin frame held tight against her dad's blocky shape. They pass Dion still lingering inside the doors; a stiff glance from Tuck keeps him in place.

'You okay, pal?'

Dion turns to me with more hurt in his expression than I expected. 'That was assault, Lorraine. Assault on an officer.' He crosses his arms, and some of the tension comes out of him. 'Not to mention it would've been better for a constable to get an ear to whatever he told you and not just...'

'Not just the tea lady?' I give him the chance to clarify, but he only stares back at me. 'Look.' I let my arms fall to my sides. 'A cop gave him a hiding back in ninety-six, all right?' 'There was a scuffle up in Bulls, outside the pub.'

Dion frowns, and a flicker of recognition moves through him. 'What, the Rat Hole?'

'That's the one. Some dickhead pulled a blade, apparently. Tuck wasn't even in the mix, but a guy like that always looks like trouble, so the guys down from Palmy dealt to him.' I set a hand to Dion's arm. 'It's nothing personal, mate. Bloody hell, he pretty much raised that girl. Imagine how he must feel.'

Dion looks back inside. 'Who, Jessie?'

No, mate. The other girl who's been chucked out like an old carcass.

'Yep.' I'll save the sarcasm for when Dion's got all the stain out of his shirt. 'And anyway, we've got plenty to go on for the minute.'

'Yeah?' The prickles start to go out of him. 'Why, what'd she say?'

Inside, the nurse at the front desk gives Tuck a good long look before he pushes the button for the doors. Then they slip into that white channel where Bea will be waiting, watching her girl through that pane of wired glass. Whatever happens in there, it'll happen soon; anyone could tell from the quick movements in that room and the glances between the doctors.

The long, thin girl. A blue hoodie covering mushroom-pale skin. All alone in those trees. What else does this place have in store for us? What else is coming, when a person can just leave a girl in a place like that?

'Lorraine?'

'I'll fill you in at the station,' I say. 'You'll want to hang tight here for a bit, I reckon. Keep yourself handy in case Tuck really gets offside with anyone. Not too handy, though.' I point to his shirtfront, then nod through the doors. 'Tell Rick I'm waiting for him.'

He frowns and blows air through his teeth, but away he goes, and I tread a tight circle under the fluorescent lights, thoughts rattling in my head like the last biscuits in the jar.

Longbush. Tārehu, the Kelson place. Tama.

Lucky thing.

The doors slide open. It's Ambrose, looking more frazzled than before. 'Christ, Lorraine.' He shakes his head.

'Still dicey?'

He nods, letting out a long breath. 'I can't say I'm keen to have that conversation again.' A breeze comes over us, the night's cool breath tickling my neck. 'What's the story, anyway?' He nods over his shoulder. 'Tuck looked fit to stomp something to death. Not in the mood to chat, I'd say.'

'No.' I squint. 'But his daughter was.' The Chief's lifted eyebrows turn his forehead into a row of cresting waves. 'We'd better get to the station and get some calls going.'

He looks to his watch. 'It's just gone half nine, Lorraine. Who did you have in mind?'

IT DOESN'T TAKE long for the Germans to get here. They've checked into their bed and breakfast in Greytown, and after an afternoon looking at what passes for antiques in this country, they're only too happy to come into the station. Only they're not German. Or Dutch.

'We are living in Forssa.' The woman, Milla Borg, smiles as if we're old friends sharing some in-joke for the thousandth time. 'It is near Helsinki.'

'Yes, it is.' Anders, her husband, nods. 'Quite near.'

'Righto.' I look between them, wondering at the Chief's geography. I won't be grabbing him for the pub quiz any time soon. 'And you're over for a little while, then?'

'Two weeks,' says Milla. 'It is our honeymoon.'

'Lovely.' I give them the least complicated smile I can manage.

'It is my third marriage,' says Anders. 'Meaning I was married twice before.'

He looks to the pen in my hand, waiting. I scribble the detail down, next to their names and the address for their B&B. When I look back up, Milla is still smiling, her features calm and even. The mood holds all the way through their account of the afternoon: the descent from Jumbo Hut—the beds could have been firmer, says Anders, waiting until I've written that down too—and how Milla nearly tripped over in the river at Atiwhakatū, but fortunately Anders was there to catch her.

'Otherwise, trouble.' Here, the man gives me a long and energetic raspberry, his tongue sliding from his mouth in a neat pink triangle. Next to him, Milla giggles quietly.

'We found her not long after this,' she says, her face clouding over. 'The girl.'

'This was around four o'clock, you said?'

'Four o'clock, yes,' Anders nods. 'In the afternoon.'

He holds his eyes to mine, and I start to understand the two previous marriages: they're the green of old bathroom tiles, with flecks of grey like seeds hidden in good bread. Milla's eyes are pretty, too. I wonder what mine might look like. Not tiles, I'd say; maybe a bargain loaf from Fresh Price.

'We called your emergency services,' says Milla. 'They advised for us to shift her to her side—for the breathing.'

'Of course,' I say. 'And what did...'

'We took photographs first.' Anders slides his phone from his pocket. 'This we told already to the other detective.'

29

'Oh, I'm not, ah…' His phone is on the table already, and they're both staring in anticipation. How would I describe my position here, anyway? Records management? Community liaison? Best to leave it. 'Yes, he told me the broad strokes.'

He didn't, but for the moment it's probably best to look like we know arse from elbow. Satisfied, the two Finns bend down to the screen. 'You may see here the vegetation having been trampled to a greater degree,' says Anders. 'This is how Milla was able to see her from the path. This girl.'

'Yes.' Milla points. 'Otherwise, she would have been quite obscured.'

'Quite obscured.' Anders nods.

They flick through the photographs, gesturing with grave excitement to the cover of ferns around Jessica, the white stems of greenery broken off, showing their brighter under-sides. I take a long breath; I need her to be someone nameless for a second. Someone I haven't seen from my niece's window most Saturdays, she and Michaela filling the footpath with laughter and screaming, the warm and messy sounds of growing bodies.

'You are okay, detective?' Milla frowns. 'Must we get somebody?'

I swallow hard. 'It's fine.' Their eyes are on me still. 'It's… she's a neighbour of mine, the girl.' I tap on the screen. 'Jessica.'

'I see.' Anders lifts a hand from the table, setting it on my arm. 'And this is not such a normal thing, here?'

'This?' I nod to the phone. 'No. Not so normal.'

I try to focus on the screen, grasping for something to say before my face gives way. Fortunately, he takes his hand back. When I flick forward to the next images, Jessica is on her side with an inflated neck pillow under her head, and a survival blanket wrapped around her in a wave of crunchy silver. Care. They took care of her, these two.

'I noticed something in the surroundings,' says Milla, 'while Anders was checking on her.' She places her own phone, identical to his, on the table. 'Some small markings just off the path. It is mostly looser gravel there, but there was something that may be of note.'

She turns the brightness up on her screen, zooming into the corner of the image. It's tough to make out at first, but it's there: a line of boot marks, not too large, with a sharp toe tapering into a V, almost like the corner of a box.

'We found only three markings,' says Anders. 'Milla checked. She is quite thorough.'

'Yes.' Milla reaches for his hand and squeezes it. 'The medical services made many footprints once they arrived, but I checked first.'

I zoom in closer on the prints. 'That's brilliant.' A lighter step, I think. A smaller person, or a larger one trying to step lightly. 'Very useful, thank you.' At that, they sit straighter, looking at each other with satisfaction. 'Could you send them to this email address, please?' I write down the station address on the pad, but before I've finished, my phone buzzes in my pocket.

'You must push to receive,' says Milla.

'Huh?' I frown, staring at my phone.

'Here.' She reaches across and moves her fingers over the screen, and the photos appear in a folder I didn't realise I had. Soon I have it all, including photographs of their passports.

'Very good.' I nod across the table. 'I'm just missing your dental records. And your last tax returns, if you have them handy.'

Milla picks up her phone, her mouth pursed and serious. 'The tax returns, yes. But as we are married just last week, these are filed individually.' She purses her lips. 'My dental office is open Tuesday to Friday, but I have an email for the...'

'Guys.' I hold my palms open. 'I'm joking.'

'Ah! You are joking!' Milla smiles wide, showing me the teeth of a well-funded healthcare system. 'Anders, she is joking.'

He nods, holding me in those circles of ocean again. 'This is humorous.'

~

On their way out, the Borgs stop at the Chief's doorway to wave goodbye. He's on the phone; he gives them a nod of thanks, raising a palm to keep them from coming in. We're nearly at the door when Milla turns to Anders and whispers an impossible stream of vowels, like many blocked pipes coming unstuck at once. The effect is not unpleasant.

'Yes, yes.' Anders turns to me with renewed enthusiasm. 'Detective, we would like for you to call us if you are needing anything further. We will be in Greytown until Tuesday

32

morning, and flying from Wellington on Friday.' He lowers his voice and leans closer. 'On the television, the persons finding the victim are always on the list of the suspects for a brief moment. But I can tell you truthfully,' here, he turns to Milla, 'we would never wish any harm on a young woman such as this.'

'Never.' Milla shakes her head.

'Thanks.' I hold my hands to my front, trying for a steady smile. 'I can assure you, you're in the clear.' I tap my pen against the cardboard backing of my notebook. 'But keep your phones handy, will you? We might need to check a few things.' Solemn, they both nod, shaking my hand. 'You've been extremely helpful.' I hold the door open; there are tears in my eyes again. 'She may not have, um…if you hadn't…'

'It's okay, detective.' Anders glances to Milla again. 'You know this girl. It is different for you.'

'From your previous cases,' says Milla.

I clear my throat, searching for the right words. *My previous cases.* Yes and no.

Mostly no.

I watch them cross the carpark and climb into their rental Toyota. They wave again as they turn into the road.

'Detective, eh?'

'Jesus, Rick.' I give a start; he has no business moving that quietly—he's taken his shoes off. He's wearing his best gold-top socks.

'Not a bad promotion. Dion will be spewing, though.'

'Can it, mate.' I shove his arm, pulling out my phone. 'You

didn't mention anything about any sodding boot prints.'

'Boot prints? They sent me dozens of photos, Lorraine.' He frowns, before a shrug rolls through his shoulders. 'Handy, that is. Bloody handy. Could be R.M. Williams, maybe. Something fancy. Not your usual Farmlands steel-caps.'

'Could be.' I squint at the glass. 'Any luck with the Kelsons?'

'Had to leave a message,' he says. 'It's nearly eleven, Lorraine. I know shepherds who take the phone off the hook after the weather.' He gives a long yawn, scratching at his stubble.

'Don't let me keep you, mate.'

He squeezes his eyes closed. 'Lee's been doing his early runs this week. Always banging the protein powder can at some heinous hour.'

Despite myself, I feel a small grin come to my mouth. 'Honeymoon over eh?' I nod through the door to the carpark. 'Maybe you could use a couple of weeks in Finland.'

He snorts. 'Never been all that keen on haggis.' His eyes stay on mine, letting me know he's joking. 'All right, let's pack it in. We'll hear from the Kelsons in the morning, and if not, we can take a drive out there.'

He turns and pads to his office, picking up a duffel bag from behind his desk. Then he notices me still staring, and his head tilts sideways like a curious collie.

'Tuck Mowbrie,' I say. 'Any history with the Kelsons?'

'Who, Pat and them?' He crosses his arms. 'Not that I know of. Isn't your niece working shifts at Seven Oaks these days? Where old Bill Kelson ended up?'

'A few afternoons a week, yeah. Just this last year.' I watch his face. 'What's that got to do with Tuck?'

Ambrose shrugs. 'It's your side of town, Lorraine. You tell me.'

'It's not like we're in each other's ears all the bloody time.'

In my mind, I know what he's getting at. Information travels unencumbered up and down Rickett's Circle, mailbox to mailbox like a well-earthed current. But it's different, hearing someone from Landsdowne saying it. He's up on the hill looking down.

'First thing then, eh?' He jabs his feet into his shoes, stopping himself at the door. 'You need a lift home?'

'Nah, I'm all set.' It sounds close to a genuine offer. And yet, it's a warm night; after the hospital a little time in the open air will do me good. 'I'll lock up.'

'Good-o.'

He yawns again, shuffling outside to the carpark. I hear the splutter and catch of his ute, and the rattle of the bike chains against the tray as he pulls out. That's how they met, him and Lee: the road cycling club, the quintessential Pākehā Sunday. Lee's mum might be Cambodian, but still. He's a bit zippier on the bike than Rick, unsurprisingly.

With the ghost of a grin on my face, I grab the keys from the back door. For a second, my gaze lingers on the doorway heading downstairs. The stacks and the boxes, those waiting rows of mute paper ready to open themselves to me, giving me the town. Tuck will be in there somewhere, no doubt. The Kelsons too, if I look hard enough. But that can wait for a fresher brain.

I lock the door and punch the code, stepping across the carpark to the footpath, tiny pebbles catching under my feet. At the corner, by the park entrance, my usual morepork mate sits in a high branch of the macrocarpa, watching me along with the rest of his kingdom. These warm streets with the weeds clinging to the cracks, these locked shops with their pie warmers waiting for the morning. It's his, all of it: our tiny stage, waiting for the lights to be thrown.

~

Tilly is under the kitchen table when I get home, a furred blur mewling into my ankles.

'All right, my lovely. I know.' I set the mail on the table. Another envelope from Arohata Women's Prison, the same as the last one. I don't need to flip it over, but I do anyway.

Patricia Prendergast.

Christ alive. If there was ever a time to reclaim your maiden name, this would be it. Three kids snatched, a good cop shot through the throat, and Patty: the kindly neighbour at the heart of the whole sorry tale. A long tremble moves through me, a bolt slipping its thread. Into the fireplace goes the envelope, nestled amongst the others on top of last winter's ash. When the cold bites in a month I'll have plenty to get the first logs started.

'Come on, then.' Fridge, rosé, ice. Jellymeat for Tilly, a little extra to make up for the lateness. The television sends its sleepy colours over me, but my mind is still stuck at the hospital: those bright hallways, the antiseptic rhythm of

36

moving feet, of wheels squeaking ever forward. Are those bodies still moving with the same urgency inside that green-white room? What is that slice of glass and wire showing Bea, and Tuck? What is it showing Michaela?

With a low murmur, Tilly leaps up onto my lap. My fingers go across her shoulders, finding her joints as she purrs. She'd have chosen Frank's old chair before, but after last year I put it out on the footpath. It was gone by the morning; I didn't see who took it.

In my pocket, a buzz. It's Dion. My heart gives a start as I slide to receive the call.

'What is it?' I lean forward. 'What's happened?'

There's the sound of wind down the line, and the automatic doors sliding. 'She's in...got her...'

'What?' I hear Tilly's paws hit the ground. 'Speak up, mate.'

'Stable. She's stable.'

Lord help us. My shoulders slump forward, and a weight comes off me; a weight I hadn't quite reckoned with. There's a long rush of air from inside me.

'You there, Lorraine?'

'Yep.' I wipe at my eyes. 'Yep, I'm here.'

'They've got her in an induced coma.' He holds his voice low. 'She had a bit of bleeding there, the back of the noggin and that. Blunt object fracture, they reckon. The exposure was the other thing, but her core temperature's steady now.' There's a pause; I can hear him deciding what to tell me. 'Another hour and it would've been a different story.'

'Milla.' I shake my head. 'You lovely, lovely thing.'

'What's that?'

There's enough ice left in my glass to chime as the rosé goes down. 'Nothing. The ones who found her, the Finns. I was just...' A breath comes into me, easier this time. 'It doesn't matter. Thanks for letting me know.'

'Yep, yep,' he says. 'Listen, it's just Bea and Tuck here, now. Michaela's gone off home.' He lets out a heavy sigh. 'I offered to give her a lift myself, but your mate wouldn't have a bar of it.'

'She walked?' I frown. 'At this hour?'

'Nah, nah. Your niece's bloke came around. Tall fella.'

'Moko.' I nod to myself, tucking the information away. A visit to Sheena's is in order; maybe Micks was feeling talkative on the drive. 'Good on him.'

'I can stay put if we need, Lorraine. But these two aren't exactly the chattiest.'

'Got it.' I can't help but smile. 'I reckon you could head home, mate. Rick's already packed it in.'

'He has?' Dion's eyebrows will be their usual furred cleft; I can picture his expression. 'Good of him to tell me.'

'We'll be chatting to the Kelsons in the morning, I'd say.'

A pause. 'The Longbush Kelsons?'

'That's it.' Onscreen, the infomercials are starting. 'They were at a party out there, the girls. With Stu Kelson and his mates.' I sink back into the cushions, yawning to myself. 'That wee one of yours will be asleep by now, I'm sure.'

'Amo just called.' I hear him return the yawn. 'He's still up, the cheeky sod.'

'Gastro again?'

'Nah, nah. Up and happy. Wanting the digger book.'

'Up and happy, eh. Good lad.' I smile to myself. 'Listen, about Tuck. You know I wouldn't take it so easy on him if he didn't have a niece in the...'

'It's fine, Lorraine.'

There are quick footsteps in the background, before he ends the call. The screen of my phone gives me the photo of me and Sheena with Bradley a couple of Christmases back. That sweet boy, those cheeky teeth shining, just bucked enough for us to start regretting the dummy. I send a text to Sheena; she'll have heard the news already from Moko, but getting it straight from me should dampen the gossip.

Jess Mowbrie found in bush. Stable now. Call in morning. Hug B for me.

I watch the screen, waiting for a bouncing bubble in response. She'll be long asleep, Sheena. These last few weeks she's been lights out before nine; the baby keeps kicking at her bladder and sending her to the loo every couple of hours. My fingers move again.

Might pick your brain on Bea & Tuck.

There's still nothing, but it can wait for the morning. I let the couch hold me, and my eyes start to lose their focus. Soft greens and reds from the television fill my gaze, its companion electricity taking me down. Down, into other colours.

Eggshell blue, the fabric of the jumper holding the pale white shape of the girl, the red tendrils of her hair sliding out from the hood and reaching for the wet earth. The green cover around her broken where they left her, the white stems of the ferns pointing the way. There, with the birds and the rocks and the wind searching through the trees. There, on her own.

On her own. Where they left her.

IN THE MORNING, I'm at the petrol station across the road from work, waiting for the girl to finish scalding my milk. She's new; the last guy was even worse. But some mornings, the drip brew in the staffroom isn't quite fierce enough for what the day has in store. Through the glass, I see Roxy from the stables pull in, her old Hilux rattling and shaking. She's got the pump hung back up before she sees me.

'Your hairy fella was having a good old whinge this morning.' She comes through the door at an angle, moving easier on one side. I've been on at her to get on the hip list, even gave her the number of my guy in Upper Hutt, but she won't have it. Not a big fan of the operating table. 'Could hear him grumbling from the road, the old sod.'

'He missed out on his supper,' I say. 'I had to duck off to the hospital.'

A shadow moves over her. 'The Mowbrie girl. It's ghastly, just ghastly.' She leans closer, huddled in conspiracy. 'Left up in the bush, I heard. The Tararuas, right?'

After a lifetime in Masterton it shouldn't surprise me, but I find myself marvelling at the efficiency of the machine. The Chief won't have had the chance to call Jamie at the *Times Age* yet; this is pure person-to-person transmission. All those websites play their part, I guess, the poxy things. Sheena spends damn near every spare minute on there.

'That's the one.' I nod along.

The Tararuas are big enough that I won't be showing any cards. It's a fair chunk of the country, that big slab of dark green running alongside Masterton. 'She's doing okay, though. Stable.'

'Oh, good, good.' Roxy holds a hand to her chest, clutching at invisible pearls. 'She's got her people in there with her, I'd say?'

'Yep.' The counter girl slides a plastic cap over the coffee and sets it down for me. 'Your nephew was there too, last night. Keeping them company.'

She grins. 'I heard Tuck gave him a bit of a whack. Dion should know better than to get too close to that one.'

'You know them, eh?' I watch her face. 'The Mowbries?'

'Tuck drove for my dad for a bit. Tractors, mostly. This is going back, mind.' She gives a small shrug. 'They had a falling out, surprise, surprise. He got it in his head Dad was cutting his hours. Bit of a spat. Bea even tried to jump in the mix, but Dad wouldn't hear about it.' Her mouth pulls flatter. 'Prone to the odd tantrum, those Mowbries. Lovely girl though, that Jess. The debating and that.'

'Five-fifty.' The girl leans against the counter, waiting. I give her coins and a loyalty card. Two more rough days and I'll be creeping up on a freebie.

'The debating, eh?' I pick up the cup, feeling the heat of the milk through the paper. 'You've been following that, too?'

Roxy chuckles. 'Jesus, you'd think I was stuck for hobbies.' She leans past me and gives the girl her pump number, holding her card to the reader. 'It's the Aquinas girls, my Monday night lot. They love a good natter, up in the saddle. After a while they forget I'm there.' Her eyes roll to the ceiling. 'Bit of an upset, apparently. Jess being picked for the regionals and all. One of the young ladies sounded right miffed. The Christiansen girl. Heather.' We turn and step outside. 'Not that I'm one to eavesdrop, mind.'

'Course not.' I return Roxy's grin. 'Still, anything else you happen to overhear, don't be shy, eh?' I watch her climb into her Hilux. 'It'd be a real hand up for us. For your nephew, too.'

'He needs it, I'll bet.' Her laugher is cut short by the truck door closing, before she winds the window down and I hear the rest of it. 'Officer Numb-Nuts, we've been calling him.'

'He's pulling his weight.' I wave and start off across the road. 'Have a good one.'

She pulls away with a long splutter. The road is thick with the Saturday morning sports crowd: station wagons and vans loaded with kids on their way to cricket and tennis, even turf hockey. The structure of the days, the weeks; hours there to be filled, to be shaped with activity, with distraction. It's been a bit much for Sheena lately, getting into the last trimester and all. Bradley's been missing a few of his hockey practices, and the coaches even threatened to drop him to the B team. I offered to take him along myself, but he wasn't so keen on being seen with his aunty. A good thing, anyway: most of the drills are a bus away, in Solway or Claireville. Unless you have Langsford money. Then you've got your own turf handy right on the school grounds, with a retractable roof to keep the elements at arm's length.

I cross the road to the station and see a ute in the carpark, new but dusty. The Kelsons, I'd say. Ambrose messaged first thing to say he'd heard from Pat and Lily this morning, and they'd be in after shifting a mob. There's a logo stencilled on the driver's door: Tārehu Station. The outline of a cattle beast around the words, its horns obscured under a film of gravel dust. My mouth fills with spit, but I keep moving.

Inside, I find them waiting in Ambrose's office, Rick nowhere to be seen.

'You all right in here?' I nod past them to the desk.

'Hmm?' A tall man turns in the chair, his eyes glassy. We've never met as adults, but I knew Pat as a boy, back when he was still Pee-Wee. He stands, blocking the light above us. 'He's fetching some coffees.' A twitchy smile comes over his mouth. 'Patrick Kelson.'

I take his hand. A firm shake, as his dad would've taught him. 'We've met before, actually. Years ago.' I take a breath;

there's really no way around it. 'Lorraine Henry.'

'Lorraine?' He frowns. 'You're the one who…'

'Yep, yep.' I nod, slicing things off before we get too doglegged. 'Not so Pee-Wee anymore, eh?' I nod upwards. He's just about grazing the ceiling, this one. Tough for a farmer, this kind of height. Dad always said he was happy being an even five-nine. No need to turn himself into a pretzel at crutching time.

'Hang on a sec. *Henry* Henry? As in Mickey and Barb Henry?'

'That's the one.' I let go of his hand, watching the information turn in him. There's something else in his expression, too. Something I can't place just yet. 'Long time.'

'I'll say.' He nods. 'I remember Mickey coming over with you and your sister, dropping off fruit cakes at Christmas.'

'My mum's. Always a little heavy on the sherry.'

His eyes crinkle at the edges. 'My father used to crack a window just to cut a slice.' He bends forward slightly, a lighter shade of colour in his cheeks. Then he seems to remember himself. 'This is my wife.'

'Lily.' She smiles from her seat, her arms held still at her sides. The Chief's got the blinds drawn, making a few thin bands of light stripe across her face. I give her a nod, and she looks to the doorway.

'Lorraine, you're here.' Ambrose carries a pair of mismatched mugs: Dion's 2006 Wairarapa Bush Meads Cup victory over Whanganui, and one from Fearon Logging. He sets them down on his desk, within reach for Lily and Pat.

'You'll want to give that a second, it's nuclear.' He dusts off his hands and closes the door behind us. There's nobody else in the station, but it helps to get a person comfortable.

'Our boy's game gets underway in a half hour, guys.' Pat folds himself back into his seat, crossing his arms. His wrists are pale as copy paper on the inside. Lily's are a deep reddish brown, the colour of a long summer—she'll be the one out mustering, I'd say, while Pat handles the books. Little Pee-Wee. 'What did you want to bring us in for, then?'

The Chief leans across his desk, hands set flat in front of him, the light winking off the top of his head. I take the short couch to the side, watching these two: Lily with her back against the chair, Pat leaning forward as though he means to take off. There's a tuft of ginger hair peering out of his collar at the chest.

'It's the semis,' Lily explains. 'That's why we're...that's what you mean, right love?' When Pat doesn't respond, she turns back to Ambrose. 'They're playing the Hastings boys. Toughest game of the draw.'

'He does all right in the hockey, eh? Your boy?' Ambrose sits too. 'I read the coverage last year, the finals and all.' He shakes his head, clucking his tongue. 'Sounded like a real heartbreaker.'

'It happens,' says Lily. 'Stuey's got a good head for it.'

Pat lets out a pointed sigh, shifting in his seat, and Lily lifts a hand to his shoulder. I notice a few loose strands of horsehair come off her as she moves. Country as steep as Tārehu, horseback's the only real way to muster; it was the same for us, back

46

in the day. Ambrose looks to me for the briefest moment, letting me see where he wants to take things. I'd read the same article too, last year: Stuart Kelson, youngest ever captain of the Wairarapa Rep hockey A-team, had missed a penalty shot in the dying seconds of the game, handing things to the team from Hutt High. There was a photo of him with the coach, the boy trying to look resolute, staunch. It's hard to hide that kind of disappointment, though, especially in the eyes. Not that the Langsford boys ever have to manage much in the way of disappointment.

'How's he been doing lately, your boy?'

Lily turns in my direction, frowning for just a moment. 'Stu? Right as rain.' A quick smile, proud. 'Been working on his fitness a lot. They reckon he'll have a shot at…'

'I asked you what this was about.' Pat lifts his chin in Rick's direction, not looking at Lily before he speaks. Across the desk, Rick sets his elbows down, his hands laced together.

'It's to do with Stuart, actually.'

At this, Lily glances past Pat to me. 'With Stuart?' I watch her face, seeing the concern in her eyes.

'He get up to much Thursday night?' The Chief gazes across the desk.

'Bloody hell,' Pat mutters. 'It's that dropkick mate of his again, isn't it? Tāmati, with the Subaru?' He shakes his head. 'We told him to cut it out with the doughies and that. Didn't I fuckin' tell him?'

'Hang on.' Lily holds a palm up sideways. 'What do you mean, Thursday night?'

Ambrose sits still, letting silence take hold. He's good at that; he knows how to create a vacuum in a room, and the kinds of information that can creep out to fill it.

'Look, it's not a big thing, having a few beers.' Pulls out his phone to check the time. 'If that's all this is, we might as well just...'

'Pat.' Lily leans sideways, squeezing his shoulder. 'Look, why don't you just tell us what's going on here, exactly?'

With the slightest nod, Ambrose passes the baton to me. 'We know he had a few people over.' I hold my voice steady and level. 'To the woolshed.'

'It was a planning day yesterday. For the teachers and that.' Pat holds himself very still. 'It's tradition. You remember that sort of carry on, Lorraine. It's harmless.'

Bile fills my mouth; I try to keep from frowning.

'That's not the issue.' Ambrose looks between them. 'We found a girl, up in the bush. Just last night.'

'The Tararuas,' Lily nods. 'We heard.'

Pat's gaze moves sideways, resting on his wife. She might have heard, but it looks like he's still in the dark.

'We've reason to suspect she was with your boy and his mates,' says Ambrose. 'On Thursday night, at your place.'

Lily leans forward, making her chair shriek. 'It was an Aquinas girl they found?' A deep frown splits her face; her eyes are wide and white. 'One of Stu's mates?'

'For Christ's sake,' Pat hisses. 'Who was she then, hmm?' His long arms fold across his chest. 'Who are we talking about?'

Was.

It's a small thing, but it snags. The Chief has noticed, too.

'Jessica Mowbrie,' I say. 'She goes by Jessie.'

'Jessie?' From the side, I can see the information move through Pat: the shoulders curling forward, the hands clenching tighter together. His neck and face drop a few shades, pink to white, his mouth hanging open enough for me to see his teeth. For a long moment, everyone is still. We're spiders under a glass.

'And she's a mate from Aquinas, you said?' Still frowning, Lily stares from me to the Chief. 'I've never heard the name. We know all the girls, really. The socials and that. Pony club, and the swimming. Most of them have been out to our place.'

'She's one of the girls from High,' says Ambrose. 'A year ahead of Stuart and his mates, actually.' He looks to Pat. 'You've heard of her, then?'

'We, ah...' He stares without focus, his lips moving in silence. 'I don't...'

'I wouldn't say so. Right, love?' Lily leans forward, setting a hand to Pat's knee. He stares down at his lap. Then, after a dazed moment, he gathers himself.

'What happened?' His voice is dry and raspy. 'You said you...you found her?'

'Not us,' says Ambrose. 'Some trampers. She'd been given a good hiding.'

The colour is coming back into Pat, his chalky pallor turning to red at his cheeks. 'And you...you think...'

'You think she was with Stu?' Lily cuts in, rubbing a hand to Pat's back. 'At our place?'

49

'We have statements,' I say. 'From others at the party.'

Behind his desk, Ambrose raises an eyebrow. It's subtle enough for the others not to notice, but I can tell he'll have words for me when they're gone. Anyone with a pulse can see something is going on with these two, and now's the time to shake the puzzle box.

'Statements, eh?' Pat lifts his chin in the Chief's direction. 'Let's see them, then.'

'It's a regular thing, is it? Drinks at the woolshed?' Ambrose picks up his own mug of coffee, watching them over the rim as he takes a long mouthful. 'Tradition, you said.'

Lily waves her hand through the air. 'Just these last couple of years. And only his close mates.' A sideways glance to Pat. 'We keep a close eye on things, making sure they're all taken care of.' She pauses. 'It's better than what they'd get up to on their own, believe me.'

'Taken care of, eh?' I shift my weight on the couch, finding a better spot for my shoulder. 'We spent a few hours outside the intensive care unit last night, watching them work on Jessica. She didn't seem so well taken care of.'

'Miles from it.' Ambrose nods.

A long moment passes. Then Lily shakes her head. 'How is she, the girl?' There's a bright shard in her expression, a vein of silver peering through the rock. 'Do they reckon she'll come right?'

'Hang on, hang on.' Pat leans forward, gathering himself. 'First of all, it hasn't been established that this girl was at Tārehu at all. And second, whatever might've happened to her, it's nothing to do with our boy or his mates, I can tell you that right now.' He crosses his arms with a huff. When Lily reaches for him again, he brushes her away, making more horsehair come off her jerkin and float around her shoulders. 'They're a good set.'

Ambrose sets his elbows on the desk, arranging himself into a more solid shape. Any of the earlier chumminess has fled his expression. 'That's your statement, is it?'

'Fuck a statement,' Pat barks. 'Come on.'

He stands to go, leaving Lily still in her seat.

'A cracked skull.' I watch the two of them, Pat standing tall in the stripes of light coming through the blinds, Lily with a lost expression. 'Someone gave her a bloody decent knock.' I lift my hand to the back of my head. 'Right here, behind the ear. She had bleeding on the brain.'

'Jesus.' Lily shakes her head; there's new moisture in her eyes. 'And you reckon it was one of Stu's mates?'

'We're done.' Pat grabs Lily's arm and lifts her to her feet. He might be the one taking care of the paperwork instead of the strainer posts, but there's still a wiry strength in him. 'Anything else, you can call us.' Then, halfway to the door, he seems to catch himself, softening his grip on his wife and pressing his mouth into something friendlier. 'Look, it's just... this is all a bit of a shock, as you can imagine. Whatever you think might have happened, we can check with our boy and see what's what. After the game, I mean.'

'After the game?' I let the words come out unalloyed. He doesn't look at me.

'Come on, then.' Ambrose stands, gesturing to the door. 'We'll give you a lift.'

'No, no.' Pat smiles wider, back in control, now. 'That's… why don't we come back another time? Lil will be out in the back blocks on Monday, but Tuesday might work.'

Tuesday. How nice, to be in charge of the schedule. I watch the side of Pat's face. As much as he might try to seem in control, he still has the air of a lanky child, looking for someone to tell him where to go, what to do. It used to be his dad, once, before the dementia and all.

'Righto.' Ambrose gives me a nod to open the door. 'Tuesday, then.'

We all stand, the two mugs for Pat and Lily left untouched on the desk. As they're coming past, I stop Pat with a hand to his arm. 'How's Bill been doing these days?'

'Hmm?' He frowns, his forced cheer becoming the low boil of spite. With anyone else I might miss it, but this is a face I've known since he was filling nappies. 'What's Dad got to do with anything?'

'Just curious.' I move into the hallway with them, smiling as gently as I can. 'I haven't seen him in ages. Since before things started to go, I'd say.'

'He's been better lately.' Lily gives Pat a warm glance, trying to ease him up. 'For a while he didn't seem to know me. Or any of us, really. He kept calling Rodney by Pat's name, and Stu was even trickier.' She smiles, pulling her jaw tight. 'He kept going on about his insulin pump, thinking it was some kind of walkie-talkie. Stu's always good about it, but still.'

'Dad's all right.' Pat moves ahead. 'We get to Seven Oaks whenever we can.'

'That's good.' At my side, I feel Ambrose glaring. 'Well, let's make sure you're not late to that game, eh?'

'Tuesday,' says Pat. 'Any time after three should be good.'

The Chief badges open the door to the carpark, letting them out into the light. It's bright; I lift my palm to cover my eyes. They walk to the ute, knowing we're still watching, giving us their best impression of a usual Saturday: Lily with her shorter gait, Pat loping across the concrete with his duck feet scraping pebbles in his town boots. They climb inside— Lily's driving—and pull out of the carpark with a splutter, their shadows poised inside the cab. Anyone can see they're about to have words; it'll be a tense twenty minutes out to Langsford. From Dion's ticket records, that stretch of road is an absolute nirvana for speeding fines, all those shiny late-model utes getting a bloody good hiding whenever some-one's arguing with their boy on the way back from boarding school. If we were targeting any other class of parents I'd find it cynical.

'His dad, eh?' Ambrose lets the door fall shut. 'What's the story there?'

I reach inside my collar, letting my fingers play over the groove in my mended shoulder. The Christmas cakes. I'd forgotten all about them. Not surprising that it stuck in little Pee-Wee's mind. Me and Debs up there on Samson, front and back with Dad in the middle, Debs holding Mum's best tin with its red and green ribbon, and me riding at the back clutching a spare handful of dad's visiting shirt. It was only a short ride across the boundary to Tārehu, and a gentle one at that. Bill Kelson always used to come out to the verandah, waving a hand to see us approaching with that sweet bounty. Even now I remember the shine in his eye, like a heading dog sizing up a mob. Little Pee-Wee would come out too, grabbing at his knees to stay upright. Pat got his ginger hair from his dad: it always came through like mandarin rind at Bill's temples.

'They shafted us, that lot. Good and proper.' I let Ambrose see what's in my expression; there's no point in hiding it now. 'We had the block next to Tārehu, and they shafted us.'

'Yeah? The Kelsons?' Ambrose frowns. 'How's that, then?'

Dad's back so straight in front of me, and Debs picking at the tin lid, clicking it open and closed until dad told her to cut it out. And Bill Kelson, ready and waiting to receive it. We never came back with anything from those trips, but Dad said that wasn't the point.

There was a point, though. Dad just wouldn't see it.

Not until later.

'Another time, if it's all the same.' I nod into the spot where the Kelson's ute was parked. I can hear the disbelief in Rick's voice, the wall this new information is banging up against. If someone with a name as old and as sound as Kelson is capable of doing someone over, where does that leave a bloke like Ambrose? I'll need more than a petrol station flat white to want to turn that rock over, though. 'Based on what those two had to say, it looks like we've got some teenagers to chat to.'

'Langsford?' Rick's eyebrows lift like foraging caterpillars. 'What, now?'

I shrug. 'You saw it, mate. They're rattled. I'm surprised Pat made it back to the truck without toppling over.' I drain my cup, the coffee only just cool enough for my tongue. 'Let's rattle them some more.'

THERE'S SOME DECENT sun by the time we reach the Langsford turnoff. Rick has to squint through the windscreen, pulling the visor down until his whole face is shaded. We've taken his ute to stay under the radar; to the untrained eye, we could be any other age-gap couple off to watch their grandson's match. I'm sure the Chief wouldn't much care for the impression, but his dome's gone smooth past his ears, and with a twice-weekly Mrs Mac's chili beef and cheese pie putting his shirt buttons to work, he wouldn't be too far off my striking distance.

'What?' He catches me smiling.

'Nothing.' I point outside. 'That's where I got my horse last year.'

'Lifestyle blockers, eh? A guy I know from cycling lives down this way. Silly bastard pays a grand every year to have twelve sheep dagged. A grand!' He lifts a fist in front of his mouth and belches. 'You seen the new auditorium here?'

'New bloody everything, looks like.'

Outside, a row of green poplars leads us through a set of shining black bars held open for the weekend sports visitors. A sign in thick lettering announces the Langsford motto— *Excellence Is Within Our Reach*—bordered by the deep green of the school colours. Beyond the gate, the common opens up in a wide expanse of grass kept at an even, smooth trim, so uniform it looks like a screensaver. If it wasn't for a handful of lanky kids lugging duffel bags at the far edge, you'd scarcely believe it.

'Lee's an old boy, you know.' Ambrose juts his chin through the windscreen. 'His folks sent him over from Wellington for sixth and seventh form after some trouble back home.'

'Look at you, mixing in.' I chuckle. 'Have you bought salad forks yet?'

He smiles just enough to show me where the line is. 'He was here a while back, mind. Before it got so fancy.'

We drive past the chapel, its wooden cross pointing up into the still blue air. 'This place hasn't always been so friendly to guys on your team, eh?' I look sideways, showing him where my heart is. 'Especially not back then, right?'

'He was never out with it, apparently.' Ambrose taps the steering wheel, keeping up with Springsteen. 'Some of his closest mates knew, but they kept it to themselves.' We pull into the shade of the chapel, the bright sun held at bay. 'The staff were pretty fire and brimstone about it, apparently. The chaplain used to look Lee right in the eyes from the pulpit during their services, especially the Old Testament stuff.' He squints through the windscreen, scanning the row of cars parked by the hockey turf. 'He doesn't like to talk about it.'

'Fair enough.' At the end of the row is the Kelsons' ute, parked with some haste across the edge of the footpath. 'Looks like those two made it in time.'

'Barely.'

Rick slows down and pulls out of the ring road, the ute's wheels sinking into the soft grass. From across the path, a tall man in a grey jacket pauses where he is, turning towards us with a hard, focused expression. The turf; he'll be ramping up for the usual warning about parking, no doubt. Then he sees Rick, and his expression shifts.

'Chief Ambrose.' He raises a hand. 'Good to see you.'

'Same to you, Graham.' I step around the car, following Rick's lead. The two men shake hands with a firm cracking sound, sharing the usual pleasantries before the Chief gets to it. 'We might need to come by for a chat later, if you're about.'

'Oh?' The man's expression clouds for a moment, his eyes snagging on me. A brief flicker of recognition comes through him, turning him grave. For a second I wonder if I'll have to get into it again: last year, Martinborough, the kids. Everyone watches the news, I guess. Not that you needed to, around here. Instead, he turns back to Rick. 'Nothing serious, I hope?'

'Hard to say just yet.' Rick holds himself still. 'You'll be around?'

'I'll be doing the rounds with the juniors, yes.' The man points to the boarding house tucked away behind the taller trees. 'It's film night, and they've chosen that superhero picture.'

I nod. 'My nephew can't stop going on about it.'

The chaplain smiles at the corners of his mouth, not quite committing one way or the other. 'Well, I'll be on the grounds in any case.' He turns and continues in the same direction, before pausing with another word for Rick. 'You're sure there's nothing I can help you with? Any particular student you might need to speak to?' He looks past us to the hockey turf.

'We're all set, thanks.' Ambrose turns, and we walk on. When we're out of earshot, he leans closer. 'Graham Young. The thumper Lee mentioned.'

'He's been around that long?' I squint back at his thin form disappearing past the tennis courts: a heron in a stiff shirt. 'I heard they had some old-timers, but that's a bloody age.'

'A place like this, you'd hardly want to mix in with the real world, would you?'

As if proving his point, a cheer lifts through the air from the hockey turf, the easy sound of shared jubilation. Through the mesh barriers I see a clutch of boys in green and white, sticks held low, slapping each other in celebration. Beyond the group, the digital scoreboard ticks over: one-two, Langsford trailing Hastings Integrated.

'There's the boy.' Ambrose nods. I recognise Stuart Kelson from the papers last year: a thin kid, tall for fifteen, with dark hair and a thoughtful expression, both of which must have come from Lily's side. He's running back to his own half, his face set in determination, an easy satisfaction in his movements. He put the ball in the net himself, I'd say.

'Look.' I nod down the line of parents, seeing Pat and Lily still clapping, their hands held aloft, faces bright with the moment. Then Pat sees us watching through the mesh, and his brows knit together, his mouth hung open as if tasting something strange. He leans down to the fence again, setting his arms deliberately across the top.

'That'll be their game ruined.' Ambrose mutters.

I'm watching Pat, waiting to see how he'll decide to tell Lily about our arrival. With as much grace as he can muster with his height, he bends down and speaks sideways. Lily goes rigid for a second, her hands gripping the fence before she recovers. When she moves again, she scans the row of spectators on our side, careful not to linger on us any longer than anyone else. Then she's back to the game, cheering on Langsford as though nothing is amiss. There's a younger boy at Pat's side, the same dark hair as Stuart but longer, his cheeks still chubby with early teenhood. Rodney, it must be. He stares openly at us, then back to his parents, until Pat points him to the game.

'Anyone else you recognise?' says the Chief.

'A few,' I say. 'It's not my usual crowd.'

There are a couple of familiar faces here and there: Mike and Sally Christiansen from the garden warehouse, and the Leongs from the roast shop cheering on their lad, Alvin. Then

I see a boy in a Langsford hoodie standing watching the game alone. Over his shoulder, a Subaru is parked in one of the student spots, deep blue and gleaming.

'That'd be Tāmati, right?'

Ambrose glances sideways. 'Good odds. Not too much competition for any other Tāmatis here.' He grins at me. 'Best if you chat to him alone, eh? You've got a way with these things.'

'These things?' *The hori whisperer.* Some things stick, I suppose.

I shake my head, and Ambrose smirks. 'Don't take it that way, Lorraine.'

I break off and move around the turf fence, hands in my poncho pockets. I get close before Tāmati knows I'm there, right next to him. I can watch him enjoy the game, clapping along whenever someone connects with a good pass, cheering the guys on by their nicknames: Salmon and Baz, Lighthouse. When you're used to safety, this padded womb of trimmed grass and a laundry service twice a week, why would you bother worrying about who's standing next to you? He's one of them, this dark-lashed boy: you can see it in his shoulders, in the ease he has, being here. And yet, he's apart, held at a distance from the watching parents and the boys on the pitch. Or maybe it's a distance he's chosen.

'Not doing too badly, your lot, eh?' I lean against the barrier, my eyes mostly on the game, but reading him.

'Yeah.' He nods to one of the Hastings players, a wolfish-looking kid with more stubble than the ref. 'Gotta keep that one boxed in, though. He's your best player by far.'

'I'm not with them.' I nod to the spectators on the other side.

'Oh.' He jabs his hands in his pockets, bringing out his keys and swinging them around his fingers. There's a question in his face.

'I was looking to chat to you, actually.'

'Me?' He frowns, smiling just enough. 'Why?'

I gesture to his keys. 'Michaela Mowbrie's one of my neighbours. You know Michaela, right? From Thursday night?' His grin shifts to a frown; his eyes dart to the game, then back to me. 'Her dad's an old mate of mine. Tuck. You'll have heard of him too, I reckon.'

There it is: the quick movement of the pupils, the jaw pulling tight. Tuck Mowbrie. Sometimes it helps, this little town of ours. Its cast of players, its names like incantations.

'I didn't, uh...I'm not...'

'Listen.' I bend closer. 'It's not Tuck you need to worry about. Not right now, anyway.' I pause and watch his eyes. 'But me and the others at the station, we do need to know what happened after you picked up Micks and her cousin.'

His mouth opens in a tiny gap, showing me the straight shape of his teeth. 'Station?'

I nod across the turf to where Rick stands. 'That's Chief Ambrose. I'm Lorraine. I work with them.'

The boy frowns in Rick's direction, then looks back to me, softer now. He knows. About me, about last year. He looks to the players, as if they can help him. One in particular: Stu seems to be getting most of his attention. He swallows hard in his throat. When he speaks again, it's quiet enough that I need to lean closer.

'It was just a few of us, out at Stu's for a couple of beers.' He stares down the row of parents to Pat, to Lily. 'Mrs. Kelson said she was cool with it. We didn't, uh…nobody said anything about…'

'No need to rush, mate.' I lean forward against the fence, bringing myself closer. 'Just tell me what happened.'

His hands knit themselves together. It's a different story with this private school lot; I doubt any of boys from High would tell me if their shoes were laced. 'The usual stuff, I dunno. We just…it was the usual guys, and some of the girls from in town.' A bright glimmer comes into his eye. 'She kept asking me to change the music on the way out. Michaela, I mean.' He snorts. 'Not big on Frank Ocean.'

'And?' I let a lighter note come into my voice. 'What did you say?'

He gives me a tight grin. 'I told her it was my car.'

'Fair enough.'

On the turf, the players are moving with a new urgency, their voices taut and strained. There's not much time left in the game, and they're all stomping and grabbing at each other, their plays getting ragged. The Hastings players all seem to push further up, a sea of blue slicing through the green.

'I was supposed to take them home in the morning,' Tāmati says. 'Stu asked me to.'

'Supposed to?' I watch his expression. 'Why, what happened?'

He shrugs again. 'They went outside for a while, and I didn't see them after that.' His breathing turns shallow and excited, watching the last play. 'I thought they must have walked to the road or something.'

'To the road?'

'Yeah.' He coughs. 'It's not that far.'

I take in his expression. If he's lying, he's more of a natural than any other teenager I've known; better than Sheena, even. His cheeks stay relaxed, his gestures loose and unconcerned. He leans forward and claps, urging the Langsford boys to keep tight. The air is full of sound: voices yelling, hockey sticks clattering together. I think back to Michaela's expression in the chapel, her lost-dog look.

They went outside for a while.

'Look, kid.' On the turf, one of the Hastings players pushes up towards the box, looking to connect a pass to his team-mate. We're all leaning closer. 'We found Jessica in the bush yesterday.'

From the crush of blue-and-green-shirts a single figure emerges, sprinting ahead with the ball at the end of his stick. It's Stu. Amidst the shrieks and whoops, Tāmati turns sideways to me, staring unfocused.

'The girl in the Tararuas?' His cheeks are pale, an image stripped of colour. 'That was Jess?' I nod. There's something happening on the pitch, but it might as well be the surface of the moon. 'Is she...' He falters. 'I heard she was...'

'She's stable.' I set a hand to his elbow, raising my voice to be heard. 'She was in rough shape, Tāmati. Someone gave her a good hiding.' He stares back at me, his eyes wet and dark. There's surprise in there, and plenty of alarm. And not just for himself. 'They left her there, mate. In the bush, on her own.' I let him take in the words. 'And if they can do it once, they can do it again.'

A loud wooden clunk sounds out in front of us, making Tāmati jump; new cheers split the air. On the pitch, Stu's teammates are wrapping him in celebration, all of them shouting and lifting their sticks. The scoreboard clicks over to two each, and the ref calls the time: three minutes left to play.

'I need to know exactly who was at the party.' I keep my hand on his arm, not too tight, but tight enough. 'We can talk here, but you'll need to give a statement. It'd be a lot easier if you came in.'

He's with me, still, all the way to those last few words. Then a shadow crosses his expression and he leans back, breaking off and staring sideways to Stu on the pitch. Inside that press of ecstatic bodies, all slapping hands and open mouths, Stu looks out to Tāmati, frowning, his cheeks paler than before. His gaze snags on me, before he looks down the line of parents to Pat and Lily.

'It's, uh...' Tāmati clears his throat. 'I should talk to my mum first.'

'What time did you see the girls leave the woolshed?' I speak over the cheers from the crowd. 'Was anyone else with them?'

He pauses where he is, halfway turned. There's the briefest glance to Stu, still held in the crush of his teammates, then back to me. 'I have to go.' He turns away from me, hunched and clutching his keys. Before I can say anything, he's disappeared into the press of parents, heading to the path for the boarding house.

On the turf, the boys are ready to restart. The ref lifts the whistle to his mouth, then pauses, looking down the row of parents. Someone is yelling out, and it's not the usual encouragement. I see Lily Kelson stride onto the pitch, waving Stu over to her.

'He's fine, love!' Pat calls after her, shaking his head. 'Just let it play out!'

Lily gets alongside Stu, holding a palm to his forehead. The boy bends down to her, giving her his most mollifying grin, but she keeps her arm tight to his forearm, her expression tight and focused. There's a shake of her head; she turns him to the sideline and marches him through the players to the gate. A pudgy guy in a Langsford jersey a couple of sizes too tight steps forward from the sidelines.

'They're tied up. I can't sub him now.'

'He's low, Walsh. Look.' Lily holds Stu's hand flat in front of him. He's got the shakes; I can see the tremble of his fingers from my end of the pitch. She points to one of the other Langsford players on the sideline, motioning for him to take Stu's spot.

'It's only three minutes, Lily.' The coach shakes his head, pointing to the scoreboard. 'It's the semis.'

'He comes off now.' Her voice is firm and unyielding. 'Let's go, Stu.'

As they walk, she unzips her pocket and pulls out a Bumper Bar, looks like. The boy takes it reluctantly, his shoulders hunched forward as though he's trying to disappear. When they reach the sidelines, Pat bends down for a word with Lily and whatever she has to say in return is enough to put him on the back foot. For a moment, Pat looks past the top of her head to me, his mouth pulled tight.

The new player sprints to take Stu's spot, and the ref whistles to restart play. The air fills with urgent cries and whoops from both sides of the pitch, but my eyes stay on the Kelsons: Stu watching from a bench, munching obediently, his cheeks still chalky and wet, and Pat tracking the play with his arms crossed. I still can't see Lily's expression, but she's got her arms around Stu's shoulders, rubbing his jersey as she speaks into his ear. Then the cries from the other side of the pitch become sharper, and there's the dull *thonk* of the ball hitting wood. A goal for Hastings, just in time for the ref to blow the end of the game.

'For fuck's sake!'

I scan the row of spectators, but I can't make out where the cussing is coming from; it might've even been the coach. On the turf, the two teams line up to shake hands. The Langsford boys all look pissed off, but they know better than to whinge outside of the changing room. Stu hunches down into himself on the bench, shaking his head. His mum leans to his side, fiddling with what looks like a transistor radio. It's an insulin pump.

I feel Ambrose beside me. 'No luck with Tāmati, eh?' He

clicks his tongue. 'We'll track down his parents, don't worry. Not a bad game to watch, in any case.'

On the pitch, the players finish shaking hands. Rodney holds up a fist for his big brother, waiting to be bumped, but Stu doesn't see him. Instead, the other players make a huddle around Stu, replaying parts of the game and eventually Rodney drops his hand, looking down the row towards us before his mum calls him away. A few other heads turn in our direction, their expressions hidden behind Ray Bans and John Jacobs.

I watch Rodney's shuffling steps, awkward and ungainly, hands tucked deep into his pockets. Then he moves away into the crowd.

WE'RE DEEP ENOUGH into Saturday that the hospital waiting room is filling with breaks and sprains. Four kids with ice packs, two of them wearing the same team colours.

'You've got to watch where the fuck you're running, Wade.' A hawk-faced woman sits staring at her phone, hissing sideways. 'I've been telling you every bloody weekend.'

Next to her, the boy swings his feet under the chair, holding an ice pack to his elbow with a serene expression. The woman gives me a vicious look as I come past, as though I'm to blame somehow.

'All right, then.' The Chief pauses in the hallway behind me, staring at the ward door as though it might bite him. 'I'll shoot back out there and see if I can grab Graham for that chat.'

'See what he knows about the debating club.' I nod. 'Apparently some of the Aquinas girls weren't too keen on having Jessica there. He might have heard something.'

'Yeah?' He squints and gives me his usual frown. 'Where'd you get that?'

'They go to Roxy's for lessons every Monday, that lot.'

'All the goss, eh?' He turns to leave. 'Dion's about somewhere if you need a lift.'

I watch him go, the fluorescent light turning his head into a shining orb. Truth be told, it's best for him to chat to the chaplain by himself. There's something in the air out at Langsford: all those boys, all those men, and I'm like a loose puzzle piece.

The same bearded nurse from last night is on the desk again. He nods me through, buzzing the door into that long pale hallway, then sees my expression. 'I went home,' he says. 'Don't worry.'

I return his grin, and the familiar smell hits my nose: bleach and iodine, the salty armpit waft of food heated too long. It's not far to Jessica's unit; I take a long breath to steady myself and push through the doors. This time there's no Tuck, and no Bea: there's only Michaela, feet tucked under her legs, knees to her chest, and a thick cardigan spread over her despite the warmth. She's staring down into her phone, hair hanging over her face, the white cable snaking under her to a battery pack. Her thumb jumps over the screen, sending images past her in a stream of colour. I'm all the way in the seat before she notices me.

'Oh.' She looks up. Her eyes are shot through with red, her cheeks like yesterday's buns. 'Sorry, I thought you were Dad.'

'Get any sleep, girl?' I give her my good ear. 'Moko gave you a lift home, I heard.'

A small nod. 'Dad wasn't keen on that other guy driving me.' She grins for just a moment. 'The cop. He's still hanging around here somewhere, I think.'

I smile back to her. 'How's your cousin doing?'

Michaela looks up and through the ribbon of glass in the door to Jessica's room, as if remembering why she's here. She clutches the phone tighter. 'I dunno. The same, I guess.' Her voice is small. 'The doctors talked to Dad and Aunty Bea for ages this morning, but I didn't really get it.' With her free hand, she reaches under her jaw, scratching slowly. 'They need to keep her in the coma for a bit. To let her catch up, they said.'

I follow her gaze to the door, seeing Jessica in that huge white bed, the cords and wires all arranged around her like she's some fussy orchid. Her colour is better than last night, at least: she's not quite so chalky in the face. In some ways, she looks in better shape than her cousin.

'It's for the best, love.' I try to sound steady. 'They know. They know what to do.'

She shifts in her seat, her eyes going back to her phone, the colour and movement filling her again. Down the hallway, I hear soft padding footsteps, and low practised voices. From inside the room, whispers filter over the chirps of the machines. All the while, Michaela's thumb taps on and on through the endless frames.

'I can text Dad if you need?' she mutters. 'He went outside with Aunty.'

71

'It's okay.' I lean back in the chair, making myself familiar, close. It's there if you're looking for it: the girl needs company. Not whānau, necessarily, but someone she knows. Past her huddled shape, I see Dion through the next glass door, coming closer. When he meets my eye, I shake my head to keep him in place. He frowns for a second, looking like he plans to come in anyway, then seems to understand. 'I was just out at Langsford, actually. Watching the hockey.'

'Mm.' She keeps on tapping. I tilt my head; the screen shows a woman brushing orange powder across her cheeks, her lips swollen and new-car shiny.

'Tāmati was there,' I say. 'Watching Stu's game.' I let the silence stretch out between us, long enough for it to gather weight. 'He mentioned a few things. About the party and that.'

Hearing his name, she breaks away from the screen, looking to the door. 'I don't know if I should, uh...' She swallows. 'Dad was saying we should talk together, all of us.'

'It's okay, girl.' I lift a hand to her shoulder. 'Whatever's happened, it's not your fault, all right?' Inside her skin is a low insect tremble. I pause, waiting until I have her eye. 'But you need to tell me about it. All of it. If you had a few drinks, whatever. Your dad doesn't have to know.' Breathe. 'Someone's out there, girl. Someone who's capable of doing that.' I nod sideways, through the glass. 'You have to tell me everything.'

'I did tell you.' She's mumbling; I have to lean closer. 'I did.'

'I know. I know you did.' I rub her shoulder, speaking low. Easy, now. 'Tāmati said something about you two going outside together. You and Jess.' She takes a long breath inwards. 'He said that was the last time anyone saw you.'

Inside these wet eyes, a flash of colour passes in a brief moment of electricity. I've done this enough with Sheena, with Bradley. Shaking the brush and waiting for the bird.

It's in there. Information. It's in there, and I need it.

'Aunty Bea blew up.' She's shaking her head, her pupils huge and dark. 'About the party. She…she would've slapped me, I think. If Dad wasn't there.' She rubs at her eyes.

'It's okay, lovey.' I keep my hand on her. 'Everyone gets up to a few things now and then. Your aunty probably just can't imagine you guys drinking, you know?'

'It wasn't that.' She sniffs, wiping at her nose. 'It was the Stu Kelson thing. She never liked us spending time with him. It was bad enough just with the debating stuff, Jess getting onto the same team and that. But going out to his place, to the farm.' She shakes her head slowly, and a wet rush of air leaves her mouth. 'She just lost it. That's why they had to go outside, her and Dad. The nurses kept on telling her off.'

I picture my bearded mate at the front desk, resigned and wary, doing his best to smile through the fatigue. I'd say it's the least of what he's seen in here.

'Just take me back. Take me back to the start of the night, and tell me again what happened.' I set my hand in my lap, waiting. 'Tāmati said you weren't a big fan of his tunes, in the car and all.'

Despite herself, she smiles for a moment. She's pretty, Michaela: she and her cousin both are. When the world gives them room to be.

'He was playing all this sad sack stuff,' she says. 'Drake and that. I dunno. It was bringing things down.' A finger comes under her eye. 'I guess Jessie didn't mind. She was up front with him, talking about books.'

'Books, eh?'

She nods, sniffing. I reach into a pocket and hand her a tissue; I've come prepared this time. She blows long and hard, emptying herself. 'Thanks.' She goes to hand it back, but I wave it away. 'It was the one from English class, that book about the guy in the fake mansion. We watched that old movie.'

I squint. '*The Great Gatsby?*'

'Uh huh.' She points into the room. 'Jessie got really into it. She kept staying after class to talk to Miss Mo'unga about her essay. Anyway, Tama's doing the same book at Langsford. They went on about it for ages.'

'What did you think?' I watch her face. 'About the book?'

'Me?' She holds herself still. 'I dunno. It was long.' A quick shrug. 'I liked Daisy, though. She was cool, the way she talked and that.'

'I like Daisy too.' I rub my jaw, feeling stiff. Conking out on the couch for the night wasn't the best idea. 'Not sure about her taste in blokes, though.'

'Yeah.' Michaela leans further back. 'I guess.'

'What happened after that, eh? Those two had their book club all the way to Tārehu?'

She rubs one hand in the other, looking into her knees. Here it comes. Whatever it is, she's looking for the best way to come to it. It's like splitting firewood, telling someone a big thing: I can feel her looking over the shape of the grain, finding the tell-tale cracks where the wood will just fly open on its own.

'It's been different, lately.'

There.

'Different?' I keep my words slow and calm. 'With your cousin, you mean?'

She nods. 'The debating and that, and hanging around with the others.' Her eyes go to the door for a moment. 'She'd never have bothered with a party like that. Not with those girls. Not before.' I hear footsteps in the hallway behind me, and I pray for them to keep moving. They do. 'She really got on with him.'

'With Stuart?'

'Yeah.' She swallows, looking to the room, then back into her knees. There's something else inside her words. 'With Stu.'

I lean against the wall, mirroring her. 'She was keen on him then, eh.'

'I think so.' She smiles, sniffing again. 'She never said anything, but I can tell with her.' Her cheeks are wet. 'That's why she was so keen to go along, even with all those other girls.' Her head moves slowly from side to side. 'But it was weird, once we got there.'

My blood speeds inside me. 'What happened, Micks?' She turns to me, then, looking me full in the face. It takes me by surprise, her eyes being this close. Something moves through them. Here. Here it is. 'It's okay, lovey.' I set my hand to her shoulder again, leaning closer. 'Whatever it is, we can deal with it. Your dad doesn't have to know.' I pause. 'Or your aunty.'

Her lips are moving, but I can't hear her. She swallows and starts again. 'They were passing around a bottle.' She looks into her knees. 'Heather and them. The Aquinas girls.'

I think back to what Roxy said. 'Heather Christiansen?'

Michaela nods. 'Jess grabbed a couple of Cody's from her mum's fridge. She reckoned she wouldn't notice, but she usually does.' A long breath inwards. 'But when we got there they had a bottle going already, and they made sure we had a bit. More than just a bit, actually.' I think back to how she smelled, that first night in the hospital. 'It was something clear, like vodka, but it tasted weird.'

My eyes stay on her. 'How was she towards Jess?'

'Who, Heather?' Michaela frowns. 'That was the weirdest thing of all. We knew she was in a huff about the regionals and that, and about Jessie getting a spot. But at the woolshed they were all being extra nice, like Stuey had asked them to put it on.' A pause. 'It was a bit much. Heather especially.'

'Yeah?' I picture the scene. I can remember the Tārehu woolshed: the tang of lanolin, the boards smooth from thousands of hours of sweat and moccasins. 'How do you mean?'

She takes a long breath. 'They were asking about Dad's driving, and about Aunty Bea working with the shearing

76

gangs and that. About her placing in the golden shears last year. All that stuff.' A pause. 'But it felt weird.'

I nod. 'It's a different group, I guess. You lot probably don't mix all that often.'

'It wasn't just that.' She lifts her head to me again. 'They really made sure we got the bottle, me and Jessie. Like, they were sending it back to us all the time. Jessie didn't seem to notice, but it was like…' Her voice trails off, before she gathers herself again. 'It felt like when someone has something to tell you, something bad, and they're taking their time with it.' She looks sideways. 'When we first pulled up, they were all sitting around the smoko table, waiting with smiles ready, before Tama even slid the door open.'

I can see it in my mind: it'd still be the same Formica table they used to have in there, and the same old Zip boiler with the pull cord, a row of dusty enamel mugs ready and waiting. They always seemed so huge, the insides of those woolsheds, when me and Debs were younger: the rafters stretching over us like the ceiling of some grand cathedral, the stale waft of the shearers' tobacco pouches, and the spicy grass smell we only figured out later.

'So, they were passing around the bottle, making sure you had plenty, eh?' I keep my voice low and coaxing. 'Then the two of you went outside, like Tāmati said?'

She shakes her head. 'Maybe Jessie took me outside, or maybe…I don't know. Fuck, I don't know anything.' A tear slides from her eye and rolls to the corner of her lip; she pulls her legs to her chest again, making herself a parcel. 'I wanted to tell Jessie about how weird I felt, about how slippery things seemed, and how my hands felt heavy. But she went outside with Stu before I could say anything.'

'With Stu?' I watch her, tucking the information away. 'You're sure?'

A quick nod. 'She wanted to show him some kind of clip or something, but there was no service. He said there was a spot he could bounce the Wi-Fi from the farmhouse, down the end of the fence. Then they went out.' Another tremble runs through her.

'And you didn't want them to?'

'I...no, not even for...no, I didn't. I didn't want to stay. Not with those girls.' A sob moves through her. 'I was trying to tell them how weird I was feeling, but Jessie just got up and left. Usually she knows. If we're at a party and one of us is too gone, or something feels dodgy, we don't have to say anything. We just know.'

I keep my hand to her shoulder, picturing the two girls coming past Sheena's place. The ease between them, the shorthand. Of course she wouldn't have to explain. I know what it is, to have that connection. To be understood.

'It's okay, girl.'

'No.' She shakes her head, making her hair fall loose. 'I should have known. Even feeling that way, I should have seen it.' More moisture slides from her eyes. 'But I woke up at home with my phone plugged in next to me and a glass of water by the lamp.'

I feel myself frowning. 'You don't know who dropped you

off?' My hand presses against her shoulder. 'Did someone call your dad, maybe?'

'Dad? Shit no.' Her voice drops to a whisper. 'He'd kill me, heading to a party like that.'

'You're absolutely sure you saw her head outside with Stu Kelson?'

She nods, wiping at her cheeks, and the words slide from her. 'It's the last thing I remember. The smell of the woolshed, and the weird taste of the bottle, like liquorice. And Jessie standing up to go with him, giving me a look to see if I was all good. But I wasn't. I wasn't.' She squeezes her eyes closed. 'Fuck. Sorry.'

'It's all right, Micks.' I press my fingers into her shoulder. 'It's not your fault.'

'I...I never meant...'

Like a chain pulled past its load, she folds into me, hands clutched to her front, shoulders tucked forward, making herself small. I feel it slipping out of her, the black feeling, the weight. My shirt is wet from her face, but it doesn't matter. She's so small, this girl, and the world has such long shadows for her. My hands go shushing over her back, and I let her cry. All the while, my gaze is locked on the ribbon of glass where her cousin lies, that pale resting thing.

~

Eventually I convince Michaela to take a spell in the cafeteria. A change of scenery, I tell her. I get her settled at a corner table with a hot chocolate and a blueberry muffin buttered beyond all reasonable standards. She looks emptied, a jam jar scraped clean.

'I'll grab one of those.' I find Dion at the coffee machine in the hallway, jabbing at the buttons with a sausage finger. He's switched his uniform for jeans and a shirt. An easier load of laundry if he encounters Tuck again, I suppose.

'First one's always too watery anyway.' He passes me the paper cup and slides another one into the machine, reaching into his pockets for coins. 'That one doing all right?' He nods past me to the cafeteria doors. 'She was here bloody early, you know. Just like yours truly.'

The coffee runs into me, thin and metallic. I nod to Dion for another one; with a begrudging shake of the head, he hands me his cup too. Two sugars, like a bricklayer. It's a welcome thing.

'Ta.' I hold my voice low. Michaela's too far to hear, but there are always other ears. 'She's shaken up, mate. Really shaken up.' I look back through the doors, seeing the girl buried in her phone again. 'Did the lab come back with the blood work yet?'

'Who? Jessica's?' He pauses. Seeing my expression, he continues, stumbling slightly. 'Right, of course. She...I meant to tell you, actually. They found a positive for GHB. Low levels, but still. Alcohol too. Not that that's any surprise.'

'Fantasy eh?' I squint, looking back at Michaela. 'Fuck me. They did the both of them.'

'They?'

I nudge him further down the hallway and give him the

broad strokes. 'Jesus.' He shakes his head. 'You don't think they meant to set them up for it, do you?'

It.

Years into a job like this, and he still has a hard time saying it. I shouldn't blame him, really. I think back to that first night, seeing her in the ward. You don't want to consider it, but you have to.

'To be raped, Dion. We're talking about rape.' I feel my hands shaking.

'All right, steady on.' His gaze goes skyward. 'I only meant...'

'The unit came over this morning for that already, the Chief said. No signs, by all accounts.'

Dion nods past me to the cafeteria, relief mixing with his prickly expression. 'The cousin?'

'She'd have said something.' My heart catches for a moment. 'No. No, I don't think so.'

I feel him staring. 'If you're sure.' He shakes his head again. 'My first thought was she and her cousin must've been getting up to silly buggers with some of Tuck's mates, getting hold of that stuff. But if the others slipped it to them, then it's a different story.'

'Tuck smokes weed, mate.' I shake my head. 'Spliffs and Red Bull, like a lot of guys doing long-haul. It's a long way from grass to that shit.'

'If you say so.' He holds my gaze. I shouldn't be surprised. Mention our side of town—mine, Michaela's, Bea's—and everyone jumps to the last square on the board. 'Listen,' Dion says, 'Our boy had a hard night at home, and Amo could really do with a sub.'

'There's nobody else.' I swallow the last of the coffee. 'We need you here with your eyes and ears open, just in case. A constable, remember?'

He sets his hands to his hips, staring blades at me. 'Right.'

A long breath leaves me. 'I'll tell the Chief no later than six, all right?' My feet are moving, taking me past the cafeteria doors to the reception. 'In the meantime, he wants you to keep yourself handy.'

'That's what he said?' I nod over my shoulder, hearing his coins drop into the machine. 'Handy, eh.' There's a long yawn before he speaks again. 'Two years' training in Porirua and all. I suppose I can manage handy. Seeing as how we've got our *best detective* in the field.'

I keep my mouth shut, reminding myself how much sleep he'll be missing out on with a young one at home.

In the foyer there's more light and it feels less like the inside of a car boot. My usual nurse must have finished his shift; now there's a slim young thing smiling so much she must be new. I pull out my phone and dial the Chief, cutting sideways across the carpark, heading for home via Bum-Bum. He'll start getting feral on me if we leave it too long between treats. I'm squinting into the blue afternoon and wishing I'd brought my sunnies when I hear a familiar voice, straining into a higher pitch.

'For fuck's sake, Bea!' It's Tuck. I haven't seen his truck anywhere, but the voice is unmistakeable. I pause where I am in the lee of the cars, hearing the Chief's faint *hello?* from the phone in my hand. 'You knew it was pushing it, that shit with the lawyers. You knew they'd never...'

'It's nothing to do with you.' She's controlled, Bea, but it won't last. Anyone could hear it: the sharper inflection, the creaking of a structure under too much weight.

There are some words I don't quite catch, then: '...everything to do with me.' Tuck, again. There's a new tenderness in his voice, now, a low coaxing mixed with frustration, with rage. 'She's in there, knocked to bloody pieces. There's no way those pricks will ever...'

'Stop! Just stop it!'

'Fuck it, then!'

There's the catch and splutter of an engine. A door slams, and I hear the quick scrape of feet over the asphalt. I move back further, into the well between two trucks, letting their shadows cover me. Just a few steps away, Bea stomps past the gap, her face pulled tight, her cheeks the pale red of early strawberries. I'm close enough to feel the sense of something being tucked away, something quickly buried inside her. She'll have arranged herself again by the time she reaches the front desk, ready to see her niece, to talk to her and Dion and anyone else without showing it.

Through the line of cars, there's the rough scrape of wheels against asphalt, the sound of a truck pulling away. I don't need to see Tuck's face: I can picture his teeth grinding, his knuckles like hatchets poking through the veneer of his skin. There's the wobble and clatter of his dogbox in the tray as he reaches the main road, and the messy crunch of shifting gears. I step out from between the cars, letting the sunlight hold me again. My collar is sticky at my neck. The Chief is still on the line.

'You there, Rick?'

There's a thud as he picks up the phone. He's muffled; he must be driving. 'Course I bloody am, Lorraine. Just left the chaplain's place.' He clears his throat. 'You saved me from an invitation to give another drink-driving lecture, actually. Top work. What's going on?'

I come to the edge of the carpark. It's not far to Roxy's stable from here. 'Few things to fill you in on.'

SUNDAY MORNING, AND my eyes spring open to the thickest part of the dark. My brain is already humming, a screen with a winking cursor. It's a new thing, these five o'clock starts. Dad said it was the same for him as he got on: stretching the days out while he still had some left.

There's nothing else for it but to leave Tilly in the warmest spot of the bed and stomp down to the station with another radioactive coffee from my petrol-station wraith. Down the stairs to the file room: computer, lamp and printer, my companion chorus of low humming machines blinking. I stretch my arms above my head and lean back, feeling the usual twinge in my collarbone.

'All right now. Here we are.' My eyes lose their focus for a moment, the concrete ceiling turning to a soft sky of grey, the steel arms of the file shelves becoming gauzy and distant.

Jessica.

Michaela. Tāmati.

Patience. Patience, and care. There's plenty in what I've seen, in what I've heard. I'll have plenty more to chew over tomorrow, once Pat brings his lot in for their chat with Ambrose. But before they do, I need to scratch this itch.

Bea. Tuck.

The stacks have something for me; I can feel it. There must be a hundred thousand pieces of paper in here on Masterton alone; twice that in the head office system.

Patrick. Stuart. Bill.

William Kelson. Dad always saw him as someone to count on, as far as we girls knew back then. Whenever they came across each other driving to and from town, they'd stop and yarn away, until Debs started with her annoyed breathing, and Dad would wrap things up before she got all the way septic. There's acid on my tongue just thinking of Tārehu. Those steep, broken hills, the pockets of scrub still clinging to the forgotten clefts of paddocks, of ranges. Sometimes their ewes would wander through the boundary fence to our blocks, canny enough to have lived out their whole lives in those wild places, their wool grown overlong, blinding them. They'd come through to the bush block, and dad would bring them in for Bill.

Our bush block. Once, anyway.

My gaze comes to rest on my desk, on the paper cup from the petrol station, on my keyboard with its grubby grey shores where my fingers rest. On the screen, the cursor blinks, patiently waiting. Then my phone vibrates. It's Sheena.

2pm ok for u aunty?

Of course. My fingers move across the screen. *I'll get the good buns.*

A bouncing bubble. *Love it. Ta.*

Two o'clock; I don't have quite as many fallow hours as I thought. I lurch myself straight and start with the digital records: Tuck first, because I know there'll be something to find. There: the assault charge from the nineties, the aggro cop up in Bulls; a caution for speeding a few years after. I try to find something on the bust-up with him and Roxy's dad, the scrap about his hours and all, but the Chief must've kept that one off the books, or at least out of the pile to scan. On a whim, I delete Tuck's name—Trevor, officially— from the search and try for any other Mowbries. There are a few from up around Kaikohe with a decent breaking and entering habit, but not much else.

Then I stumble on an old entry for a B. Mowbrie, from nearly twenty years back. It's a call about an alleged assault. I click ahead and see the full name: Beatrice Mowbrie, twenty-one at the time.

'Bea?'

I've always known Bea as someone quick out of the blocks when it comes to a temper—not as bad as her brother, of course, but not far off—but imagining her on the wrong end of an assault charge is a bit much.

At the end of the record is a single phrase: *Officer attended.*

No charges progressed. There's one more detail that really knits my brows. The address. *Longbush Station.*

It's Tārehu.

Bea, out at Tārehu.

The digital records don't show anything else, not even the name of the officer attending, or the complainant party. It's no matter: it's one of ours, meaning it'll be in the stacks somewhere. My gaze falls on those tall surfaces of green steel, their cardboard spines in mottled browns and whites, like teeth pulled from so many thousands of patients. I get up and pull the basement windows further open, letting in fresh air and birdsong. My fingers brush against the edges of the files as I move, feeling the weight of the information. The rough date's all I need: the assaults and batteries for that year occupy a couch-length part of the stacks, and my coffee's still warm.

Out they come, these sheafs wrapped in twine, or others with long-suffering rubber bands cracked and ready to fall apart at the merest touch. I work my way through, looking for Bea's name, hearing the sounds of the late summer morning grow louder outside: traffic from the road, car doors slamming, and the occasional voice. Some of the files are heavy enough that my collarbone complains, but we've got a girl in the intensive ward, and this is my task. I'm nearly at the end of the papers, my fingers dusty with print, when I find it.

'Dickerson.' A loud sigh escapes me. 'Bloody typical.'

Eugene Dickerson was a graduate officer sent over from Porirua for an ill-fated five-month posting in the Chief's team. He had a habit of disappearing for whole afternoons at a time, and Rick could never get him on the radio. It would've been tolerable had some keen-eyed taxpayer not noticed him in the cinema at eleven o'clock on a Monday morning, watching the newest *Star Wars*. The silly prick was in full uniform, even wearing his hat. A single call to the local paper and that was that.

He wasn't big on taking notes, Dickerson, but what's in there will give me enough for a good old neighbourly chat to Bea. It was late morning on a Thursday in December, and Dickerson got the call to pay a visit to the Tārehu Station woolshed. The notes mention a shearing gang, and a wool handler, one Beatrice Mowbrie, tossing a handpiece at a shearer after a scuffle with a rousey. It sounds like the kind of thing my sister Debs and her man Billy might have told me about when they were still working the boards: long days, a grey sea of bad-tempered sheep to get through; everyone's blood running good and hot. I turn the paper over, looking for the name of the shearer—the shearing comb opened up his knuckle from the index to the middle finger, apparently—but there's nothing on him. Or the rousey who kicked everything off, for that matter.

'Fuck's sake, Dickerson.' I shake my head. I've half a mind to find a number for him and give him a spray. 'You wrote down which knuckles, but not the owner of the knuckles?'

The paper does list one other familiar name. *Officer spoke with Bill Kelson. Parties agreed not to take things further. Knuckle bandaged and work resumed.*

Knuckle bandaged and work resumed. Sounds like an

average morning for Billy's lot. I'll say this for Dickerson: he might have been skimpy with the details, but his spelling's better than what I'm usually dealing with. I make a copy of the report and set it on my desk, flicking through the rest of the pile to make sure there's nothing else waiting for me.

Bea. Bea should remember a thing like that, I'd say. Bill too, if I can catch him on a morning where his noggin's cooperating. Might be easier said than done, these days. I pull out my phone and type a text to Rick.

Know anything about Bea Mowbrie getting into a scrap on the Kelson place? Dickerson took some notes back in 2002.

Before I hit send, my palm starts to itch. Bea Mowbrie. Does Rick really need a reason to shift her higher on his list of local miscreants? I could always keep it to myself, a little spark of information tucked away, ready if I need it.

No. It won't do. Shit, if we'd put our heads together earlier last year, I might not have ended up in Prendergast's shed with my collarbone busted up, pissing into a fertiliser drum. Not to mention Keith would probably still be on his throne in the roast shop. And Bradley would still have his dad. I hit send, tapping the phone against my palm.

They're absolutely shit notes, I add. *Just in case you were wondering.*

I keep on tucking the papers back in their places, replacing some of the worst rubber bands. Then my phone chimes. *Dickerson, eh. No surprises there. Doesn't ring any bells.*

Sheena might know a thing or two about it, or Moko maybe. It's going back a good while, but if there's a shearer out there with a scar across the knuckles, it'll have been a story at some point. Debs might even have told Sheena the story over her morning Milo. There were always plenty of stories about handlers and rouseys going at each other.

Through the open window, I hear the crunch of tyres over the loose gravel, doors opening and shutting. It sounds close. Could be dog walkers; they sometimes use the station carpark in the weekends. Then the footsteps come closer. Sounds like more than one person. I turn around to give it my good ear, and a knock sounds against the front door, loud and insistent against the glass, before the buzzer sounds.

'Jesus.' I squint up the stairs. 'On a Sunday?'

I stand as still as I can, waiting for them to go, but whoever it is keeps on knocking and buzzing. They might've seen the basement windows cracked open. I feel like my rock's been flipped over, my dusty sanctuary thrust into sunlight.

'All right, for Christ's sake.' I climb the stairs out of the basement, feeling my weight with each step. Upstairs, the hallway is still dark, leaving me hidden in shadow. Across the foyer, a group of faces peer through the front door, bathed in the bright morning. Four in total. A woman holds her hands to the glass, making a box for her face. She sees me, beckoning me to come closer. I stay where I am, catching my breath after the stairs, and slide my phone from my pocket, opening my chat with the Chief.

You'll want to come in. My fingers move over the screen. *The station.*

I move across the foyer to the Chief's office, looking around for the keys. The woman outside taps the glass again, as though I'm going to take off on her. She's bloody impatient for someone who charges by the hour. When I get the door open, she shifts her hand to her forehead, still squinting.

'Horiana.' I watch her expression. 'Been a while, eh?'

Behind her shoulder, Lily Kelson holds her arms tight across her chest, a wide pair of sunglasses hiding her eyes. Pat's looming tall behind them, the sunlight turning his face to crinkles. Tucked between them is their boy, Stu, doing his best to looked relaxed.

'That it has,' says Horiana. 'Your niece been doing all right?'

'Sheena's sound, yep.' I push the door open wider, feeling a call vibrate through my pocket. It'll be the Chief. 'You lot better come in.'

AMBROSE PULLS UP not long after the jug's boiled. I hardly have time to hand the mugs around—green tea for Horiana, which draws a blank expression from Pat—before he comes through the back, face a little flushed.

'Lorraine.' He's got his weekend jeans on, at least. No stubbies. His attention turns to the others on the couch, then lingers on Horiana. 'Miss Paul. Doing all right, are we?'

'Āe.' She holds his eye just long enough. The last time they were in the same room it was the District Court, and Horiana was grilling Rick about pulling a client of hers over on suspicion of driving wasted, and why he'd stopped the same guy four times in a single week. The charges ended up sticking, but not before she'd made the Chief squirm. 'Well enough.'

Rick gives a small smile. 'I see you're dressed for action,' he gestures to her suit jacket, 'so let's get to it.' He digs around in his pocket for his keys. 'I wasn't expecting you lot until tomorrow, but no time like the present, eh?'

At the far end of the couch, Lily leans forward. 'Our son would like to give a statement.' She looks sideways to Stu, an arm set to his shoulder. 'He wants to help.'

'That's right.' Pat brings himself forward too, matching Lily's gesture, his expression earnest and doglike. Between them, Stu seems braced: a structure liable to fall over if left on its own. None of the confidence I saw on the hockey pitch. Here, he just looks trapped. Then the boy looks from the Chief to me, and his expression grows warmer.

'I...' Stu clears his throat. 'I thought it might be helpful. About Thursday and that.'

'It would be, mate, yep.' Rick points towards the interview rooms, holding an arm out to show the way. 'Whenever you're ready. Not a bad game yesterday, by the way. Feeling better?'

'Oh.' Stu mutters. 'Yeah, much better. Cheers.'

Clutching their mugs, Lily and Pat go to stand. 'Just the lad would be best,' says Rick. 'And the lovely Miss Paul, of course. Can't forget her.'

Horiana grabs her case and stands, her features impassive. 'It's all right.' She holds a palm up for Pat and Lily to stay where they are. 'We'll be fine.'

'Hang on, he...they can't just...' Pat frowns. 'Can they?'

'We'll be fine,' says Horiana, firmer now. 'Just sit tight.'

Past Pat, Lily's eyes catch mine for a second, full of tender feeling. There's the low boil of concern in her movements, the need to shield her boy from this place. She looks to the

94

Chief, then to me, and she seems to relax slightly. She rubs Stu's back, whispering something into his ear, before he stands and comes to us. We come through the doorway to the interview room, and Ambrose shifts everyone to their spots. The door clicks shut.

'You too, Lorraine?' Horiana gives me a tight smile. 'Records management has never been more important, I guess.'

'Lovely as it is to chat, Miss Paul, how about we hop to it, eh?' Ambrose clicks over the record, speaking aloud in the usual preamble. In my pocket, my phone vibrates. It's Dion.

Doctors just came around. Stable. No change.

I hold the phone up for the Chief. 'Our officer at the hospital.' He nods, looking to Stuart. 'Giving us an update on Jessica's condition.'

The boy's gaze flickers from the Chief to me, then back again. 'Is she...Tama said, uh...' He shifts in his seat. 'I mean, I heard she was...'

'My client has prepared a statement.' Horiana's vowels come out firm and flat, the sleek sheen of the professional. She unzips a thin black folder, sliding it across to Stuart and tapping at a spot with her pen.

'He has, has he?' Ambrose crosses his arms, leaning back in his chair until it complains. 'It that right, mate? Those are your words, there?'

'Yes, officer. They are.' The boy holds his gaze across the table, the fluorescent light above us turning his eyes to young apples. A tremor goes through the Chief's jaw.

'Away you go, then.'

Stuart sets his hands out on the table, one on either side of the paper. I lean forward, squinting to make out the words. It's better if I watch his face, seeing what else I might find.

He starts out with what we know already: the debating team, meeting Jessica at the practice evenings, and how he'd invited her for the planning day drinks. How he'd sent a friend—Tāmati, but he stays nameless in this telling—to give her a lift out to the woolshed with her cousin.

'How'd she come into the mix, then?' The Chief cuts in. 'The cousin, Michaela?'

There's a long pause. 'They do everything together, those two. She came along to the practice evenings and that.' Stuart looks to me. 'They even...'

'Let's finish up with the statement, Stuart.' Horiana taps the paper with her pen, a dry sound slicing through the silence. 'Go on.'

Gathering himself, the boy presses on. Jessica and Michaela had arrived at the woolshed and mixed in with the others—again, there are no names, but we'll have time for that later—and Stuart had come in and out of the party, making sure everyone had drinks and snacks. Then, after a couple of hours or so, he says, the two cousins had gone outside, by the gear shed. Here, I notice him look past me and Ambrose to the door, just briefly, before his attention goes back to the sheet of paper. He'd seen the two girls there, he says, before he and a few others went out the back to their cars. When they came back inside, one of the Aquinas girls, Heather

96

Christensen—she gets a name, now—was taking care of Michaela on the old woolshed couch. She'd vomited, apparently, and Jessica was still outside, looking for a place to pee. After a while, Heather had agreed to drive Michaela home, and Stuart had given her the address. Michaela wouldn't go without Jessica, so Heather agreed to drive down the row of trees and look for her before they left. It was no use trying to call her, Stuart explains: the reception was still too patchy out there.

'Even with the new antenna up by the old lime works?' The Chief asks.

'That thing's useless.' Stu shakes his head, grinning briefly. 'Everyone knows that.' He looks sideways to Horiana, and his smile dissipates. 'Anyway, that was the last thing I remember. We didn't see Heather or Michaela again, and the rest of us just assumed they'd found Jessie too.' He holds my gaze. 'I thought Heather had dropped them both off at Michaela's place.'

I look to Rick, then back across the table. 'What'd she say about it, then?'

Stuart swallows hard. 'Heather? I...nothing. We never...it was the planning day, the next day. Everyone was off school, and I stayed home to clean up. I just thought...we all just thought she'd found Jessie and driven her back.' He pauses again. 'It wasn't until you spoke to Mum and Dad that we realised.'

'Realised what?' The Chief stares over the table.

'That...that she'd only dropped Micks home.' He falters for a second, his eyes clouding over and dropping to the table. Then Horiana nudges him, and he reaches into his pocket. 'It was only today, walking from the woolshed to home, that I found this.'

In his hand is a resealable plastic bag with a phone in it. It has a pink cover and a sticker on the back with the words 'Lost in Translation' beneath a turkey-looking man and a much younger woman in a wig the exact shade of pink as the cover. I can feel the Chief staring at the side of my face.

'It was by the fence,' says Stu. 'Between the woolshed and the windbreak trees.'

'And you just happened to find it this morning?' The Chief picks up the bag with careful fingers. He slides a thumb along the side of the phone, pressing once, then again. The screen stays black.

'That's right.' Horiana nods. 'Early this morning.'

'Was that before or after you decided to come in?' I watch the boy's face as I speak; the angle of his mouth, the way his chin pulls tighter.

'My client...'

'It was why we wanted to come in.' Stuart leans forward. 'It was too important to wait.'

'Is that right?' The Chief squints. 'Good of you.' He glances to me, letting me read his expression. Bullshit. He's heard it, and I have too. Whatever affinity he might have for the Kelsons, he's still got ears. 'We'll need to take a drive out your way, I'd say. You can talk us through it again, and show us exactly where it all happened.'

'All right.' Stuart sets his hands on the table and pushes himself up.

'Not now, kid.' I nod back to the chair; he looks sideways to Horiana.

'My client's given a thorough statement,' she says. 'We've come here willingly, let's not forget.'

I ignore her, pressing on while the boy is distracted. 'You mentioned Michaela throwing up. Any ideas why that might be?'

Stuart looks to Horiana again. She nods for him to answer, and he sits. 'She'd been drinking. With the others.'

'With Heather Christensen?'

He nods. 'But I think they'd had something before they showed up.' He swallows, staring into his hands. 'My friend who drove them, he...'

'Tāmati, right?'

There's a brief tremble in his expression; he looks to the microphone. 'That's...yep, that's right. He said they were drinking in the car, both of them.'

'They seemed drunk when they arrived, then?' The Chief leans forward. 'Did you notice anything?'

Stuart's eyes fill with a distant expression. He seems genuinely to be recalling, this time. 'She...they both seemed a bit out of it, actually. A bit hyper.'

'Hyper?'

He nods. 'Micks especially. She was yelling over the music, and she broke a chair.' Despite himself, he smiles. 'We had a laugh about that. They're all poked, those old chairs.'

'Did you notice them sharing drinks?' I hold his gaze. 'The girls?'

'Who, with Heather and them?' He frowns. 'I think so, yeah. Heather had brought a bottle.'

The Chief scratches at his jaw. I can tell he's fighting a yawn. 'A bottle of what?'

'She's vodka, Heather.' The boy shrugs. 'Usually, anyway. But sometimes she...'

'Is this relevant?' Horiana crosses her arms.

'The same bottle, you said?' I ignore her, grabbing the kid's attention back.

'I...' A longer pause. 'I think so, yeah.' He frowns. 'Why?'

I watch his expression, looking for anything I can latch onto. It's real, this confusion: there's something pure, unvarnished, in his expression.

'Heather missed out on the regionals this year, didn't she?' I speak slowly, letting him understand. 'She'd have been miffed about that.'

'The debating team?' He frowns, his eyebrows forming a deep cleft. 'I guess so. Heaps of girls tried out, though. She wasn't put on because she couldn't...'

'We're getting off track here,' Horiana cuts in. 'Let's stick to the evening.'

'It's relevant.' The Chief leans forward with his elbows against the table, giving me a glance to hang back. 'It's relevant because they found traces of GHB in Jessica's system.' He pauses, letting them take it in. 'That's fantasy, Stuart.'

'Fantasy?' His mouth hangs open; he shakes his head. 'That bodybuilding stuff?'

'All right.' Horiana goes to stand. 'That's enough. If you

want to proceed further, you'll need to...'

'If anyone brought shit like that to my place, I'd know about it.' Stuart points to the tabletop, his nostrils flaring. 'They'd know better than to mess about with that.'

'Stuart.' Horiana sets a hand to his arm.

'No, fuck that.' He shrugs her off, then seems to catch himself. 'Sorry, Miss Paul. I'm...no, listen.' He turns to us again. 'Everyone knows I'm not into any of that, all right? They know.' He points a thumb to his chest. 'Graham...Mr. Young trusts me to keep the boys focused, especially after last year.' Here, he stops himself. There's sweat beading at his temples.

'Focused?' I gaze across the table. 'What do you mean, last year?'

'All right, Lorraine.' Ambrose holds a hand up. 'Let's just cool it for a second, now. I've spoken with Graham. I know all about it.' His expression is a blank wall; I get the feeling I'm a second away from being sent to fetch biscuits. 'You've been helping him a lot, he said. Sounds like it's made a real difference, especially with the younger guys.'

The colour starts coming back to Stuart's face. 'I'd hope so, yep.'

I give him time to breathe. 'You'd be doing us a huge favour, giving us the names of everyone at the party.'

'Lorraine.' Rick frowns at me. 'Why don't you let us...'

'Of course.' Without pausing, Stu lists off six names, including Heather and Tāmati. Roxy's mentioned a few of them already.

'All right, then.' The Chief reaches for the recorder button. 'Good for now?'

'Hang on.' I know I'm pushing things with Rick, but it can't wait. I lean forward, silent until I have the boy's total attention. With the door closed, it's absolutely still in the room; I can hear the fabric of Rick's jeans as he resettles his leg, and the impatience in his breathing. 'You said they both went outside together, Michaela and Jessie. But only Michaela came back inside the woolshed.'

He nods. 'That's what happened.'

'Well,' I clear my throat. 'We have a statement from someone else at the party that you were the last one seen heading outside with her.' He frowns. 'With Jessica, Stuart.'

'Someone else at the party?' He looks to the Chief, then back to me. 'You mean Micks? She was out of it, I told you. She…'

'You'll need to give us the details,' Horiana points to the table. 'My client's given his statement. That's his account of Thursday night, Lorraine.'

'Well, it doesn't quite tally, does it, mate?' I lean back, careful with my shoulder.

'Lorraine.' The Chief shakes his head.

'Well?'

Stuart breathes in, quick and shallow. 'She went outside with Micks.' He looks to the door again, seemingly reaching for someone to help split the problem, but it's all on him. 'They were outside for ages. We went out the back to the cars to get some stuff.'

'What stuff?' Ambrose cuts in.

'Some jerseys.' Stuart swallows hard. I can hear the insides of his throat. 'It was chilly inside. For the girls and that. When I came back in, Heather was dealing with Micks. Just Micks.' When he looks to me again, his eyes are wet. 'I thought she'd driven them both home. Honestly, I did.'

'That's enough, Stu. That's plenty.' Horiana stands, looking to the boy for him to do the same. 'If you two have anything else, you can contact me directly. Stuart has a big week ahead at Langsford, and he won't do well to be distracted.'

'A big week, eh?' I let it come out of me, now. 'Can't have any distractions, then. Not at Langsford.'

Ambrose jabs the recorder hard enough for me to get the picture, and the red light flickers off. Looking dazed, Stuart climbs to his feet. I wait for him to get close before I speak. The Chief is staring absolute murder at me, but now's not the time to hold back.

'You asked how she was doing.' I hold my voice low, making the boy lean closer. 'Jessie. She took a bloody good knock to the back of the head, kid. I don't know if they told you, your mum and dad.' I lift my hand to my head, shifting my hair to let him see. 'Enough to crack the skull. Right here.' My fingers point to the hard curve behind my ear. Then I reach out and tap him in the same place, until he understands.

'That's enough.' The Chief pulls the door open. I feel his hand on my shoulder, his fingers tight to me.

'Another hour on her own in that bush and we'd be burying her, Stu.'

'I...'

All colour is drained from him; he can only stare back at me with huge eyes. There's a safety he's used to, a sense of comfort. And this isn't it. Fuck it. Let him feel it. Let him feel a fraction of what Jessie must have felt.

'Get over here.' The Chief pulls me to the side, rough enough to send a flash of yellow pain through my shoulder. Through the open door, I see Pat stand, leaving Lily still seated on the couch. 'It's my call when to wrap up an interview, Henry. And I've made that call.' His voice is hard and low, but clear enough for everyone else to hear. Maybe that's the idea. 'If we have any issues knowing which stack to use downstairs, or getting the right fucking coffee filters, then it'll be your cake to slice. You understand?'

My collarbone is crying out; his fingers are locked around my arm. I nod.

'If that's everything, Chief?' Horiana floats to my elbow, doing her bit to cut through Rick's attention. After a long moment, the slate in his expression breaks up and falls away.

'Yep. We've taken enough of your time, I reckon.' He nods through the door to Pat and Lily. 'I was thinking I'd take a drive out to the farm later on, to take a look at the shed and that. Does that suit?'

'You okay, Stu?' Lily lifts an arm around her son, holding him tightly. The boy gives a small nod, still looking at me with a soft expression. Horiana mutters a few words, and they move to the door.

'You'll give us a time, at least.' Pat stands, squaring up to the Chief. 'We can't just sit around all bloody day waiting.'

'Four, then.' Rick checks his watch, pushing the door open to the carpark. 'Happy?'

With a glance to Horiana, Pat nods. They file out, Pat moving with unhurried steps, Lily tucking Stuart's head into her shoulder. Halfway across the carpark, Pat seems to notice Lily cuddling their boy. He adjusts his steps to move a hand between them until Stuart is standing straight on his own. Then the Kelsons climb into their ute and Horiana gets into her silver Toyota. Inside the truck, Stuart wipes at his eyes. It's quick, but I see it. Someone else is in there, too. Rodney, the brother; I make out white buds in his ears. He'll have been in there the whole time. I wait until the door has swung closed, watching them through the glass.

'That was a bit much, Rick.' I move one hand over my wrist. 'Even for you.'

'Even for me?' His hands go to his hips. 'Fair play, Lorraine. You went miles beyond your brief in there, pushing the boy like that.' He stands up straight, venom flickering in his expression. 'You had your chance to play detective last year, and look what bloody came of it. A good man in the ground, for nothing.'

My throat closes up. 'For nothing?' A sob slides out of me, splitting my words. 'Three bloody kids, eh? That's nothing, is it?'

'You know what I mean.' Rick shakes his head, quieter now. He uncrosses his arms, breathing low. 'Shit, Lorraine. I just...you don't know this lot like I do, all right? They're bloody hard workers, the Kelsons. Always have been.'

I take a long breath. There's enough blood in my head for me to stay upright. 'You're right,' I mutter. 'I don't know them like you do.' We stay where we are, listening to the ascending whine of the Kelson's ute as they pull into the road. 'At least tell me what you were on about with Stu, everything with the chaplain and all.'

The Chief sighs, a heavy sound for a Sunday. 'A plasterer was touching up the new shower block one weekend last year,' he says. 'Found a bag of pills taped in the roof cavity. MDMA, apparently. The school kept it to themselves.' He nods through the door. 'The boy's been helping Graham keep an eye on things, making sure there's none of it about.'

'Yeah?' I picture the way Stuart's pupils had flared at the mention of the GHB. Such young anger. The kind you can't mask and can't fake.

In my pocket, my phone vibrates. It's Sheena. She's on the way to mine already.

'Shit. My niece.'

'What?' The Chief turns to me. 'The baby, is it?'

'No, it's…' I feel like there's a new stone at the very centre of my body. Or maybe it's an old one. 'It doesn't matter. I just need to get home, that's all.'

'Come on then,' Rick nods to the back, his features assembled in what passes for a half-hearted apology. 'I'll give you a lift.'

'It's fine.' I hold my eyes firm to him. 'I'm sound.'

SHEENA'S ALREADY THERE when I get home, on her knees in Frank's old planter box, next to Bradley. Our boy sees me first, looking over his shoulder with a flat expression, a smudge of soil on his cheek. Then he nudges his mum, and she turns around with a handful of silverbeet, the deep green swaying thickly.

'Working on a Sunday, eh?' Sheena grins. 'Lord's day of rest and all. What would Uncle Frank have said?'

'He'd probably tell me to stop drowning the lettuce.' I point past her to the leafy globes resting in the soil like a row of buried heads. 'Can't bloody help myself. Here,' I grab a hand and help her to her feet, setting a hand to her belly. It feels tight and warm. 'How's she been treating you, our little one?'

She sets her hand over mine. 'Early start, but no surprises there. Coffee's the hardest thing, eh boyo?' She smiles to Bradley. 'Just like it was with this one.'

Bradley returns the grin, a little hesitant, still. He squints as he looks to me. The sun is high and strong, but it's more than that.

'I got your favourite, kiddo.' I lift the paper bag, making it crinkle. 'From Kuripuni.'

His eyes stay on me, ignoring the offering. It's as though I'm something he's just found in his digging, some mud-borne creature he can't yet name.

Time. That's all it is.

'You sure you're all right, Aunty?' Sheena squeezes my arm. 'Is it the Jessie stuff?'

'Something like that.' I wipe at my eyes, gesturing across the lawn to the porch. 'Come on, then. There's ginger beer in the fridge.'

'He…uh, we might've made a start there already.' Sheena giggles.

'Just while we were waiting,' says Bradley.

Laughter, and bright colours in their eyes. My heart gives a leap. After everything in the station, everything in the hospital, it's a balm to see these two. A man's hand tight around my arm, and his expression making me smaller. All those assessments and papers, all those thin glances. A dead phone, and oblique statements from a terrified boy. And yet here there is laughter and warmth.

'That's all right.' I take Sheena's hand as I walk, feeling more like myself than I have since I saddled up Bum-Bum on Friday. 'It's all for you two anyway.'

~

While I chat to Sheena, Bradley picks through my books, a third raspberry bun in his hand, taking care—mostly—not to get icing on my Dickens. Last time he made a decent effort with the illustrated Tolstoy, but this time he cuts straight to the good stuff: Frank's old *Footrot Flats* weekender editions. It'll be thirty years next February, and I still haven't had the heart to drop them off to the Salvation Army.

'What's hydatids?' It's the kid's fifth question in as many minutes.

'A dog disease,' I call out through the doorway; I know exactly which strip he's looking at. 'They get it from eating offal.'

'Offal?'

'It's been good, having the shifts at Seven Oaks,' says Sheena. 'They've been decent about the baby, mostly. Not so much bath duty anymore. Not the heavy ones, anyway.' Sheena breathes in sharply, setting a hand on her belly. I go to stand, but she shakes her head. 'Just a kick, Aunty. Don't get excited.'

'Corgis, mum.' Bradley speaks up again. 'That's a dog, right?'

'The Queen's dogs, yep.' Sheena keeps her attention on her glass of ginger beer. When she picks it up, the beads of water on the outside slide down onto her fingers. 'The little ones.'

'Oh.' There's the sound of a page turning. 'Like a chihuahua?'

'You ever see Bill Kelson in there?' I reach into the fridge for the bottle and refill her glass.

'Bill?' She frowns. 'Only for tea times. He's a bit far gone for me. They wouldn't risk it, the dementia and that.' The glass comes to her lips again. 'He's still strong enough to be a hassle if he gets turned around. One of the guys sprained a wrist at bedtime last month, giving Bill a fright.' She allows herself a tiny grin. 'Serves him right, in a way. Some blokes are bloody rough undressing the old ones.' Her eyes go to mine. 'Why's that?'

My hands go to my mug. 'Not sure just yet.' I fill my mouth with coffee, wondering how much I can say. You tell one person around here, you might as well print mailbox flyers. Even with whānau. Especially with whānau. 'It's the Mowbrie stuff. Jessie and Bea.'

Sheena nods, a new brightness in her now. She'll have been waiting to get to the topic; I can't hold it against her, really. 'I heard they were out Tārehu way, those girls. A party or something, right?' Her sombre expression softens into something almost playful. 'You could hear Bea yelling about it from our verandah.'

'Yeah?' I think back to what I heard between them in the carpark. 'What, with Tuck?'

She shrugs. 'Whoever it was, she was giving them a real lashing.'

'What's a miso-jinnist, Mum?'

Sheena rolls her eyes. 'Aunty's got a dictionary, Brad. A good one, actually.'

'Third row at the end.' I hear his grabbing it off the shelf, then the thin sound of the pages turning. I could give him a few real-life examples by way of illustration, but now isn't the time. 'Listen, girl.' I lower my voice and scoot forward. 'You ever hear of Bea having a bit of drama in the shearing gangs? This would be going back, now. You'd have been at high school, I reckon.'

'High school?' She laughs. 'I wasn't exactly keeping tabs on the Mowbries back then, you know. Better things to spend my time on than that lot.'

'No, I know.' I shake my head. 'I just wondered if you or Moko might've heard about anything.'

She purses her lips in thought, exactly the way Debs used to do: making the top lip poke out in a little roof over the bottom one. 'It's been ages since she worked the sheds, hasn't it?' She grins. 'Ages since she worked anywhere, that one. She might as well be bolted to the couch.'

'Still.' I return the grin, letting her know I'm not having a go. 'It's horrible, what's happened. Just horrible. Imagine, your kid getting dumped in the bloody bush like that.'

There's a pause in Bradley's rustling from the lounge, before he continues his rummage through the dictionary. It's not much of a stretch for these two to imagine all kinds of wretched things. Not after last year.

'It's not just Bea, either.' Sheena nods, seemingly lost in thought. 'Moko said Micks was pretty out of sorts when he dropped her off the other night. Way quieter than usual.'

'Not surprising.' I wait for my niece to speak. There's something else lingering on her tongue; just like with Michaela, I can feel it.

'They'd been going at it a bit lately, you know.' Sheena's brows go up. 'More than just the usual teenage stuff.'

'Who?' I clutch my mug tighter. 'Micks and Jess?'

'I heard them a couple of times, out hanging the washing.' A tiny frown comes into her expression. 'Moko heard it too. Bea's place is just a few houses away, you know. It carries.'

I picture Michaela outside the hospital room, the pale screen lighting her face.

'More than just the usual stuff, eh?' Through the doorway, I can hear Bradley practising the syllables. *Me-sodge-gin-ist*. 'What did you hear, exactly?'

Sheena shakes her head. 'Nasty shit, Aunty.' She leans closer, letting me see a couple of new greys where her hair is parted. Keith would've whipped out the dye bottle at first sight, but Moko's more of a take-it-as-it-comes type. 'Micks was saying something like, Well, at least I know my mum. At least my mum still calls me.'

'Jesus.' I feel my brows furrowing. Everyone around here knows the story: Bea getting herself hapū by a fruit picker from down south, Timaru way. Jessie's never met him, the poor thing. As far as she's concerned, Timaru might as well be Jupiter. Not like Michaela's mum, running that café in Woodville with the black pudding toasties. 'Even for sixteen, that's vicious.'

A grave expression creeps over Sheena's face. 'I thought about heading over there to see if Jessie needed a cup of tea, but Moko told me to leave it. More trouble than it's worth, he reckons.'

Tuck, he means. Even for a guy Moko's size, trouble is shorthand for Tuck.

I reach for another bun, taking a bite as I turn the new information over in my head.

'Mum! The dog's doing yoga!'

Sheena grins. 'That's a word you know, eh boy?' She giggles again. 'Moko was giving it a go a few weeks ago. Had it on YouTube and everything.'

'Moko? Yoga?'

'He gets tight in the hips.' Sheena sets a hand over her side. 'Keith used to as well. It's pretty common with the tall blokes.' We sit in easy silence, listening as Bradley flips through the pages in the next room. Then I notice Sheena staring.

'What, girl?'

'Just tell me, Aunty.' She leans closer, her hair falling across one side of her face. 'Something happened this morning, right?'

I could cover things with a smile, but she's too close for that now. Instead, I give her the details: the lashing from the Chief, the words he'd had for me. By the end, I feel emptied.

'Oh, that prick,' she whispers, shaking her head. 'That absolute fucking prick.'

I hear Bradley go still next door. 'What's wrong, Mum?'

'It's nothing, kiddo.' I wipe a finger under my eye again. 'We're just...'

'If you hadn't climbed out of that fucking file room, my boy would still be in that place. Not to mention the other two.' I meet her gaze; there are blades in her expression. It's been a whole year, now. More, even. And yet the feeling is still in her. 'And that bitch would still be living next door.'

Here, she points through my window, across the lawn to the slanted shape of the old Wikaira place.

'I don't need reminding, girl.' My eyes go through the door to my log burner in the lounge. For a second I think about opening it and showing her Patty's letters, but that would really sink the afternoon.

Sheena grabs my hand and squeezes it. 'A bloke like that is never going to get out of your way on his own, Aunty.' She shakes her head. 'It'll take a good hard shove.'

On the table, my phone rings. It's Dion.

'Hang on a sec.' I pat at Sheena's hand to let me go, pick up the phone and collect myself as best I can. 'Hey, Dion. Everything all right?'

'Yeah, all good.' I can hear his squeaky intensive-care footsteps. 'I just ducked out for a second. They're both here, still.'

'Bea and Tuck?'

'Hmm? Nah, nah. Tuck and Michaela.' He stifles a burp. 'Bea's gone home for a bit. Said she needed some clothes and that.'

'Gotcha.' I motion to the phone, and Sheena nods in understanding, reaching for the rest of her bun. I move outside, my free palm keeping the sun from my eyes. 'Any change?'

'Nothing yet,' says Dion. 'Doctor said she's still stable.' There's a longer pause; I can feel his question before he asks it. 'Listen, did…did you or Rick plan to come by at all? It's just, Amo needs to sort out some stuff for work, and I…'

'Sorry, mate. Rick's off at the Kelson place for the afternoon, and I'm at home.' I walk past the planter box to the fence, out of earshot from Sheena. 'I could try for tomorrow?'

'Tomorrow, eh.'

'Listen.' I lower my voice. 'If you get the chance to chat to the girl, give it a try, eh?'

'Who, Michaela? Tuck's been giving me the death stare just for standing in the same fuckin' hallway.'

'He has to head out sometime,' I say. 'He'll be back on his long-haul routes again soon, I reckon.'

There's a long pause. 'What have you heard, Lo? Why should I try the cousin?'

I look back inside. Through the kitchen window, I see Bradley come in with another question for his mum, the heavy brick of my Collins Unabridged straining his wrists until Sheena takes it from him.

A good hard shove. All right then.

'They'd been going at it, Jessie and Micks. Some pretty nasty stuff, apparently. About Jessie's dad and all that.'

'Shit. Righto.' Dion sucks air through his teeth. 'Anything else?'

'Actually, yeah.' I step across the lawn, the dry blades of grass scraping the soles of my feet. There's the thrum of a cicada on a fencepost, the noisy industry of the world. I hold my voice even lower. 'He had her cell phone. Stu Kelson.'

'You found it on him?'

'Nah, nah,' I say. 'He turned it in at the station this morning. But he was the last one seen with her, Dion. And he's given us a story a bullock could fall through.' I think back to his lost expression across the interview table. Half-truths and omissions, a working sketch of the evening with great big blank patches. Patches the size of whole people, even. 'He's hiding something, mate. They all are.'

'Bloody hell.' I hear the disbelief in Dion's voice; I can picture his head shaking from side to side. 'The hockey star, eh? The papers'll have a party with that one.'

Then there's the squeak and snap of a bottle from behind the fence, and the sound of liquid pouring. It's close. Close enough to have heard this whole exchange.

'Shit.' My mouth hangs open. 'Hang on a sec.'

With the phone pressed to my chest, I go to the fence and stand on tiptoes. It's Hika, horizontal on his long-suffering deck chair, one hand on a tall jug of cloudy liquid fizzing with ice. He's got his shades on, but not much else: a pair of Hawaiian Speedos from fifteen kilos ago are doing a heroic job, but one can only expect so much.

'Come on then, e hoa.' He nods from behind his shades, lifting the jug in my direction. 'Plenty to go around here. You bring over some Gordon's and we'll be away laughing.'

A chuckle escapes me before I can catch it. 'Sheen's here with the boy. And anyway,' I glance sideways, 'I haven't been on the gins for a while now.'

'Suit yourself.' He seems to know what's on my mind. With a shrug, he leans down to fiddle with his radio and James

Brown starts crackling away as he reclines. 'Few more hours in the day yet if you lot change your mind.'

I watch his shades, trying to get a read on just how much he might've heard. The Kelsons' visit will be all over town soon anyway, plus we've got Heather Christensen lined up for Tuesday. Still, there are some things that would be better kept close to the chest.

'You all good there, lovey?' Hika's eyebrows clump together, their careful plucked shapes like commas fighting.

'Āe.' I do my best to smile. 'I'd better get back to it.'

'Don't let the Chief work you too bloody hard, now.' His voice slides through the fence as I turn away. 'Better things to do.'

Still smiling, I lift the phone back to my ear. 'You still there?'

'Where else would I be?' Dion takes a sip from something. He'll have damn near emptied the coffee machine by now, I'd say. 'Not at home with my boy, that's for sure.'

'Just see if you can chat to Michaela in the meantime. But don't tip your hand.'

I slide the phone back into my pocket. Through the fence, I hear the clink of ice hitting a glass, and a squeak of protest from the deck chair. The radio's on to Santana now: 'Black Magic Woman'. It was one of Frank's favourites. He and Hika sang that one together a few times, even. More than a few, now that I think on it. I pause where I am, the dry blades of grass pressing into my feet.

Suit yourself.

Backyard or not, I should've known better than to get into that stuff on the phone. Privacy's a foreign word in Rickett's Circle, in Masterton. They're whānau too, Hika and Michaela: on her mum's side, up the coast near Kairākau.

A long breath leaves me. A worry wart: that's what Frank would say. It's a Sunday, and with these two here, there's still enough of the afternoon for me to make something of it. I'll get a pot of decaf on the stovetop for Sheena, a spoonful of condensed milk each. If Bradley fancies reading a while longer I could even see about a game of Scrabble.

It can wait, all of it. Nobody's going anywhere.

TO MY SURPRISE, I wake up feeling bad for Dion. It must've been the time with Bradley; seeing him always leaves me with a bigger heart. I text for him to take the morning at home and head to the hospital myself. It must be tough, with his little boy and all: I can remember what Sheena was like at that age. Debs and Billy used to miss some big moments being away shearing all the time; she'd damn near double her vocabulary after two weeks with me and Frank.

Bloody lifesaver, types Dion. *Got a washing pile you wouldn't read about.*

No worries. Any luck talking to Micks?

I get the bouncing bubble for a while. *Nah. Quiet all arvo. Back to school today, and Tuck said he's driving timber up Taupō ways.*

Just me and Bea; I'll be able to run a few things past her. The shearer with the split knuckles, for starters. And if I play my cards right, her shouting match with Tuck in the carpark. We might even have something by the end of the day.

Something useful.

I pour myself a strong brew and head past the stables to the hospital, giving Bum-Bum a good long scratch on the way. It's another morning of hard, frank sunlight, the kind of day that would send Dad up into the verandah for the hottest hours. I'm coming past the old hospital building, hugging the shade where I can, when I see Bea's car pull in from the main road. Jessie must've been in the ward all night on her own. It's to be expected, I suppose; Bea can't exactly stay there around the clock. I walk towards her, putting a few words on my tongue to get us started off nicely, but instead of coming towards the hospital, she beeps her sedan locked and heads over the road to the dairy. After a moment's pause, I follow her. It won't hurt to catch her away from the ward.

Bea crosses the road without looking, making a logging truck cycle down a gear with a passive-aggressive whine; the driver shakes his head through the open window as he comes past, but mellows when he gets a better look at her. She keeps herself tidy in the waist, Bea: she's one of the few who can put in a daily innings on the couch and not just graze her way through the fallow hours. It's easy to forget, but she's not much older than Sheena: five or six years, a short enough gap to have mixed with some of the same crowd. She steps up onto the footpath, arms wrapped around herself as if it were August, not March.

In the dairy, I find her grabbing a bright green can of energy drink from the fridge.

'Morning, Bea.'

She gives a start, pausing in place before she heads to the counter. 'Hi.' Her eyes go to the drawer behind the till. She nods, and the guy produces a packet of Bensons. 'Heading somewhere?'

'Coming in to see your girl, actually.' I watch her movements. She holds her card to the reader, her cheeks puffy and tired. 'Dion said she was much the same. Stable.'

'Stable.' She sweeps the smokes and the can of drink into her handbag. 'Sounds almost like a good thing, coming out of your mouth. My girl, being stable.' When she looks at me again, I can make out the red veins under her foundation. 'Not like she's been chucked in the fuckin' trees like a bag of dirt.'

'Hang on, now.'

She shoves past me, all spittle and elbows. The chap behind the counter gives me a blank expression, then goes back to his phone and the compressed static of a crowd cheering. I turn and follow Bea as close as I dare, across the footpath to the road's edge. There are cars coming, but she doesn't seem to have noticed.

'Bea!' I grab her arm and pull her back onto the footpath as a ute slides past, its horn bursting through the air, a team of dogs on the back all leaning and barking.

She jerks out of my grip, her eyes wide and furious. 'What are you even doing, coming here?' A hard finger pokes into my chest. 'Keeping tabs on my brother? Is that it? You should be out there looking for the snivelling little pricks who put my girl in there.' She steps closer, pushing me back a step; there are flecks of white leaping from her mouth, and all the while, cars fly past us in the road. 'And then that bastard copper has the nerve to try to get alongside my niece, eh? Waiting until she was on her own?'

'It's okay, Bea.' My hands come up. 'We're doing every-thing we can. You know that.' I'd touch her, but it definitely wouldn't help. 'Dion was just following something up.'

'Yeah?' She squints. 'What, exactly?'

With a long breath, I turn us away from the road. 'The Kelsons gave a statement yesterday.' Careful, now. 'About the night of the party.'

'The boy, you mean? Stuart?' Her eyes dart past me into the road. 'The one who asked her out there?'

'That's right.' I choose my words, searching for something that won't send her palm into my cheek. 'We're talking to anyone who might shed some light on what's happened, Bea. Anyone who might know more about the state of things between Micks and Jessie.'

'The state of things?' She balls her hands and lifts them to her hips. 'They're best mates, Lorraine. You know that. Everyone does. You see them every other day, don't you?'

With quick fingers she pulls the smokes from her purse, unwrapping the cellophane and jamming one between those white sharp teeth. She's about to put the pack away when she catches herself, and holds the box out for me. Despite everything, there are still ways things are done: a fresh pack of smokes, a neighbour.

I shake my head—no thanks—then say, 'I do, Bea. I see them enough to know they'd had a row.' With a long pause, I watch her expression. 'About Jessie's dad and all.'

I expect her pupils to flare again, but there's just the same grey surface: the weight and the fatigue, the impossibility of what's happened. What's happening. Her mouth is slightly open, the smoke hanging from her lip like a half-formed thought. There's hesitation in her, an impulse she's wrestling with both hands. Then she turns away and stomps back into the road. This time she looks out for traffic. It's something, I suppose.

'Bea.' I follow her across the road and into the hospital carpark, not quite able to keep up. 'I know it can't have been easy. I know it's...'

'You don't know a fuckin' thing.' I hear tears coming. 'You don't.'

'All right, tell me. Tell me, and I can help you.'

She stops, still facing away, her slim frame tucked between the rows of parked cars. A breath of smoke slides sideways from her mouth and clings to her shoulders. We're standing in about the same spot where she and Tuck were arguing. I try to recall what Tuck said exactly; truck window open, engine screaming.

You knew it was pushing things.

'The Kelson station. Tārehu.' I speak into her back, and she

123

turns around. 'It was a surprise for you, wasn't it. To hear they'd gone out there.'

She frowns and takes another drag, letting the smoke curl around her mouth. 'Too right it was.' Her gaze stays on me. 'They don't know any of that lot.'

I feel myself squint. How easy it is, trading caricatures. There's such venom in her, now: in the sideways pull of her mouth, in the hardness of her expression.

'It's more than that, though.' I move closer.

There's something cornered in her now. 'What are you talking about?'

'The row you had, out at the Kelson place,' I say. 'With a rousey and one of the guys from the shearing gang. The year before you had Jessie.' Her eyes go wide and clear. 'Bill Kelson had to come and break it up, didn't he? After you split some bloke's knuckle with a handpiece?'

Her mouth draws tight. 'That's what you've been looking into?' There's a short scrape against the pavement as she moves forward. 'Some little silver-spoon fuckwit nearly kills my girl, and it's *my* sheet you're digging up?'

I hold myself straight, turning my good hip to her; if she tries anything, I'd rather take a hit on that side. 'It was the same station, Bea. The same woolshed.' Her expression could melt steel. 'You never thought to mention it?'

'Fucking hell, Lorraine.' She turns to go. 'Just do your job, whatever the fuck it is, and leave me out of it.'

'Bea.'

Her wrist comes across her nose, just like Michaela's. With

a practised flick she sends her half-smoked cigarette across the hood of a parked car. I stay where I am, the acrid waft of smoke in my nose. With short, jerky steps, Bea reaches the entrance and disappears into the building. I can hear the traffic sliding past behind me, a river of sound, endless.

I SPEND THE afternoon going over the photographs Ambrose took out at Tārehu, but nothing jumps out at me. The woolshed looks just like I remembered, like every other woolshed in the country: flaking roofing iron and old windows twisting in their frames. Alongside the shed, a sagging seven-wire fence borders a grazing paddock where a tidy-looking filly in a shade jacket stands, staring past the camera to Ambrose with huge dark eyes. It's Lily's horse, Rick tells me. Apparently she's a rider from way back—grew up on one of the nearby stations.

'She's a Brooke, you know.' Across the other side of my desk, Ambrose folds his arms. He seemed reluctant to come downstairs at first, but it's the only place to really spread everything out.

'As in Arthur Brooke?' I squint, learning back in my chair until it squeaks.

'Her dad. You've run into him?'

A sour taste fills my mouth. 'Once or twice, yep.'

'Their place has been in the family since they broke the bush, pretty much.' A wry smile comes across his mouth. 'Old Bill Kelson would've been happy as a sandhopper, his boy marrying into that blood.'

'He would, wouldn't he?' I fold my arms and look to the ceiling. My usual spider has shifted corners.

'You all right there, Lorraine?' Dion slides a file back onto the shelves. 'You've got a weird mug going.'

Names, faces. A horse. The land. 'It's nothing. We're all set for Heather and the others tomorrow, yeah?'

'Graham reckons it'll be the easiest time for it.' Rick nods. 'Most of them have got PE, so no big loss. Just, uh...' He clears his throat. 'Just try to hang back this time, Lorraine.'

'I bloody loved PE.' Dion smiles.

'Course you did.' Rick slaps him on the shoulder and heads for the stairwell. 'We'll try the other lad tomorrow, too. Tāmati.' He lifts his fist to his mouth, stifling a burp. 'Meantime, I'll drop by the hospital and see if I can get Bea back onside.'

Smirking, the Chief climbs the stairs, sending low shakes through the building. When he's gone, Dion is still staring at me. 'What?' I ask.

'I've no idea what you were aiming for, winding her up outside the dairy like that.' Dion shakes his head. 'With her kid in the ward and all.'

'We could fill a whole row down here with what she's not

telling us, mate. She and the Kelsons both.' I lean forward and slide my phone from my pocket, bringing up my chat with Sheena. 'You can see that as well as I can.'

He shrugs, checking his watch. 'I'm off then. That Bashir bloke at the timber plant wanted someone to check his camera setup. The forklift joyriders and that.'

'Lucky you.'

'Long as I'm out of that bloody ward.'

I hear him plodding up the stairs. My fingers move across the screen.

You've got a shift at Seven Oaks yeah?

There's a long pause. *Five start. Y?*

I gaze down the stacks, letting my eyes lose their focus. All these shelves coated with dust, their sheafs of paper coiled and waiting. Paper and ink. Impressions, hunches. Stories.

Mind picking me up?

~

Sheena parks in her usual spot, waving away my offer of a hand getting out of the car.

'I'm hapū, Aunty.' She heaves herself to her feet. 'Not bloody IHC.'

'All right.' I back off, raising my hands. 'It's for her sake, you know. Not yours.' I set a hand to her belly. 'You're a lost cause anyway.'

Her giggle echoes across the carpark, making a couple of the rest-home residents turn in our direction like fairground clowns, mouths open and waiting for ping-pong balls. We'll be interrupting their doze. One of them, a fuzzy-haired woman in a knitted blanket despite the sun, waves to Sheena, smiling wide.

'She's almost gone, that one.' Sheena returns the wave, whispering sideways. 'It's been all downhill for her these last months. The son moved to bloody Canada.'

'You can just push me out to sea, you know.' I grab her hand. 'When the time comes.'

'Oh, can it. You're still out here chasing ratbags.' She squeezes my hand, nodding to the waving woman. 'We'll go through the back. I'll sign you in as though you're visiting her.'

'Why the cloak and dagger?'

'It's the Kelsons,' Shena mutters. 'Pat and his wife don't want anyone seeing Bill without their say-so.'

'Without their say-so?' I hear the disbelief in my voice. 'He's that poked, is he?'

'Good days and bad.' She shrugs as we come up the steps. 'I get the feeling it's mostly Lily.' A cloud crosses her eyes. 'She got all hōhā last time she brought her boys in to say hi. Bill had pissed himself just before they pulled up, and nobody had the chance to sort him out.' She opens the door and tucks me inside. 'She was worried someone might see him like that. You know her type.'

Her type. Pākehā, she means, but now's not the time to get sniffy. 'I get it.'

The smell of cabbage and talcum powder hits my nose; the place is half-frigate kitchen, half-nursery. A haggard woman in a cleaner's smock comes past with a knowing look.

'He's down the end, there.' Sheena leans closer, whispering as she clutches my hand. 'Best not to let him get between you and the door.'

There's a slow twist through my stomach. 'Okay.'

'One of the others can give you a lift home after, if you need.'

'The walk will do me good, girl.' I find her cheek, and she moves down the hall. There's an endless procession of chins to wipe, of rubber dinner trays to clear away. It's good, her having something like this. Regular hours, a routine. Bradley hasn't seen much of his mum working these last few years, and he should know where his coco pops come from.

I move from doorway to doorway, keeping my feet soft and quiet. At the end of the hall, a tag reads *W. Kelson*. The name is printed out on thin temporary paper, its metal sleeve scratched and worn from so much coming and going. I stop in place, staring at the letters and listening to the low chorus of time accreting: muffled footsteps and running water, and a radio playing talkback. Dad came in here for a bit himself, actually, not long after Debs died. He didn't exactly take to it.

What would he say, knowing where I am? Knowing who I'm here to see?

A door clicks open from the far end of the hall, filling the air with voices. Too loud and distinct to be residents. I push the door open with a low creak, and there's Bill in an armchair the colour of mustard facing a small television in the corner. The news is on; I can't tell if he's heard me. There's a new smell in my nose, something musty, like old lawn clippings. In the hallway behind me, I hear the voices go past.

'Bill? I...' My eyes snag on a framed map hung on the wall over the bed. Elevation lines and paddock names: *Corner Bush, Big Bluff, Dog Leg I and II*. It's a map of Tārehu. At the easternmost corner of the map is Dad's old block. Our old block.

When I tear myself away, I find Bill turned around in his chair, his slate eyes taking me in. There's silver stubble across his chin, and a droop in one cheek rendering him not quite symmetrical.

'Hi, Bill.' I muster a smile and move forward. 'How have you been?' He stares back, his expression as blank as an empty page. 'You won't remember me, but I...'

'Back already, eh?' As different as he looks, his voice is the same: like fencing wire creaking tight around the post. 'Did they close early?'

'Close?' I watch his face, seeing the unvarnished expectation, the childlike sense of a promise being kept. 'Yep, they did.' It was the same with Dad in those last few years: always yes, never no. 'You were right.'

'Lazy beggars.' He chortles and turns back to the screen. It's something about fuel levies, the reporter's voice droning on. 'Always been keen to knock off early, even when you're waiting on a tyre.' A cough rattles through his chest. 'It's that Irish blood. His father was the same.'

I move further into the room, a square box about the size of my kitchen. The smell becomes stronger, but it's manageable—and he's got a window. It'd be a coveted spot, this one; Pat and Lily must've forked out.

'How about a cup of tea, eh?'

'The girl will be around in a bit. I wouldn't bother.' Then he purses his lips, and his expression brightens. 'Did you bring any?'

'Any?' I pat at my pockets. There: inside my jerkin, I feel the tiny square of my last toffee. It'll be risky with teeth as old as Bill's, but it's all I've got. 'Here.' I hold my palm open, spreading it flat like I would with a horse. 'Your favourite.'

'Tops, darl.' He takes it with a shaking hand, his knuckles pointing through papery skin. 'Absolute tops.'

His fingers grasp at the lolly, shaking and struggling with the twists of waxy paper. I reach out and unwrap it for him; he opens his mouth and turns to me, waiting. Who am I, here? Are these misfiring neurons giving him a sister? A daughter? Jesus, a wife?

Whose phantom am I?

'Here we go, then.' I slide it into his mouth, watching him feel with his tongue for the smooth shape. 'Good?'

'Lovely, just lovely.'

He leans back, making the armchair creak. A soft sucking comes from his mouth, the television low enough that it catches in my ear.

'You've been sleeping all right?'

'Weather's on.' He holds up a palm between us, eyes fixed to the map onscreen: those friendly isobars and the blue dots for rain, the concentric circles for the pressure and shifts in wind. 'Mob of two-tooths to bring in first thing,' he mutters. 'Gang won't crutch them damp.'

We watch the screen in silence, until the forecast moves southward to Nelson. Mum had the same rule: no television at the dinner table, except for ten to seven every night.

'Looks like it'll be a clear one.'

'Mm.' Satisfied, he leans back further, the ginger ends of his hair pressing against the fabric of the chair. I don't remember it ever being this long; none of the farmers ever let it grow over the ears. I wonder if he even realises. 'Clear enough.'

'I was thinking, the other day.' I do my best to sound nonchalant, familiar. 'About the shearers. The summer mobs and all that.'

'Buggers left crayfish in the shed bin one Christmas.' Bill clucks his tongue. 'Only found the poxy things once we came back from the coast. You remember the pong, darl? How Pee Wee wouldn't go in?' He lets out a dry, rueful laugh. 'Absolute sods, the lot of them.'

'Silly bunch.' I shake my head, smiling. At least I know who I am, now. My gaze moves over the room, snagging on the divots in everything, the scratches of paint flecked away in a thousand collisions. He's big in the shoulders, Bill; I can see how he'd be a handful if he got himself turned around. 'Then that cop had to come out one summer.' I choose my words carefully, thinking back to the file. 'The girl who tossed the handpiece. Remember that?'

'Lordy.' He slaps his knee, chuckling to himself. 'Nearly had a charge on our hands, there.' Another cough works its way up and through his chest, thick and heavy. 'No surprises, though. A girl like that, from her family. It happens.'

'Her family?'

He turns to me. 'They're kettles on the boil, that lot. You know that, darl.' A long shake of the head, almost reverent. 'Bugger all to be gained where the Mowbries are concerned.'

A new bright feeling moves through me. An engine ticking over, a weatherboard nailed snug against its neighbour. It's in here somewhere, in this burly confused man pinned in his boxy room with its spirit of cabbage and sleep hanging in the air.

Information. For me, and for Jessie.

'Too right, love.' I pat him on the hand, not too familiar, but enough to keep him focused on the memory. 'He never deserved it, either. The shearer.' Easy, now. 'The split knuckles.'

'Oh, I'm not sure about that, love.' He sucks on the lolly, then bites; there's a crack as the brittle caramel gives way to shards. 'It's in every lad's blood to tomcat from time to time, but he put himself in a mucky spot, you know. The baby and all.'

'Hmm.' I nod back to him, my mind racing. 'And the other one, the rousey. When did...'

'She shouldn't have been in the sheds anyway.' A deeper shake of the head, now. 'Not that kind of work, even in the early months.' He clucks his tongue, looking at me harder. 'You could tell just from being on the boards something was bubbling. Always is, with their lot.'

'Still.' My mind is racing. 'It's a good thing he didn't want to press the charge. Would've thrown the whole gang out of schedule.' I watch his eyes move. 'Turned out for the best, didn't it? With the shearer? I forget who...'

'You didn't bring it, did you?' He's sitting up straighter, now, his expression like silt spreading through water after a landslide. 'You forgot. Again.'

'Hmm?' I lean away, seeing the cords in his neck pull tighter. He teeth shine through his open lips, their incisors sharp. 'I did, darl. I gave it to you already.'

'I told you.' He leans forward. A switch has flipped, here. This is the old Bill, the Bill who stuck us for our block, who did us over. 'Didn't I tell you?'

He's faster than I expect. His hand shoots out and grabs my wrist, hard. I try to twist away, but he has me. He stands, as tall as Pat, maybe taller. I feel his size in this room, this cell. I'm back in Martinborough, here, clawing at the high window and listening for footsteps across the grass outside. I push at him, but his hand is a rat trap.

'Bill,' I hiss, looking to the door. 'Bill, you let go now.'

'All bloody day I'm in here.' There's a new fragment in his expression, now; something is breaking in him, falling down and away. 'All day, with no one. No one.' He grips me tighter, twisting my arm sideways until my vision flashes white. 'And then you...'

'Mr. Kelson?' A voice sounds from the doorway. 'What's the matter here?'

His attention splits for a moment. With a hard twist, I

wrench my arm from his grasp. There's already a reddening band of skin, and a bruise in the mail. I stretch out my fingers; it doesn't feel like anything's broken.

'Who are you?' A younger woman stares at me, a tea trolley in the hall behind her.

'Sorry.' Stammering, I duck sideways, out of Bill's reach. 'I was, uh…I was looking for my niece. For Sheena.' I breathe hard, moving quickly to the door, past the bed and the station map. 'Sheena Henry.'

'She's doing the dinners.' The woman looks between us, taking in Bill's state. 'Wait in the hall, I'll fetch her.'

'No, it's…it's fine.' I try for a smile. 'I can manage.'

'No one comes.' Bill stays where he is, his tall shape bordered by the bright window. His cheeks are wet. 'No one.'

The woman nods for me to make room, then steps closer to Bill. Her arms go out, practised and steady. 'We'll need to sit, Mr. Kelson. Sit for a nice cup of tea.' Her voice is honeyed. 'There we are, now. There we are.'

There we are.

I slip into the hall, still holding my wrist, and find the door to the goods entrance. In the carpark outside, the smell of old fat slides up my nose; a trap must need emptying somewhere. But I'm outside. I breathe as deeply as I can bear, taking the steps two at a time, until I'm on firmer ground. My feet take me away, and the sunlight holds me in its closed fist.

IT TAKES TWO and a half rosés to get me back to myself. There's still enough warmth in the evening for some time outside on my chair, feet up on the edge of the planter box, my toes curling over the grains of wood in Frank's old railway sleepers. I can hear Hika's music through the fence, but I don't much fancy a chat. Not right now.

The wrist has calmed down a bit after some ice in a tea towel, the red band of raised skin dulled to a lighter shade. It's bloody tender, but nothing I can't sort out with a few Panadol. By tomorrow, Ambrose and Dion might not even ask about it. Hopefully—I'm not sure how I'd explain it.

The broad shape of that man, and the dormant strength inside those hands, still. Sixty years hauling strainer posts and tucking wool bales into their place: it'll take more than a few years pissing yourself in Seven Oaks to drain that away.

Just like Dad.

The bad taste on my tongue is more than just the nine-dollar rosé. Jesus, I might even have sympathy in me for him after everything he did, everything he took. It was bloody clever, actually. After three decades and a belly full of wine, I can say it.

I can say all of it.

They'd come to see Dad in person to get him on board. Bill Kelson and Arthur Brooke: two of the oldest farming families sitting on our verandah drinking tea with too many sugars while Dad heard them out. It wasn't too long after Debs and I had moved into town. The wool price had bottomed out, and with Labour taking the axe to all of Muldoon's safety nets, there were plenty of farmers eating porridge and chops for dinner. Bill and Arthur would've been able to guess just from the state of the ute that dad was in a tight spot: tyres running near-bald and a rattle from the muffler. They picked their moment, those two, to pitch him on planting a joint pine block at the westernmost boundary of our place, with a consortium from up north paying in advance for logging access. The numbers weren't great, but Dad was good and stretched, and it didn't take a lot to get him nodding along. He got our lawyer in town to check things over, of course. The bloke was a Brooke by marriage, but that didn't matter. Not at the time.

Things went all right for the first couple of years. The consortium payments were enough to keep the roof up; they even went away to the coast for a few days one Christmas, just the two of them. The block they'd planted—Big Bluff—had never been the best grazing anyway. Too steep for cattle, and an absolute prick to muster, even with our best horses. Dad was only too happy to shut it up and forget about it for a bit.

It all came out the next year, when Debs and I visited for Mum's birthday. It took a bit of a nudge, but eventually Mum told me. The projected timber price had dropped below the contracted threshold, which gave the consortium the option to back out of the deal and take back their payments. Dad was worrying himself into a stick about it, and Arthur and Bill were apparently furious, too. The three of them dragged it out as long as they could, with Dad calling the bank manager every other week to beg for breathing room. In the end there was nothing for it: we'd have to put some acres on the market. It was the worst possible time. Interest rates were criminal back then, and nobody had the cash to make any offers.

Then Bill Kelson came around with a bottle of Grant's and a proposition. He'd been chatting to Arthur, and they'd come up with enough capital to buy out the pine consortium and take its place in the deal. But, he said, to make it work they'd have to double the size of the block, most of which would come from Dad's land. They'd take care of paying what Dad owed the pine company, so long as he agreed to plant an extra eighty hectares on the same terms as before.

They knew he had no other option. And sure enough Dad went for it, and we culled the herd to make room. The same Brooke lawyer took care of the paperwork again, and things ticked along. Dad got used to not being able to push a mob through that part of the farm, and he started getting cheques in the mail again, this time from Bill and Arthur's trust.

Then the timber price dropped again: low enough for Bill and Arthur to recoup their own payments to Dad. This time there was no bottle of Grant's and no footsteps on the verandah; there was only an envelope in the mail. Eventually even the bank manager stopped returning Dad's calls. By the next winter, we'd run out of options and Dad had to put the whole place on the market, not just carve off this or that paddock. It was for the best, Mum reasoned. Me and Debs were both getting things started in town, and every day was starting to feel like winter.

So, auction day. And guess who turned up, ready with their accountants? Bill Kelson and Arthur Brooke. They even had enough bollocks between them to shake Dad's hand afterwards.

Tough luck, Mickey.

Mum and Dad ended up with enough for a house in Greytown with a lawn for the dogs, and a bit left over for Debbie, to help her get set up for baby Sheena. That was about it: our block got divvied up between Tārehu and the Brooke station, with Bill Kelson taking the lion's share. A bigger slice for their kids to come into—Pee Wee and Lily at the top of the list—and one less neighbour to help gather the hermit ewes whenever they pushed through the boundary fence. Mum tried hard to put a brighter shade on things, and even seemed to enjoy the part-time teaching job she found, but Dad was never the same. That townie house with its quarter-acre section, the neighbours always calling about the dogs barking: it was like he was wearing someone else's shirt. The horses were the hardest thing. Seeing old Samson go was like sending a son off for dog tucker.

And now.

Now Bill Kelson gets to go to sleep with that map on the wall. *Corner Bush. Dog Leg I and II.* He even stole our names for the paddocks, the prick.

And somewhere in those grifted acres, Jessie found herself in a spot of real trouble.

~

The sun's coming over Hika's fence, leaving just the grey-blue twilight to creep over the garden and the trees, over the dregs of the day. At the far edge of the lawn, the magpies are crooning. Something furry brushes against my dangling fingertips. I hear a low chirp from Tilly.

'Hello, lovely.' It's simpler, of course, not having land. This is probably all a person should need: two rows of lettuce, a cactus glasshouse and a parking spot nobody ever uses. 'Teatime, is it?'

I spoon some jellymeat into Tilly's bowl and roll some sausages into a pan. Over the sizzle the phone rings.

'Lorraine?' It's Ambrose. 'Where have you been?'

'What? I'm at home, Rick. What do you...'

'I've been trying you for the last half-hour.'

Jesus, mate. Pick a lane.

I look out the window to the blue shapes of the garden.

Everything is growing dimmer, darker. 'I left my phone inside.'

'Doesn't matter.' I can hear his footsteps scuffing over gravel. 'Lily Kelson called. It's Stuart.' A car door slams, and his voice changes, growing tighter and more serious. His cruiser sparks to life in the background. 'He went out for a training run from Langsford and hasn't come back.'

'They're sure he's not just taking a longer run?' I switch off the element; the sausages are spluttering. 'It can't have been more than a few hours, Rick.'

'They've been out to check all his usual routes already,' says the Chief. 'Drove damn near to Mount Bruce, they said. Nothing.'

My eyes lose their focus. In the watery murk, I see the shape of the fence between my place and Hika's, the wooden slats portioning the night between us. It's solid, this fence. But not so solid as to keep someone's phone call from being heard.

He had her cell phone. Stu Kelson.

'Okay.' I feel ice in my belly. 'I'm coming now.'

'I'm already on my way to you.'

I hang up the phone and grab the edge of the bench, ignoring the throb in my wrist. I can feel myself breathing.

I WRAP A couple of sausages in bread and butter with some Watties for the road. The Chief's much too distracted to care about me stinking up the cruiser.

'They took a drive already, you said?'

'Huh?' Rick frowns sideways.

'Sorry.' I swallow my mouthful. 'They've been out to look for him already, right?'

'Whole bloody boarding house is out there with their flashlights, Graham said.' We pull through the outskirts of town and Rick guns the engine, making the neat fences and new-build houses slip past us in a blur of grey and white. 'Pat's been checking all his old smoking spots down by the river, just in case.'

'He didn't strike me as the smoking type, Stu Kelson.' I get my next sausage ready, tweaking my wrist as I move. 'Tobacco or otherwise.'

'Nah. But still.'

The motion's not doing great things for my guts, but I force myself to finish the second snarler: it could be a long night. I stare through the windscreen into the last of the daylight, slivers of sun clinging high against the hillsides like the edge of a golden blanket being pulled away.

A fence, and a deck chair. Santana playing low and lazy, and a full jug. Enough open air to let my words—unthinking, careless even—travel to waiting ears.

He's hiding something, mate. They all are.

'You all right there, Lorraine?' I feel the Chief watching me across the cab, staring at my bad wrist. 'I'd slow down, but Lily Kelson's called me twice since we started the drive.'

'All good.' I could share my hunch, I suppose. I could cleave off this gnawing thing and halve its weight. But I'll need a little more trust in the ledger for that. 'Give it heaps. I'm just...it's nothing.'

We come to the turnoff, back past the lifestyle blockers with their pristine utes, and through the tall steel Langsford gate. Everything looks different in the dark, the vivid green of the commons turned to a flat void between the hunched shoulders of the classroom blocks. Rick wasn't kidding: the whole school does seem to be out looking for Stu, all the footpaths and leafy nooks lit up with flashing pockets of white light from the boys' phones.

'There's Dion.' The Chief nods to the auditorium carpark. 'He must've hoofed it out here.'

It's a relief, seeing Dion's broad shape under the auditorium lamplight. Even if he's not best pleased with me right now, his familiar presence helps to still the churning in my guts. He's chatting to Graham, the chaplain, both men wearing serious expressions. As we pull closer, I notice a third person hidden in their shadow. Lily Kelson, hands welded to her hips, shaking her head like she's working a disobedient dog. When I open my door, I catch a stream of choice words coming from her.

'...responsibility to ensure the safety of our boys, Mr Young. That's what our thirty grand a year's for, isn't it?'

The chaplain takes a half-step back, his hands held up and open. 'We're taking this extremely seriously, Lily. You know that.' He turns to us, his expression flooding with relief. 'Chief Ambrose. Your constable's been most helpful.'

'Helpful?' Lily frowns. 'All you've done is natter on like a couple of bedwetting old pricks. All while my boy is God knows where, and everyone is...'

'How long's it been?' Rick speaks directly to Lily. It puts her back for a second. 'When would he usually come back?'

Lily pauses, her features softening. 'He called home at Milo time, like always.' There's a tiny brightening in her eyes: pride, and love. A son. A dependable boy, a leader. And he's hers to stand beside.

'He went out around quarter past eight,' says Graham, holding his back straight. 'That's second prep for majority of the boys, but the rep players get a dispensation to train, providing they're back and showered before nine.'

'And they're back, are they?' The chaplain's silver eyebrows curl at the sound of my voice. 'The others?'

'Ages ago.' Lily crosses her arms, exhaling deep and long.

'I spoke to the other lad.' Dion points to a group of boys standing just out of earshot, heads bent down to their phones. I recognise Tāmati watching us out of the corner of his eye, trying not to be seen. 'He said Stu wanted to put a few more sprints in near the main road.'

'Tāmati?' I squint. 'He's not a rep player, is he?'

Graham's nose twitches. 'He runs with Stuart most nights. They keep each other steady, those two.'

'My boy doesn't need help staying steady.' Lily shakes her head. 'You know that.'

'All right, now.' Rick moves between them. 'Let's stay on track, shall we?' He checks his watch. 'I've got quarter to eleven, so we're only talking about a couple of hours, here.' He looks between Lily and Graham. 'Are there any particular spots the boys head to around here? To blow off some steam, let's say?' A knowing glint comes into his eye. 'The share-milkers next door have been calling about those smashed-up computer monitors down by the river where their heifers graze.' He gives me a look, then turns back to the chaplain. 'Any chance Stu might've felt like busting something up? After yesterday and all?'

The ghost of a smirk travels between the three men. Boys and breaking glass. We've all been there, they seem to be saying. Even the chaplain, the dusty old stick, is puffing his chest out, trying to mirror Dion and Ambrose.

'Stuart felt much better after yesterday.' Lily steps forward into the centre of the men, speaking directly into Rick's chest.

'He was telling us how good it felt to help the investigation, and to share what he knew about everything with that girl.' She holds her eyes to Rick's, her voice laying a film of acid under her words. I could help, but I stay where I am. 'Before you start tossing around insinuations on where my boy is or what he might have done to himself, you'd do well to remember he came in on his own steam.'

The chaplain lifts a lanky arm. 'All right, now. Let's not...'

'It's all right, mate. We're all on the same page here.' Rick edges Lily away from the others, bending lower to her. As they move, Lily's eyes find mine, full of the hot dark shine of trapped feeling. It needs to go somewhere. Privacy and space: Rick will need her to simmer a bit before he'll get anything useful. I leave Dion chatting to the chaplain and approach the circle of boys standing to the side. Tāmati keeps staring into his phone with his hood up, even when I get next to him. Alvin, the Leongs' boy, is the first one to speak.

'Hi, Mrs Henry.' He's got a smile just like his dad's. Even if he's a bit shy around his mates, it still comes out as easy as anything.

'Doing all right, Alvin?' He nods back to me, looking to Tāmati. The other boys are staring too, waiting for Tāmati to respond. There's a sense of something interrupted in the air between them: a story only half-told, something I could almost grab with my own hands. I decide to keep my mouth shut and wait. It doesn't take long.

'We spoke to the big guy already.' Tāmati stays hunched

into his screen. He's flicking through his texts, I think. 'He can fill you in.'

'He can, eh?' I catch Alvin's eye and nod him sideways. 'I reckon you could just as easily fill me in yourself, eh? Just for fun?'

Alvin nudges his mate, and they break off, heading for the yellow lights of the boarding house behind them. The third boy follows, and so does Tāmati.

'Just a second, mate.' I grab his elbow, hard enough for him to get the picture. He stands in place, frowning at my hand, his eyes still reflecting the light from his screen. The other boys' footsteps scuff through the dark.

'I told you.' He mutters. 'We already spoke to the…'

'Don't fuck me about, kid.' I lean closer, making myself unavoidable. His nose crinkles up; I'm hoping the sausages are covering up the rosé. They were pork and rosemary from the Fresh Price discount bin, so my chances are good. 'I don't give a toss what you told Dion. You can tell me again.' I relax my grip, but keep him where he is. 'Now, you both went out for a run, right?'

He looks to the chaplain to intervene, but his back's turned. My fingers close tighter around Tāmati's wrist until he grimaces. 'That's…ow, fuck. That's right.' He pulls in a quick breath. 'I told him already.'

'What time?'

There's less hesitation in him, now. 'Ten-past eight, I reckon.' He pulls his hand closer into himself, and I let go. He doesn't seem in the mood to take off anymore. 'We were

going to head just to the road. It's about five, there and back.'
He pauses, looking at my middle. 'Kilometres, I mean.'

'Got it. Thanks.' I watch his expression. 'What do you mean, going to?'

'He, uh…' The boy coughs, then continues. 'Stu changed his mind. He wanted to do some sprints, after all. The straight bit, up near the main road. It's an even hundred metres with no corners or anything.'

His gaze drops to the ground. I can tell he wants to look at his phone. And not just to kill the time. 'You don't do the sprints, then?'

'No.' His head stays bowed. 'Not tonight.'

I bend lower, angling my face to his. His eyes are wet, and he's scared enough that his whites are showing. I think back to his expression at the hockey game: the way he'd tracked Stu's movements, lingering on him even when he was off the ball, ignoring the others. When he lifts his face, there's something softer in him.

'It's okay, Tāmati.' I set a hand to his elbow, gently now. 'Something happened, didn't it? You can tell me.' I speak quietly. Behind us, Lily is still giving Rick another earful. 'It'll help us, Tama.' I move closer to him. 'It'll help Stu.'

'We…' He sniffs, and a hand comes under his eye. 'Look, I only came with him just past the gate, all right?' He points past me to the black steel shape looming tall in the dark. 'I came back early.'

'Why?' I watch his shaking hands. 'Did something happen?'

The boy hesitates, looking to the chaplain again. Then he

turns back to me, his expression more open than before. 'It was about Thursday and that. Everything with Jessie.' He pauses, and I let him gather himself. Easy, now. 'He said the cops...he said you guys had told him about some stuff in Jessie's blood test.'

'The fantasy.' I nod. 'It's true, kid. Her results showed traces of GHB.'

The boy stares at me with a lost expression. 'Stu was asking me about it. About Heather and that, especially.' His expression flickers in calculation. 'Something about a bottle.'

I watch his mouth as he speaks. The jitters, the hesitation; it seems real. 'It's something we're looking at very closely,' I say. 'If you had any ideas about it, now would be a good time to...'

'He kept going on about her,' Tāmati cuts in. 'Heather, and the debating stuff. The regionals. How she seemed about missing out.' The boy takes another long breath, deep in his chest. 'He wanted to know if I thought she was cooking something up, her and the others.'

'And?'

He looks to his feet again. 'I told him I didn't know. And I said anyway it wasn't such a big deal if someone did bring something like that.' With a long breath, he continues. 'That's when he lost it. He was saying how we owed it to Jessie to tell them if someone had done something like that. To Micks, too.' A single bead of moisture slides from his eye, rolling down the side of his nose to his mouth. He lets it stay there. 'I couldn't get him to calm down, so I came back. I sat outside the boarding house on the bench for a bit, until the bell for ablutions.'

Waiting. He doesn't say it, but he was waiting for Stu to get back.

'You don't fight all that often.' I keep my fingers on his elbow. 'Do you?'

'With Stu?' He sniffs. 'Not really. Most of the time we're on the same vibe.' His eyes flicker up to mine. 'That's...I mean, we're on the same page.'

I let myself smile. It's a good thing I've got Bradley to keep me up to speed. 'So, you would've seen him at, what, eight-thirty?'

'Quarter to nine, maybe.' He nods. 'By the first corner, at the end of the trees, there.'

'And you reckon he went off to run sprints?'

He wipes at his cheeks again. 'He does that sometimes, to get it out of his system.' A small frown clouds his expression. 'He'd get a high reading before bed sometimes, if the Milo was too strong or whatever.' He points to his pocket, standing in for Stu's. 'Put in a few sprints to bring it down.' A long moment passes. When he speaks again, it's quieter. 'You don't think anything's happened, do you?'

I keep my hand on his arm. 'No, I don't.' A surface of words, that calm and impossible sheen. What else can a person say? 'I'd say he'll be letting off some steam, like you said.'

He stares into my face. He wants to believe me, I think, but something's in the way.

New lights shine behind us, slicing open the dark. I hold my hands in front of my face, keeping the high beams out of my eyes. There's the sound of an engine slowing, and a ute pulls up next to Lily and the others. It's Pat Kelson with Rodney, and Rodney's driving. I pull out my phone for Tāmati.

'Put Stu's number in there, would you?' The kid frowns, but does as he's told. 'All right, don't go anywhere now.' I leave him where he is and head for the others.

'Dip those lights, kid.' Ambrose waves towards the truck as Pat climbs out.

'Checked all the usual spots.' Pat steps with purpose to the footpath, looking more like a foreman than a worried dad. 'Nothing. I reckon we should try down past the golf course. That was always a great spot for a few durries, back in the day.'

'Jesus, Pat, he's not out having a fag!' Lily's voice breaks into a sob.

'Come on, now.' Pat moves to her, his arms encircling her shoulders. 'He'll be off somewhere, that's all. You know how he can get.'

'We're doing everything we can.' The chaplain gives a satisfied nod.

Lily bristles and smacks away Pat's hand. There's a series of hissed syllables between them; nothing I can make out. Dion leans away from the scuffle and ambles over, trying to mask his relief at putting some distance between him and the situation.

'You drove your car, right? The Nissan?'

'Yeah, why?' He frowns, then looks back to the group. Lily and Pat have stepped away from the others, their voices getting louder while Rodney stares from inside the truck. Rick stays with the chaplain, professionally disinterested; only the slightest crinkles of his forehead give away his irritation.

'Need me to drop you home or something?' says Dion.

Ambrose looks in our direction, and he seems to read my mind. I can see the impulses warring inside him: reluctance fighting necessity. If he had his way, I'd be nowhere near this. But at this time of night, getting his way isn't top of our list. With a slow nod, he points to the gate, gesturing with his thumb to Pat and Lily, then to himself. I nod back to him, letting him know I understand.

'No.' A breeze runs over me, cold for the month. 'Not exactly.'

~

I explain everything to Dion as we drive.

'They had a tiff, eh? Stu and Timothy?' For once, he's driving slowly; I've told him how my guts can get. 'And what, you reckon he ran all the way into town, eh? To see Michaela?'

'Tāmati.' I clear my throat. 'And sure, it's possible. You've seen how fit he is.' I pull out my phone and dial the number Tāmati gave me.

'His phone?' Dion frowns as we come through the corner towards the straight section before the main road. Ahead of us, a truck sails through the dark, its orange lights like a tall apparition. 'Lily tried that already.'

'I know,' I say. 'But it's ringing.'

I hold the phone to my ear, the hope smoking in my chest like a stick of damp kindling. It would be so easy, so neat. He's gone to Michaela's on his own steam, to chat about Thursday. He's feeling like an explanation is called for, like he owes her something. It could have happened. And with Tuck away on one of his long shifts, it might even be safe.

'Nothing?' Dion pulls up at the intersection.

'Shush, for fuck's sake.'

I look out the passenger window, trying to focus. Then the briefest glimmer catches my eye, just before the call clicks over to voicemail.

A light. A light on the side of the road.

'Wait.' I turn in my seat, making my collarbone twinge. 'Back up a bit.'

'What?' We slow down and pull to the verge. There's the sound of dry grass rubbing against the bottom of the car. 'What is it?'

'Just back up.'

Dion waits for a car to pass, its headlights sending a bar of refracted white over his features, showing me his grimace. Then he reverses in the road. It's quiet outside. I pick up my phone and call the number again, holding the metal square tight in my damp palm.

'Please.' I'm whispering to myself. 'Please be something else.'

There. A square of white light laid out of the gravel verge, just past the Langsford turnoff. I look down at the phone in my hand, and out at the white square on the roadside, still glowing. When I click to end the call, the other light goes dark.

'Lorraine?' Dion is talking, but I'm underwater. 'What is it?'

WE TAKE A drive past Tuck Mowbrie's place, but it's dark and no one answers my knock except his dogs. So, Bea's it is.

At the Chief's suggestion, Stu's phone is bagged and tucked away in Dion's backseat. I don't know if anyone's told Pat and Lily; for once, it's a relief to have Rick deciding. At Bea's place, there's light flickering through the curtains: the always-on television. Dion goes to climb out.

'Hang on,' I set a hand to his shoulder. 'Maybe I'll take a first crack at this one, eh?'

Dion pauses, looking from me to the house, and a spark leaps through his expression. 'The Chief told me what happened, you know. With the Kelsons, the interview and that.' He turns in his seat, squaring up to me. 'You think it's a good idea, you making calls like this?'

I feel my head shaking. Sure, let's make this a pissing contest;

it's not like there's a kid missing. 'Just…just trust me, mate. You already got offside with Tuck once, and he's got a better memory than most.'

Dion stares back at me, unresponsive. There's a hot feeling crawling through me, clenching my hands tight together. Time. This is time we don't have.

'Fine.' He points through the window to the house. 'Go.'

'Actually, um.' I nod ahead in the road, past the carrion husk of Moko's old Commodore. The rods went just before Christmas, and it's been picked apart since. In the lamplight it looks like the remains of some mythical beast. We're only a few houses down from Sheena's, but her windows are all dark for the night. Thank God. 'Maybe you want to park out of the way a bit.'

He snorts to himself. 'Righto, Lorraine.'

While he finds a spot, I take a second to gather myself at Bea's garden gate, looking down the path alongside her house. She keeps everything tidy, Bea: she's been paying Bradley ten bucks every two weeks to keep the lawn under control with her old push mower, and an extra five if he gathers up the lawn clippings. Last month she even had the arborist out to keep her two oaks from dropping limbs: a team of three guys were there most of the morning. She's had a new deck put in out the back, too. Hard to say where she gets the coin, exactly, but it puts my crappy little verandah to shame. You'd think you were in bloody Landsdowne, looking at her place.

A cold shiver runs through me. The phone on the road. That lonely glowing square of light, tucked down in all that darkness, in all that forgotten space.

Breathe, now. We don't know anything. Not really. He could've just dropped his phone. It could be anything. It could be nothing.

When I knock, I knock quietly, as if somehow it'll excuse the hour. I'm prepared to wait, but it's only a moment before a shadow passes through the blue light pulsing inside the lounge windows and the door clicks open. It's Michaela, in a pair of trackies and a huge pink jumper.

'Lo?' Her eyes spread wide in her head. She looks over her shoulder into the hallway. 'What are you, uh…did…what's happened?' A frown comes over her. 'Did Jessie come to?'

'It's not about your cousin, girl.' Past her, I hear the sharp squeak of a shower being turned off, and a voice calling out.

'Micks?' It's Bea. 'Who's that?'

'Come in.' Michaela motions me inside. 'It's just Lorraine, Aunty.'

I move inside, and she closes the door behind me. The house is hushed and quiet. A small part of me relaxes; it'll be harder for the street's avid ears to reach us here. The hallway smells like new carpet, and beneath that, the hot buttery smell of something in the oven. A pie, Goodtime steak and cheese, most likely.

'Yeah?' Bea appears at the bend in the hallway, a towel tucked tight around her middle. Her face and neck are crayfish-red; she must've been damn near poaching herself in the shower. Her fingers go to her throat, scratching a row of fresh white lines above her clavicle. 'What's the story, then?'

'Listen, girl.' I turn to Michaela. 'You haven't heard from Stu Kelson, have you?'

She stares back, her cheeks puffy with fatigue. The days at the hospital must be weighing on her. Her eyes flit to Bea before she speaks. 'No.'

'Why would she have?' Bea puts herself between us, an angry sausage slipped from its casing. 'What, you think they're on fuckin' speaking terms, eh? After what that poxy little shit and his mates did to my girl?'

My hands come up to keep her where she is. It was a good call, Dion staying in the car. He'd be one puzzle piece too many. 'Something's happened, Bea. I...listen,' I force a smile, neighbourly and harmless. 'Is there any chance we could sit down with a cup?' I nod to the kitchen. 'I've been running around a bit tonight.'

'It's through here.' Michaela moves past me. 'I'll get the...'

'No.' The movement surprises even Michaela; Bea grabs her by the arm, hard. Then she seems to catch herself, and lets go. 'No, it's...it's just gone midnight, Lorraine. We need to be back with Jessie first thing.' With shaking fingers, Bea readjusts her towel. 'You just say your piece and let us get to bed, eh?'

Inside the wooden border of the doorway, Michaela looks trapped. She looks to the floor, one hand rubbing her arm where her aunt grabbed her.

'They can't find him.' I watch Bea's expression. 'Stu Kelson.'

'So? She frowns, shaking her head. 'What's that got to do with us?'

158

I stare back at her, but her expression gives me nothing. Her eyes are hard, and the colour of slate. 'I'm guessing your brother's pulling a haul, is he?'

There's a pause. 'That's right,' Bea nods. 'He's doing Taupō and back all this week.'

In my good ear, I catch the low murmurs of the television from the lounge: discount lawn furniture. Anyone would think this was one of a thousand houses on our side of Masterton, getting settled for the night.

'What time's he usually get started, then?'

Bea holds my gaze for a long moment. She moves closer, close enough for me to smell the soap on her. 'You didn't answer me.' Her skin is seal-slick, her shoulders coiled and ready. The redness in her neck seems to be ebbing away. 'What's any of that Langsford shit got to do with us, Lorraine?'

I take a breath. The hour feels even later than it is. 'I thought...*we* thought maybe he'd reached out to you, Micks. That's all.' I watch the girl's expression. 'But obviously not.'

'Obviously.' Bea turns to her niece, gesturing to her with an open palm. 'You'd say, wouldn't you, girl? If you'd heard anything from that little shit, or his little shit mates?'

In Michaela's eyes there's something undetermined. 'Of course.'

'All right then.' With a sigh, Bea turns back to me, wiping moisture from her temple with her wrist. 'We'll tell you if we hear anything.'

She reaches past me, clicking open the front door. As it opens, I see a handful of photos tacked to the back. There's one of a younger Tuck with the girls at the beach. Castlepoint, it looks like. He's got one on each shoulder, holding them steady in the white churn of the surf. The water's only waist-high, but it could still grab them. It's the only time I've ever seen him without his beanie on: his hair hangs thick and dark to his shoulders, a wet tendril curled halfway around his neck. He's got a hand around each girl, and he's grinning to split his head apart. They can't be much more than three in the photo, or four at the most. Jessie and Micks, both small enough for Tuck to reach around their waists, almost, with just one big hand. Small enough to need him to keep them steady and still: to keep those two sandy parcels of smiles and fears and loves in place and upright.

I'm halfway out the door before the question bolts through me. 'I was chatting to your uncle yesterday, girl.' I smile, doing my best to sound normal. 'Hika. He was out the back in his Speedos. You know the ones, right? Hardest working togs in the world, I'd say.' This would be comfortable territory to share a few giggles, once upon a time. Here, now, all I get is the same blank look from aunt and niece. 'You heard from him lately?'

'Hika?' Bea frowns. 'Uncle's putting it strong, Lorraine. More like our girl's mum's cousin, whatever that is.'

'Once removed, then.' I look to Michaela, searching for a glimmer of recognition. 'So that's a no?'

'I don't think so.' She shakes her head: a new confusion now. A real one, I think. 'We don't see him all that often.'

'He didn't even come by after last week, Lorraine.' Bea holds the edge of the door. 'Not a call, nothing.'

We stand where we are, the three of us. There's more of the cool breeze coming over my shoulders, creeping into the house to fill the vacuum. The kind of night Jessie lived through, up there in the bush. Behind me, the street is quiet.

'If there's nothing else?' Bea starts pushing the door shut.

'All right.' I step backwards into the cover of her porch, and her motion light clicks on, revealing a thin cloud of moths and midges. 'Let me know if you hear anything.'

As the gap closes, I catch one last glimpse of Michaela staring out. Her eyes are as wide as when I first knocked, and as dark as they were in the ward when she told me about the bottle and the blackout. But there's something else, now: the low tremble of fear. Not for herself, I don't think, but for someone else.

Someone close.

Transference, displacement. A bath poured too full, and the water with no place to go but the floor.

I move slowly to the street, letting my thoughts race ahead. Dion's parked just outside Sheena's. In my distraction I nearly trip at the gutter.

'You all right there, Lorraine?' He pushes open the passenger's door, setting his phone on the dash with a clatter. 'Still nothing from Langsford. They're calling around Stu's dayboy mates in town, just in case he's parked up with them.' He stifles a yawn. 'His phone could've just fallen out as he was running, you know.'

'You're closer to sixteen than I am, mate.' I slip inside his car and let my head fall back against the rest. 'You know any teenagers who can go ten minutes without their phone?'

'S'pose not.' He shrugs, nodding down the street to Bea's. 'That lot wasn't much help, then?'

My eyes stay closed for a long moment. Dion's question rattles around inside the car, mixing with whatever nameless music he's got on the radio. The quiver in the girl's lip, and the white scratches through the red skin at Bea's neck. There's something there, strung between them, wrapped around them.

When I open my eyes again, I can see better out into the night. Its depth and form. I can see the distance a night like this can hold.

'Lorraine?' I can feel Dion frowning. 'You still with us, over there?'

'Indulge me for a second.' I sigh and point ahead into the road. 'If it comes to nothing, we don't even need to tell Rick.' He's still frowning but he sparks the engine. I lean sideways, looking to the dashboard. Three-quarters of a tank. It'll be more than enough. 'We need to check the bush.'

'The bush?' His eyebrows clump together, then settle as he seems to understand.

'The Tararuas.' I zip my poncho to my neck. 'Where they found her.'

WE TAKE A right at the timber plant, heading north to the ranges. I can't make them out in the dark; there's only a jagged void where the stars end. Alongside us, the floodlight on the plant's steam vent illuminates a thick plume of grey dissipating into the empty space.

I keep my eyes to the road, watching as the car's headlights show us fences and sheds, fruit trees sheltering the low wooden houses dormant with the hour. We lurch over the railway tracks, and at the next corner a glowing pair of eyes flash next to a corrugated iron tank. A pet sheep grown improbably fat lies against the packed dry earth, a giant lump of yellowing wool. Dion's turned off his music after a few timely scowls from yours truly; it's quiet enough that I can hear his stomach murmur.

'Left the muesli bars in the patrol car.' He lifts a hand to his mouth, stifling a yawn. 'You're not going to spew or anything, are you?'

'Course not.'

I give him a glance, just enough that he won't linger. It's always these night-time drives that bring everything back. I can feel Prendergast's steering wheel under my hands again, his car snaking slow and careful through the corners as Bradley jammed the gears into place and Hēmi watched. A year. It's only a year ago, but already it feels like something that might've happened to someone else. Even after all the articles in the paper, the details seem flimsy. Those bloody letters from Patty are the only thing still making it real.

'Not far now.' Dion winds down his window. I can hear the wheels grumbling at the road. 'Hear the river, there?'

'Yes, Dion, I can hear it.'

'What's the bloody matter, then?' I can hear his frown without having to look.

'We're not on a bloody camping trip, mate.'

The window slides apologetically back into place. 'I know.' A long pause. 'It's just...it's a mint spot, out here. Dad always brought us up here for Christmas and that.' He gestures through the windscreen. 'Two weeks at a pop, me and the cousins just swimming and eating.' He snorts. 'Bloody river would be icy, even in December.'

I muster a small smile, just for him. 'Something for your boy when he's older, eh?'

He looks across the inside of the car, giving me my smile back with interest. Outside, the ranges loom even taller as we approach the Holdsworth Lodge carpark, the thick block of shadow growing like a cresting wave. It's late enough in the summer that all the Wellington tents have gone, leaving the gravel wide and empty in our headlights. Dion parks as close to the start of the Atiwhakatū loop as he can, pausing halfway out of the car to check his phone.

'It's Amo,' he says. 'Wants to know if it's a fridge night or an oven night.'

'Huh?'

'My lasagne.'

'Oh.' I push the door closed with a crisp thud, the sound even more final out here in the dark. 'Fridge, I reckon.'

'Yeah, thought so.' The tip of his tongue slips out of his mouth as he types. I pop the boot, and he helps me make sense of the collected flotsam that confronts me.

'Here.' He fishes out a yellow plastic boat flashlight and a tartan blanket. 'She's seen a few picnics too many, but she'll do.'

'Thanks.'

I pull the blanket around my shoulders and tuck it into the collar of my poncho. It smells like budget mayonnaise and takeaway chips. Somehow, I feel oddly comforted. Dion grabs a pair of Red Band gumboots and tugs them on, then digs around for a second pair.

'Amo wears a bigger size than you, but you'll be all right with those socks.'

There's room for a whole second set of toes when I pull them on, but they'll have to do. The track can get pretty mucky and my runners won't cut it; anyway, if a blister from a pair of gumboots is all the night has in store for me, I won't have too much to whinge about.

I point us ahead, and Dion shines the flashlight across the gravel to the gate marking the start of the path. There's a wooden Department of Conservation lean-to on one side of us with a battered intentions book hanging from its metal holder, the breeze spinning it slowly on its string. There won't be too many trampers heading up the trails this late in March, but it could be worth checking on the way back for names to call. Anders and Milla—they'll be in there, I'd say; they struck me as rule-following types.

'Reckon those could be recent?' Dion nods at a row of tyre marks in the gravel, horizontal across the gateway, as though someone pulled up to block the entrance.

'Could be, yep.' I bend down to take a look. 'Christ, who am I, Columbo? It's all just bloody gravel to me.'

His giggle is incongruous in the night air. 'I guess so. Still, it's something.' He bends down next to me. 'The tread looks newish. Couldn't be too many people I know.'

We move through the gateway and along the first flat section of the track, the air around us still open to the sky, before we reach the trees. There's the low murmur of the stream at our side, like a voice in my ear. I keep my eyes to the yellow beam of Dion's flashlight, noting the rises and dips in the gravel; we could have a decent walk ahead of us, and I don't need another fall to add to my list. The path is crisscrossed with scrapes and boot prints, and there's a long scratch in the stones on the far side where someone must have dragged a branch.

'Tell me about this hunch again, would you?' Dion yawns with a wet sound. 'Tuck's supervisor already confirmed he was on the Taupō run, right?'

'Yep.' That was another call I was happy to let the Chief make. After the visit to Bea's, I wasn't in the mood for chatting with the grumpy old bastard at the haulage outfit. 'I dunno, mate. I just…his phone, lying there in the gravel. And Tāmati, the way he was describing it all. I don't know.' There's ice in my guts again. 'It's just a feeling.'

'Scared, eh? The kid, out at Langsford?'

Those saucer eyes peering out from the shell of his hoodie, and the way his mouth had hung open, making a little cave of tongue and teeth. His expression telegraphing some distant storm on the way, the electricity already warping the air.

You don't think anything's happened, do you?

'Yeah. Scared.' I clear my throat. 'Listen, let's just take the walk, all right? Just to where they found Jessie. Rick'll probably call us any second now, saying Stu's popped up at a mate's place or something.' There it is again: comfortable words all stacked on top of each other, a sturdy wall keeping out barbarians and doubts. 'Okay?'

'Course.' Dion sets a big hand to my shoulder, comforting in its weight. 'Plenty of worse places we could be, eh?'

In the open air, I could nearly agree. Then we step beneath the reaching arms of the trees and into the bush proper, and the stars blink away for good. The thick lattice of leaves and branches reaches over us, and all we have is our footsteps.

167

~

It should be an hour to the spot, even at my pace. With all this inky dark and my too-big Red Bands, it takes us nearly two. The track rises and falls, bringing us over a handful of swing bridges as the stream zig-zags beside us. The night is even thicker here; I've had to keep a hand on Dion's jersey for the last twenty minutes, my gaze held tight to the track, watching for roots and loose stones. Then we come over another swing bridge. My hands feel the twist and coil of the cables as we traverse the open space, the rapids hissing with haste and mystery beneath us.

'Hold it.' I set my hands to my knees, bending forward to catch my breath. 'Just give me a sec.'

'We're close, right?' Dion shines the flashlight up the path ahead, turning the trail markers into a row of flaring orange triangles. 'The callout records said it was less than a kilometre off the hut, didn't they?'

'You know they did, mate.' I stand up straight, leaning back to give my spine a break.

'All right.' He raises his free hand. In the flashlight's glow, I see the hurt in his expression. 'Didn't mean anything by it.'

'Sorry.' I let out a long breath. 'I'm just...I'm starting to realise how thick it was, coming up here. We didn't even bring any water.'

Dion grins. 'It's cleaner than any tap water you'll find, this stream.'

'You think I'm scrambling down there?' I point down the

bank to the water below. 'We don't need another call to Search and Rescue.'

'Still don't trust the new hip, eh?'

I tuck the blanket tighter around my shoulders. 'Fifteen more minutes and we'll pack it in. Then Pat bloody Kelson can sleep easy knowing we've turned every rock.'

He waits for me to take hold of the back of his jersey again, his breathing still clear and easy, unhurried. All those training runs for the rugby season: the sod must've really been putting in the work. Then we set off down a narrower section of the path. It's tight going in places, though the earth is packed with enough gravel that everything's stable. Funny the places your tax dollars end up.

'What is it you've got against that lot, anyway?' Dion points to a thick root snaking across the path, waiting for me to wheeze over it. 'The Kelsons, I mean.'

'What, besides the obvious?'

'What do you mean?' I can't see his expression in the dark, but I should take him at face value. He's never been big on sarcasm, this one. 'What's so obvious about it?'

'The whole Langsford act.' I pick my footing in the yellow light. 'Thirty grand a year, Lily said. You heard that, didn't you? And showing up to the station with Horiana Paul. That'll be another thirty right there, probably.'

'Didn't your niece use her, last year? The drug stuff, after Keith?'

'Yeah, but.' My feet feel heavy. 'Well, it's more than that. Bill Kelson, Lily's dad…look, let's just say there are a few burrs in the plank from back in the day, when we farmed out at Tārehu.'

'When you farmed?' His voice lifts with incredulity. 'Shit, Lorraine, that's taking us back, isn't it? That's before Lily was even a Kelson.'

'Trust me,' I feel the knives under my words. 'They're all the same stripe, mate.'

He shines just enough lamplight to see my face, before turning it back in front of us. Then I feel his hand on my shoulder, holding me in place.

'Lorraine.' His voice sounds different. Hushed and urgent. 'Look.'

I follow his finger into the beam of light. Ahead of us on the path is a running shoe, a reflective stripe flaring bright along one side. With careful steps, we move forward, doing our best not to disturb anything.

'Here, look.' He pulls out his phone and points it into the mud, taking a quick series of photos. 'Two different sets of footprints.'

'Shit.' My breath catches inside me. 'It could be his.'

I try to think back to Saturday's hockey match. The boys were all wearing turf shoes; this is a standard trainer. Still, it looks like about the right size for the boy.

For Stu.

There's a hush over us, now. I grab the flashlight and point it through the trees. Trunks and leaves, small shrubs and ferns dotting the distance between them. And everywhere the flashlight beam isn't pointing, thick, thick dark.

'I didn't bring any evidence bags.' Dion clucks his tongue. 'They're back in the car.'

'We don't know it's evidence yet.' I pull air into my lungs, my chest feeling like a tire pumped too tight. One breath, then two. There. 'Come on.' I point the flashlight at the footprints. 'We can follow them.'

For a second Dion looks like he's about to call dibs on the flashlight, but he seems to think better of it, and we move slowly along the path, following the prints. The larger ones seem to disappear, before they return at the side of the path.

'Someone being dragged.' I point to the marks. 'Look. Whoever was in these boots had to hug the side of the track to make room.'

'They're different from the prints the Borgs found, aren't they? Not so pointy, right?'

There's broken vegetation at the side of the path, stems stripped and naked, and leaves pulled from branches. 'Whoever was missing a shoe, they've come this way.'

'We're nearly at the hut, Lorraine.' Dion whispers, pointing through the trees. 'It's just up there, I think.' He grabs my arm, hard. 'Listen, let's not get too far off the path, eh? I know we're on the flats, but still. Plenty of people have gotten turned around in easier spots than this.'

I pause in place. He's right, but now's not the time. 'We'll go until the tracks stop, all right?' A weight sits inside me, some base magnetism pulling me forward. 'We have to check, Dion. We have to be sure it's nothing.'

In the thin electric light, his features look even more boyish than usual. Then he nods, and we press on. The river's steady murmur recedes behind us. Soon, all I can hear is the sound of our breathing, and the whisper of the branches above.

'They were carrying something here. Look.' I point to a spot in the earth where the prints become simpler, turning from two lighter sets to one deeper set, easier to follow. Then, at the next rise, I shine the flashlight ahead, sweeping the beam down into a hollow, following with my eyes. There's a sharp jolt inside me. I feel the hot rush of panic, and the freezing certainty of what I'm seeing.

'Dion.' I can barely speak.

There will be a before and an after to this. I can feel it.

'Oh, Jesus.' He pushes past me, crashing through the undergrowth. I should tell him to be careful, to not disturb anything, but my mouth is welded shut. 'Hold that light on him!'

It takes me an age to get there. I'm going as fast as I can, but in some submerged, reptile corner of my brain, I know it won't matter. Not now.

At the bottom of the hollow, Stu Kelson. His arms looped around a stout tree and tied behind him, his legs folded uselessly under him, his head hanging forward, slack and unmoving. He's pale. As pale as Jessica was that first night. Paler, even.

'He's not breathing.' Dion calls back to me, trying to get a response from the boy. Stu's wrists are held at a sharp angle at either side. The rope, an orange nylon blend you could find in the boot of any car, cuts hard against his skin. 'Stu! Come on, mate!'

I stand where I am, watching. The night, so large and anonymous, hangs over us. Dion holds a finger to the boy's neck, but I can tell before he speaks that the news isn't good. He looks to me, shaking his head, his eyes wide and disbelieving in the beam of the flashlight. Then, he goes to reach for the rope at Stu's wrists.

'No, Dion.' Finally, I reach him. My hands go to his shoulder. 'We need to wait.'

'Fucking hell.' The words tumble thick from his mouth. 'We can't just...'

'We have to, mate.' I speak loud enough to reach him. 'He's gone.'

My gaze lingers on the boy's face, the lips swollen and dark with blood, one eye completely closed over, the other open just enough to give us his pupil. There's something under my foot. When I raise my boot, I see a black metal square about the size of a pack of smokes, a clear plastic wire running from it. His insulin pump; I recognise it from the hockey match.

'What do we do?' Dion runs a hand under his nose. 'What the fuck do we do?'

I motion for him to stand, and we take a step back. I shine the light around us, looking for any sign of another person, but there's nothing. Whoever was here, they've been gone long enough for the air to leave no trace.

'Check your bars.' I keep my hand to Dion's arm, squeezing to let him know I'm still here. It's all I have to keep me on my feet. 'We need to call Rick.'

AT FIRST, EVERYTHING happens piece by awful piece. Then it happens all at once.

I'm not even sure what we did, me and Dion, waiting for the others. I remember walking back to the main track, and him saying how cold he felt. We sat on a fallen log gone soft with grubs, the picnic blanket wrapped around the two of us, with just the sounds of the trees. Dion found a single bar of service up near the hut, but he couldn't bring himself to make the call, so in the end I did it. I remember the way Rick answered the phone, the sense of expectation in his voice. Then, once he'd taken himself somewhere quiet, somewhere away from Pat and Lily, I told him. The second time through, he heard me.

The chaplain was still with them, thankfully. I can only imagine what he must have said.

By the time Rick made it to the lodge carpark with the gear from the station, the Wellington forensics team wasn't too far off. They must've broken a speed record, driving over the Remutaka Ranges. Somehow, Rick convinced Pat and Lily to stay with Graham back at the carpark while he came up the track to meet us with the team. We could see their lights through the trees, and walked back up the main path to point the way. Walking ahead of the Wellington team, his features made ghostly by his headlamp, I'd never seen Rick look so tired, so bent with duty. We huddled together, me and Dion, waiting to show them.

~

I get an hour of sleep towards dawn, collapsed on the couch in my bush gear, Dion's tartan blanket still wrapped around my shoulders. Rick reckons they won't need me until the afternoon, so when my eyelids fall closed, I let them stay that way.

Trees and shadow. A plume of silver smoke rising into the dark. There are stars, yes. But the mountains only eat them.

Orange rope, and a boy coiled inside it. A day ago, he was thumping the interview-room table, certain enough to be indignant. A day ago, he was tucked into his mum's side, held in the carpark's hard frank sunlight.

A day ago, he was.

Stu Kelson.

Jessica Mowbrie.

'Aunty?' Familiar fingers grip my shoulder, and I hear my

coffeepot splutter in the next room. My eyes crack open.

'You'll burn it.' I go to sit up. 'It wants taking off the stove, girl.'

Sheena holds me where I am. 'It's okay, Aunty.' She lowers herself beside me, lifting my head as she moves. 'Moko's on the case. Aren't you, love?'

'Āe.' There's a whole loving world held inside that single syllable. 'Don't you worry.'

We sit in silence for a long moment, my head on my niece's thigh. I blink, letting a little more of the daylight into my eyes.

'What…' My tongue feels like something exhumed. 'What time is it?'

'Just gone eight.' Sheena's still holding my hand. I sit up and lift it to her belly, and she lets it stay there. Right on cue, the wee girl gives me a good hard thump, then another. That's it, little one. That's it.

'Jesus, Aunty.' My niece clucks her tongue. 'It's awful, what's happened.'

I lean back against the couch, keeping my head as still as I can manage. She won't probe for details; that's not what this is. Her head will be full of what we're all thinking, but she'll keep it to herself: Tuck Mowbrie with his broad shoulders and capable hands, his frothy temper, his hard loyalty. Maybe I'm thinking the same thing.

Then I hear the fridge door open, and big hands rummaging for a sugar spoon. Moko, you lovely thing. I blink, and a steaming mug materialises on the coffee table.

'Felt like a two-sugar morning.' Moko edges away, standing in the doorway and looking to Sheena. 'I'll get out of your hair, eh?'

'Wait.' I point to the chair by the fireplace. 'The rest of the pot will need a good home. Just...just sit with me. Both of you, just sit.'

The big guy does as he's told, falling backwards into the chair with a loud whoosh of air. Sheena lifts a hand around my shoulder, her fingers pressing gently against the base of my neck. It's like there's honey in my brain.

'Where'd you learn that, then?'

'One of the guys at Seven Oaks studied massage at the Polytech, before they cut the course.' She smiles to herself. 'Does wonders with the geriatrics, he reckons.'

It hurts to laugh, but I do anyway. 'You're not too old to leave here with a smacked arse, girl. Hapū or not.'

'Look out.' Moko slurps at his coffee, holding up the cup like a courtroom exhibit. 'See, love? See what you get when you broaden your horizons beyond instant?'

'You can drink whatever you like.' Sheena rubs the top of her belly. 'I'm on decaf until game day anyway.'

With a long groan, I sit up straight and let my eyes adjust. Sheena hands me the coffee, and I swallow half the mug before I know what I'm doing, the hot sweet liquid burning through my gullet, flooding every chamber.

'Another pot, I'd say.' Moko gets up and busies himself at the stovetop.

'Jesus, girl.' I press my palms into my cheeks, whispering

mostly to myself. My hands rub my eyes until I see flashes of white. 'That boy.' His expression on the hockey pitch, pale-cheeked and damp at his forehead, letting his mum—his brave, strong mum—usher him to the safety of the sidelines. I feel Sheena's hand on my shoulder again, before her head comes against me. She breathes long and slow, and soon, I'm doing the same. 'I should get to the station,' I mutter. 'It's going to be a mad one.'

'A shower first, I reckon.' She rubs a hand across my shoulder. 'For the Chief's sake.'

I lean back against the couch, my niece's hair in my nose, and the morning sounds of Rickett's Circle coming through the open window. Car doors and morning radio, lawnmowers and birds. The waiting creatures, the sleeping creatures. You'd never think the world was on its side, hearing all that. You'd never suspect a thing.

THE USUAL CHARACTERS are hanging around outside the station when I arrive: the goateed guy from the *Times Age* with a tie tucked under his Swandri, and a gaggle of rubberneckers watching from the park bench across the road. Then I notice the *Dominion Post* van, and a young woman, a girl, really, tapping a pen against her notepad, waiting with an eye on the station doors.

'Sure you'll get on all right with that lot?' Moko pulls to the curb, squinting through the windscreen. 'Here, why don't I walk with you, just in case?'

'I'll be all right.' I pat his hand. 'You get on home, eh. That wee girl could come any time.'

I climb out of the car, but he waits anyway, making sure I've crossed the road to the station at least.

By the time I reach the footpath, the Wellington reporter

has her microphone in my face. 'Miss Henry, can you tell us anything about the discovery of Stuart Kelson's body?'

I duck my head, but the microphone follows me. Before everything last year, they'd have thought I was one of the cleaners. Thanks to that *Woman's Weekly* feature, everyone seems to know me.

'Is there anyone you're...'

'Give her some room, for fuck's sake.' The goateed guy gets an arm between us, shepherding me to the door.

'Cheers, Jamie.' I keep my gaze down, pushing through the scrum with his help.

'No worries.' He nods inside the building, waiting until I've got the door open. Behind us, the girl is huffing and puffing, arms crossed tight inside her suit. 'You'll give me a yell when you've got something, yeah?'

'Yep, yep.'

I let the doors close, leaving them where they stand in the bright daylight. My shoes squeak lonely and wistful across the station foyer. It's dark in here; the Chief will want it to stay that way, after the night he's had. I find him and Dion in the kitchen, both hunched over the biggest mugs we've got, their elbows making twin pyramids against the tabletop. Their voices are hushed and low.

'Lorraine.' Rick nods, then points a thumb over his shoulder. 'There's more in the pot, there.' He slides his mug in my direction. 'I'll take a top-up. We both will.'

I busy myself at the bench. 'The Wellington team still onsite at Atiwhakatū?'

'Finishing up now,' the Chief checks his phone. 'Should have everything through this afternoon, they said.'

There's only one question, but it hurts to even think it. 'Lily and Pat?'

An even deeper hush folds over us, speaking those names. Dion shifts his eyes to mine. He looks like he's slept less than I have.

'They left not long ago,' says Ambrose. 'You can imagine how that went.'

He doesn't have to say anything. It's all there, in the angle of his shoulders, in the dry rasp in his voice. It's been one of the hardest nights in memory, this one.

'We took statements from the neighbours by the haulage place,' says Dion. 'They saw Tuck pull in around six. His ute was still there when they went to bed just after eleven.'

'And the delivery logs?' I set their mugs down on the table and pull out a chair. 'What do they show?'

'It all checks out.' Rick gives a slow nod. 'He dropped the load off just after midnight and came back for his ute just before six this morning.'

'Long night for him, then,' says Dion.

I lift the mug to my mouth. Bea's face in the doorway, and the way she'd told Michaela not to put the jug on. Those white marks raked into red skin, and the towel tucked so tight around her body. There's more there.

'We'll need them to come in,' I say. 'Tuck and Bea both. Michaela too, if we can.'

'No shit. Already made the call to the hospital,' Dion nods.

'Bea's going to come in with Tuck as soon as he wakes up.'

'All right, mate. No need to get septic.'

'Two-thirty, she said.' Rick crosses his arms, looking to me across the table. There are shadows in his face I haven't seen in years. 'What made you think of it, Lorraine?'

'Hmm?' I know what he's asking. I've felt it since I walked into the room.

'The Tararuas,' says Dion. Then it gets even quieter in the room. When the fridge motor clicks on, its rattling grumble makes me jump in my seat.

'Talking to those boys,' I say. 'Tāmati especially. I don't know. Something about it just...he seemed scared, Rick. Properly scared. Even if he didn't know what to be scared about.' The boy's expression tucked inside that hoodie, feigning nonchalance. There was so much care there, so much thought. I wonder if Stu knew. He had to, surely. 'And then the phone on the road. I just had a feeling.'

'And Bea seemed jumpy, you reckon? At her place?' The Chief frowns.

'Definitely.' It's like there's sand in my throat. 'But I can't say why.'

In the low light, his face looks thin and gaunt. 'What a fucking mess.'

'You've got time to rest, Rick.' I watch his expression. 'Before the Mowbries come in.'

'I'll be all right.' His eyes slide halfway open, like lift doors past their service date. 'Don't worry yourself.'

We sit in silence, the three of us with our thoughts. Soon,

my mind starts to wander, and pieces of the scene announce themselves. 'It was the pump, wasn't it?' That metal square under my foot, so small amidst the leaves and the dirt. 'He'd had a decent hiding, that boy. But nothing that would do him in otherwise.'

'Stu,' Ambrose croaks. 'We can say his name, Lorraine. If we're saying Jess Mowbrie's name, we can say his too.' He sighs long and loud, keeping his eyes on mine. 'That's what they reckon. The report will confirm it, but they already said as much. A diabetic coma.'

'And not long before we got there,' says Dion. 'An hour, maybe two.' His hands come together, his thumb and forefinger rubbing the flesh of his palm. 'Jesus, if we'd only driven a little faster.'

Or if we hadn't wasted time arguing about who would knock on the Mowbries' door. Jesus.

'Don't, Dion.' Rick reaches a hand across the table, setting it over Dion's forearm. 'There's only one person responsible here, and we'll get to that soon enough. It's a lucky thing you two found him at all.'

A lucky thing.

Dion nods, wiping beneath his eye. I lift my hand to his shoulder; I can guess what's on his mind this very second. Those pale wrists, pulled so sharply behind his body. The way he'd hung forward, so thin. A boy, still. Small despite his height, and in need of shelter, of protection.

A boy.

'All right, then.' Rick pats Dion's arm and stands, stretching his hands up above his head. 'We've got an hour before Bea and Tuck.' He nods to Dion. 'You'll want a fresh shirt at least, mate.'

'Yep, yep.' Dion yawns.

'Wait, don't you think, uh…' I look between them. 'After the hospital and all, don't you think a smaller group would be a better move?'

The Chief shakes his head. 'We've accommodated them at every fuckin' turn, Lorraine. I've had it. Dion's in the room.' The kitchen becomes busy, now: we're all standing and moving. 'We've got the girl coming in after that. Heather.'

'Christiansen?' I hold my hands open. 'She'll only just have heard about Stu, Rick.'

'Then she'll know how serious this all is, won't she?' The Chief walks out of the room without waiting to see if we're following. 'Maybe we'll get a little less bullshit than usual.'

Pointless to argue after the night he's had. Instead, I slink downstairs to my desk and let them both get ready for what the afternoon has in store. It's a relief, smelling the paper and the dust, the usual shadows opening their arms to welcome me home. I sink into my chair, but before I can feel any of the usual calm, my phone vibrates. It's Sheena. My mind leaps to contractions, to busy wards and blood loss.

'You all right, girl?'

'Aunty, there's…' She's whispering; I have to switch the phone to my good ear. 'A truck pulled up outside Bea Mowbrie's place not long ago. Blocked the driveway, Moko reckons.'

'A truck?' I lean forward against the desk, my blood speeding in my veins. 'Should we send someone?'

'Nah, nah.' I hear her speaking to someone in the background. Moko, it sounds like. The feeling in my chest slackens, knowing he's there. 'They left already. Moved on once they realised nobody was home.' There's a long pause on the line. 'They had a gun in the back, a twelve gauge.'

'Shit.' It could be anything; it could be nothing. 'Did you recognise anyone?'

'Some bearded guy, Moko said. There was something written on the cab door, though. Longbush Station, or something.'

'The Brookes.' I feel something click into place. 'It'll be Lily Kelson's people.'

In the background, I hear Bradley's bright voice, babbling away. 'Anyway, he sorted them out,' says Sheena. 'It's all good.'

'Who? Moko?' I can't help but grin. It'll take more than a bunch of Brooke shepherds to shift that one, especially on Rickett's Circle. 'Good on him.' I stand and start the climb upstairs again. 'We could put someone outside, girl. On the street, for the afternoon at least.'

'I wouldn't worry,' Sheena says. 'But maybe fill Bea in, just in case.'

'All right.' I pause between steps, hidden by the stairwell. 'All good otherwise? The baby?'

'Yeah, course.' There's the clatter of the cutlery drawer, and Bradley asking for Colby, not Tasty. 'Last time it got too melty, remember boy? And you couldn't even...I have to go, Aunty. Text me later.'

THE CHIEF BRINGS Bea and Tuck through the back, out of sight of the reporters and rubberneckers. Michaela's with them too. It could complicate things, but she has her own questions to answer. Whatever goodwill Bea might've had for us before, it's evaporated now: she sits across the table, arms folded tight over her chest, hard-eyed and mute. Tuck won't even sit down at first; it takes Michaela to get him to stop pacing behind the table.

'How's she doing this morning, your girl?' Rick nods to Bea, doing his best not to let the night show on him. 'The doctors sounded hopeful, last time we came in.'

'Her colour seemed a bit better,' says Dion. 'I heard they might even...'

'The answer is no, all right?' Bea keeps her voice low, and her arms crossed. 'No, we didn't have anything to do with that boy.' Her eyes go from Rick to me, then back: searchlights sweeping. 'Now, if that's all you had for us, we can save everyone some time, and I can get back to my daughter.'

I watch Michaela as Bea speaks. At the mention of Stu, her gaze drops to the tabletop. She's wearing the same pink hoodie she had on last night, her body lost inside it. It looks like she hasn't slept either, her cheeks slack and pale. She keeps her hands jammed into her pockets, as though she's trying to keep as much of herself out of sight as possible.

'Let's all just take it easy, all right?' The Chief holds his hands open. 'After everything that's happened, of course we'd want to talk to you. You especially, Michaela.'

The girl nearly jumps out of her seat. 'Me?'

'Through me first, mate.' Tuck jabs a thumb into his chest. He's not long out of the shower; his hair is still slick under his beanie. 'Minors and all.'

'Sure, sure.' Rick leans back, looking quickly to Dion, then to me on the couch. 'Have you had any contact with Stuart Kelson over these last few days, Michaela?'

Tuck sets an arm around his daughter's shoulder, wrapping her up. She goes to speak, then pauses, looking to him. In a quick, firm movement, he nods. 'No,' she says.

'You didn't seem too surprised when I came around last night.' I'm talking to the girl, but I'm watching the others. 'It seemed almost like you were expecting someone to come and ask about Stu. Is that about right?'

'Expecting?' Tuck spits out the syllables like he's tasting old milk. 'Fair play, Lorraine. You're only a few houses down.

Shit, this lot can hear your niece change the channel from the verandah.' At this, a small grin breaks through their veneer. 'Haven't we been seeing a lot of you, lately? Our girl, especially?'

'Been a daily habit, pretty much.' Bea scoffs.

'True enough. I guess we have been chatting a fair bit, eh?' I give them enough of a smile for the line to go slack between us. I can feel Rick staring, wondering where I'm going. 'Like our last chat at the hospital, right Micks? Outside Jessie's room, while your mum was off at home?'

The girl's eyes go wide in her head. 'I...I don't...'

'What's she on about, love?' Bea twists in her chair, staring at her niece, then to me. 'What do you mean, Lorraine?'

'Did you tell them? Eh?' I lean forward, nodding to Bea, then to Tuck. 'About feeling like maybe someone had dosed you up, out at Tārehu?'

'Dosed her up?' Tuck lays his arms across the table. I could fit a closed fist up each one of his nostrils.

'Go on, girl.' I wait, but Michaela just stares across the table, lost. Whatever rapport I'd built is burnt now, but there's no time for anything else. 'You're saying they didn't know?' I sit up straighter and make myself stern. 'You're saying you didn't fill them in about the GHB, eh? And they didn't go looking for Stu to teach him a lesson?'

'Jesus, they gave you that shit too?' Tuck turns to his daughter, all nerves and spittle. 'Why didn't you say anything?' He grabs her by the shoulder, hard enough to make her wince. 'Those little pricks can't just...'

'Leave it.' Bea doesn't even have to turn her head; the words on their own are enough. Tuck brings his arm back to the table, but his eyes stay vibrating in their sockets. Bea stares across the table at the Chief. 'Like we said already, my brother was running a load to Taupō last night.'

'Call Derek Lau,' Tuck mutters. 'He'll confirm it.'

'We did already.' Rick looks to Bea. 'But what about you?'

She wipes at her cheeks. 'I was watching my girl breathe through a tube, mate.' A sob breaks through her voice. 'Like every night this whole fuckin' week. And now you lot call us in here just to…'

'Not every night,' says Dion.

Across the table, Bea turns scarlet; her lips are quivering. 'There's no shower in the ward, you thick cunt. What am I supposed to do? Use the basin?' Her eyes narrow. 'While you're hanging around looking through the door, eh? Is that the idea?'

'Hang on a second,' Dion squirms in his seat. 'That's not…'

'All right, all right.' Tuck leans forward, elbows against the table, and sets a hand to Bea's arm. 'It's been a rough few days, Chief. You know that.' There's something new in his expression, now. A brighter feeling; the promise of an open door. 'You know just as well as I do, that boy was due a good kick up the arse. His mates too.' He looks to Michaela, but the girl's eyes stay in her lap. 'But this stuff, up in the ranges? Tied up and left to die? No. That's not how we handle things.' He leans back against his chair and crosses his arms, moving slow and steady. 'We've given you everything we know. You can

189

check with anyone you need. Anyone at all.' He looks sideways to me, making me feel smaller. 'If you want to play games, trying to get us offside with each other, you can do it another time.'

With that, he pushes his seat back, nodding to the others to follow. He gives me a decimating shake of the head as he gathers himself. Disappointment and deflation, a role poorly played. This is the end of something. We'll live near each other, sure, but we won't be neighbours. Not after this.

'Hang on, mate.' Rick stands.

'Open the fucking door,' Tuck barks. 'Now.'

Bea and Michaela stand and follow him, the girl wrapped up in her aunt's arms. I feel the Chief looking at me for direction. Past Tuck's stout shape, Bea looks thin, fragile almost, like she'd collapse if not for her brother. But I know how she can put him back on his heels. She's shown us, in the room.

And out of it, too.

'One thing before you go.' I move to Tuck's side.

'I'm picking up a load at four, Lorraine.' He lets out an exasperated breath and looks to his watch. 'You know Derek. He doesn't exactly...'

'Saturday, at the hospital. In the carpark.' I watch their faces. 'You said Bea knew it was pushing things too far, the stuff with the lawyers.' Past Tuck's shoulder, the colour drops out of Bea's face again. Only this time, it doesn't come back. Her mouth hangs open, showing her sharp white teeth. 'What did you mean by that?'

Tuck's eyes narrow to mail slits but he keeps himself

steady. 'I've no idea what you're on about.'

'The papers, you said. Right before you drove off.' I move closer, putting my arm between him and the door. 'What papers would those be?'

A new silence grows around us, holding us in place. Tuck can only stand and wait, his arms loose at his sides. Past his shoulder, a deep frown splits Michaela's features. This is news to her, I can tell.

'The door.' Tuck holds his gaze on me. 'Now.'

He leans closer, his fists clenched tight. I stay where I am. It takes more brass than I've got, but I manage it. 'Listen, now. Forget where we are. Forget these two.' I motion to Rick and Dion. 'This is me you're talking to.' My feet carry me closer. Before I know what I'm doing, my hand goes to his forearm. I can see Bea's face now, staring all the way through me. 'It's been an absolute cunt of a week, all right? For all of us, believe me.' I keep my voice soft, trying to catch Bea's eye. 'But your girl's going to come right, trust me. And when she does, we can all get back to things.' Breathe, now. Breathe. 'If you've done something, something to do with that boy, there's still time to come back from it. Here, now.' I look to Tuck again. There's a weight moving between him and Bea, a landslide shifting and settling. 'But after today, it'll be different. After today, we might not be onside.'

Under my fingers, I feel the tension inside him, all tendons pulled tight, his heart slamming in his chest. For a brief moment, I see something in his expression, before the hard surface of slate comes back.

191

'Call Derek Lau.' Tuck keeps his voice steady. 'He'll tell you where I was. As for my sister, she should be there when Jessie comes to. Like you said.'

I stay where I am a few seconds longer, as though it'll make a difference. I should know better, really. After a lifetime in Masterton, I should know a mind made up when I see it.

'All right then.' I nod. Rick reaches through us and unlocks the door. As they leave the room, Michaela gives me a kicked-puppy stare. I've torn up all of the shorthand between us, and yet part of her has something to give me. Not here, though.

'This way's best.' Rick gestures over his shoulder to the back of the station.

'No,' says Tuck. 'Let them see. We're helping, aren't we?'

'Hang on.' I try to catch Rick's attention. 'I'm not sure that's the best idea, guys. Not after this morning.'

'What, that shit with the Brookes?' Bea snorts. 'We're supposed to be crapping ourselves because a couple of farm boys drove past?'

'It's not just that, Bea.' I watch her expression, unable to tell how much of the bravado is real. 'They had a gun.'

'So you say.'

'It's fine, Lorraine.' Rick strides across the foyer and unlocks the front door. 'Leave it.'

'Leave it? Fuck me, am I the only one with my head screwed on here?'

'Chief?' Dion leans between us, speaking just low enough

192

for the Chief to hear. 'She's right, mate. We can't risk it. Not with—'

Ambrose gives a sharp shake of his head, pushing the doors open and setting off a scramble from the waiting cars. The *Dominion Post* girl jockeys for position with Jamie, the local reporter, elbowing her way to the front of the steps. There are utes parked everywhere, including one I don't recognise at the far side of the road. I feel a lurch in my chest. I scan the cars for any sign of the Brookes, but the windows are too dark to see inside.

'Get the truck.' Bea points Tuck around the side of the station. 'We're all right.'

With a quick scan of the reporters, Tuck nods, striding away with purpose, but not moving too quickly. He pulls his sunnies from his collar and slips them on. The reporters jab their phones and recorders in Bea's face, asking her about Stu, about Jessie. Bea just stares out between them, holding Michaela close. Then the ute with the tinted windows opens up, and a mid-forties couple emerge with a young girl. I squint, holding my palm above my eyes. It's Mike and Sally Christiansen from the garden shop; the girl must be Heather.

'Shit, they're early.' Dion looks from me to the crowd. 'Make room, everyone!'

'Rick.' I point to Bea and Michaela. They're getting hemmed in by the reporters, and a couple of cameras have appeared, their big square eyes pointed at the crush. 'This could get tricky.'

'It's fine,' Rick nods to the gate. 'Here he comes. Just keep yourself handy.'

Tuck pulls through from the back, bringing his ute alongside the kerb so the crowd has to shift. Then he reaches across the inside of the cab and cracks the passenger door for Bea, moving through the crowd with Michaela held tight to her. I don't know where to put my attention. The reporters follow Bea, moving in a complicated shuffle, one single yapping creature. Then somehow the Christiansens are alongside them. I see Heather through the press of shoulders, right behind Jamie; she's trying to get Michaela's attention. The Wellington reporter shoves her way closer, reaching her microphone towards Bea. It's enough to distract her. For a moment, close to Tuck's ute, she lets go of Michaela, leaving her on her own. Then a shrill, clear voice cuts above the fray.

'You did this! You did this to him!' Through the gaggle of bodies, Heather lurches towards Michaela, grabbing her by the shoulder. People press closer to them, and when I see them again, Heather has a fistful of hair; Michaela's head jerks sharply back and she yelps in surprise. The cameras move back as she falls to the ground, opening up space to capture the scene.

'Rick!'

I wade into the fray, keeping my good hip ahead of me, and hearing more screaming from Michaela as Heather brings her closed fist down around her head and shoulders. Sally and Mike are trying to get closer, but they can't get through all the flailing arms. Then, past Jamie, Bea reaches through the press of shoulders. She takes Heather by the collar, all her lean strength coiled in one swift movement, her feet planted and steady. On the ground, Michaela holds her arms above her head, whimpering. Bea gets Heather's head up just enough to reach. The blow comes clean and tight, her arm popping forward as her fist crosses cleanly into the girl's nose.

Even with all the shouting, I hear it crack.

There's a hush, a fragment of a second of stillness, before everyone is moving again. Heather falls to the ground, but Bea is still on her, her fingers locked tight to her collar, looking to get another punch in. A broad guy himself, Mike gets his hand to her shoulder, and is pulling her towards him when Tuck slips to Bea's side, crouched in a boxing stance. Before Mike knows he's there, Tuck doubles him over with a fist to the gut; with a loud whoosh of air, he goes down too. As Tuck spins around, the circle of onlookers shrinks back.

'Hold on, everyone!' Rick has his arms out, and is moving between the two sides, trying to put himself in the way. He motions for Dion to do the same. 'Let her go, Bea!'

'She's broken her nose!' Sally moves forward into the gap, past Mike on his knees. She reaches for her daughter, her features pink with outrage. 'Look!'

As she reaches them, she bumps one of the *Dominion Post* guys, who drops his camera with a heavy clatter and a string of new curses.

'Stay back!' The Chief turns sideways, hands held out to make room around Heather's bloodied form. Then, as Sally reaches him, he trips. He falls with his arms held up awkwardly, too many bodies in the way for him to get his hands where they need to be, and there's a moment, there in the hot confusion of arms and spitting, of bared teeth and scuffing shoes, where I can see it happening. The angle of the fall is all wrong, Rick's arms pinned high and useless, his heavy torso coming down like a load of logs giving way. I move forward to reach him, but it isn't enough; he hits the pavement, and his head strikes the sharpest edge of the camera.

'Rick!' I kneel down, waving to Dion to make room. Tuck too, for that matter. 'Jesus, someone…someone call an ambulance.'

The Chief's eyes are half-open and rolling; there's already a thick finger of red sliding from his temple down into his collar. Behind me, I hear Tuck yelling to the others to get in the truck. There are slamming doors, then a woman, Sally I think, yelling at Dion to keep them here, to not let them go without being charged.

'Make some fucking room!' I push the reporters back. Jamie crouches beside me in his Swandri, holding a practised hand to Rick's neck.

'Keep him still, now.'

I feel Dion's hand at my shoulders. 'It's coming, Lorraine. The ambulance is coming.'

I keep talking to Rick, there at his side under the carpark's bright arena, feeling the eyes on me. My hand goes to the side of his head, and I feel a line where the bone drops away, the smooth surface interrupted so strangely, like broken eggshell. We sit there, holding him together and keeping him still. His mouth is moving, but I can't hear anything.

'I'LL SAY IT if you won't.' Dion shakes his head slowly, hands loose against the steering wheel as he drives. 'What a clusterfuck.'

'A what?'

'A cluster—'

'No, mate, I heard the words. I'm just not au fait with your terminology.' I lean back against the seat, feeling every hour of this poxy day hanging heavy across my shoulders. 'If you're saying it's been a jar of arseholes lately, I'd have to agree.'

'Like I said.' He grins just as much as he can get away with.

I let my eyes fall shut for a bit, focusing on my breathing like those YouTube guys in the tight sweatpants have been telling me. Dion's driving at about half his usual pace; he knows I'd never make it out to Longbush with my guts intact otherwise. The road curves and bends under us, taking us ever closer to

Tārehu. Pat and Lily Kelson: they're about the last people I want to bother right now, but we have to talk to them.

I have to.

There's a low digital burble inside the car. Dion lifts his phone to his ear, muttering a hello, then a series of yeps.

'The hospital?' My heart stumbles.

'Lee.' He breathes in, deep and long. 'Fourteen stitches, he said, and a hell of a concussion. Rick won't be home until next week at least.'

'He's not in the same ward, is he?' I stare sideways. 'As Jessie?'

'Nah, nah.' He lifts a hand to his mouth, belching as discreetly as he can manage. 'Not quite the same level of urgency, Lorraine. Even with a knock like that.'

I stare out into the road, letting my mind wander. It was urgent enough when it happened, urgent enough that I never want to deal with anything like that ever again. The hot smell of iron in my nose and the rolling of his eyes, something cut loose from its tether.

A man laid out against the concrete. A boy, pale and tied, with all life drained away. A girl discarded in those same lonely trees.

It can happen so quickly, all of it.

'Listen, uh...' Dion clears his throat, speaking as though someone else might overhear us. 'I think we should put a call in.'

'What?' I watch his face. 'To Wellington?'

He nods, looking grave. 'We're short, Lo. Shit, we were short before this. I mean, fuck, you're not even a...and me,

I'm only…' His words fall away, leaving only the creak of the steering wheel's rubber casing rubbing under his hands. 'Now we've got the Christiansens wanting charges, and who knows how many of Rick's leads still to follow up.' He shakes his head. 'We don't even know who to call at the papers, if we ever manage to crack any of it.'

'The papers?' My tongue clicks all on its own. 'That's what you're worried about? Jamie Clayton was right there, mate. Christ, he's probably washing Rick's blood out of his Swandri right now. I wouldn't worry about him needing the details.'

'Well, sure.' Dion frowns. 'But Sally Christiansen, she said she…'

'I spoke to her, Dion. After they got Rick sorted. Told her we'd have to go ahead and charge Heather if she wanted to go press against Bea.' I think back to the scrum. 'It was all on camera, her girl rag-dolling Michaela Mowbrie. The whole bloody lot of it.'

'Yeah? And she went for it, did she?'

I shrug. There was more indignation than fear in Sally Christiansen's face when they left the station staffroom, her girl's nose held in place beneath a tea towel full of ice from the staffroom freezer. Mike seemed to get the message though; or at least, he looked pissed off enough to know the bind they were in. We might hear from them still, but it isn't exactly at the top of my list.

'Let's just hang tight, the two of us.' I give him the calmest expression I can muster. 'I'm not sure now's the time to bring anyone from the city up to speed.'

'I should've been there for a discussion like that, Lorraine. If charges were on the table, a constable should've been present.'

'We're a little bit past that now, don't you think?'

Dion grips the wheel tighter. 'What about the reports? It's going to be a real pain in the hole, Lorraine, everything happening on station property and all.' He looks to me out the corner of his eye. 'I can do my best to type it up and all, but I don't know how we'll manage it.'

'Spit it out, mate.'

His chin drops to his chest. 'We need a detective, Lorraine.' Silence. 'A real one.'

Through the windscreen, the road curves slow and easy through a cleft carved in the hillside. There's a clutch of native trees on the inside of the bend, their thick branches sending shade out over the patrol car. They never seemed this tall when I was younger. Some part of me must be refusing to believe how long it's really been. Jesus. Thirty years. Thirty years since Dad had to sell up, and fifty since Debs and I moved into town to plant our own feet. It's been long enough for these new natives to turn the land into something else. And yet, there's still the same old churning in my chest, seeing these hills with their broken patches of bush, their steep faces of dry summer grass like waving strands of gold.

Up ahead, the road opens up into a long straight section. We come past my old driveway, the gate long bolted and padlocked. Then, at the end of the stretch, is the gateway to Tārehu Station.

'One thing at a time, eh?' If I really try, I might even sound halfway confident. 'Let me worry about the reports.'

~

It looks different than I remember, the gateway. When we were younger it was a simple cattlestop: rusted metal bars submerged into the ground, the bottom of dad's truck rattling and shaking every time we'd come over. Not that we came over all that often, mind. Now, there are stone pillars on either side of the gateway, with a lacquered wooden sign—rimu, it looks like—spelling out the name of the station: Tārehu. I have to stifle a chuckle; back in the day, everyone knew the stations. Something like this would be like hanging a nametag on the sun.

'Bit flash, isn't it?' Dion looks bemused. 'Looks like a bloody cheese ad.'

'It's not enough to just sell lamb anymore. You have to sell a story.'

I can't tell if the Kelsons have refitted the cattlestop, because there's a bulldozer parked sideways across the gateway, blocking anyone from driving in. Or out, for that matter. Through a gap in the pillar and the dusty yellow flank of the Caterpillar, I can make out the glint of another vehicle. There's a flash of reflected sunlight as the door opens, then the muted thud of it closing. It's a ute, new but dusty.

'What's the story?' Dion nods to the bulldozer. 'You think they meant to park that thing there?'

There's more movement through the gap in the gate: a

bearded guy, early forties I'd say, lifts a phone to his ear, staring with a flat expression at our patrol car. It's Harry Brooke, I think. Lily's younger brother. There's a shotgun cradled in the crook of his spare arm, barrels broken open. I can't see if it's loaded.

'I'll take a first crack at him, all right?' I take a long breath and push the door open, ignoring the expression on Dion's face. 'Come on.'

Blinking in the hard sunlight, I move slow and steady around the bonnet of our car, making myself easy to see. Not that it's a stretch these days.

'Hello?' I call through the gap, as though I'm talking to the dozer. There's a long moment of silence before the guy appears in the gap. He's closed the shotgun, and his palm hovers near the stock. I feel Dion stop sharply in the gravel besides me.

'Lorraine.' There's a crunch under his feet.

'It's okay.' I keep my eyes forward. 'It's Harry, right? Harry Brooke?' The guy just stares back. It's mostly a rhetorical question; with these wolfish features, he could only be a Brooke. 'I knew your dad, back in the day. It's Lorraine. Mickey Henry was my dad.' I clear my throat, pointing a hand behind us, up the hill and into the trees. I could be pointing anywhere. 'We used to farm out here too.'

'Used to, eh?' Harry squints. 'I think I've heard that story.'

'Well.' Breathe, now. This isn't the job. 'Things are looking different these days, eh?' I nod to the gate pillar and step forward, nearly to the bulldozer treads. 'Listen. Your nephew.' I shake my head. 'It's a terrible thing, mate. A terrible thing.'

He doesn't say anything. Instead, he just stares from me to Dion and back. He's got his dad's eyes, I realise: Arthur's dark irises, like currants in a bun. It's hard to see what's in them. Pain and malice, anger, hate. Harder still to see who it's all for.

'We're here to see Lily and Pat.' I try to keep myself steady. 'Few things to follow up.'

'I'd fuckin' hope so, woman.' His lip quivers inside the black thicket of his beard. There's a tiny break in his voice, before he swallows it down. 'For Stuey's sake.'

I feel Dion move forward at my side. 'Mind putting that back in the truck, fella?'

Harry steps closer, his spare arm lifting the shotgun into view. It's not pointed at us, exactly, but it's close enough. 'I would, yeah.' He stares through the gap. 'So long as there's someone out there laying hands on my family, I'd mind it quite a bit.'

'All right, guys.' I lift a hand to Dion's shoulder; there's tension coming off him in waves. 'We've all got our jobs to do. Let's not get too bloody high noon, shall we?'

Moisture beads at Dion's temples, and his mouth hangs open and ready. We stand where we are, staring through the gap and waiting. Eventually Harry lets the shotgun barrel drop just enough.

'It was you two who found him, they said.' He's quieter now; I have to turn my head to the good side to hear him. 'At Atiwhakatū. You went up there.'

'That's right, Harry.' I hold his gaze. 'We did.'

'Any ideas, then?'

An ocean of implication moves beneath his words: the Mowbries and their kind. Our side of town. Workers, not owners.

'That's why we're out here,' I say. 'To see your sister. And Pat.'

He keeps on eyeballing Dion. There are worse people he could be taking his grief out on, I suppose. Then, over his shoulder, I make out a boxy vehicle moving down the road and through the trees. It looks like the Kelsons' ute. They're coming slower than I remember anyone driving these roads, a dust plume lifting behind them in a steady low cloud. The sound reaches us like the sound of distant surf.

'Wait here.' Harry nods, turning with the gun and walking back past his truck, his steps slow and methodical.

'The rifle,' Dion whispers. 'It's in the safe in the boot.'

'No, Dion. Jesus, no.' I speak sideways to him, keeping my eyes ahead. 'The rope's halfway cut already, mate. You want to make it worse?'

There's the quick yellow sting of hurt in his expression, but I don't have time for it. The Kelson ute pulls to a stop just short of Harry, the wheels crunching in the gravel. When the engine switches off, I can hear the bleat of a lamb near the creek alongside us, followed by a long croaky response from its mum. *Here I am. Here I am.*

'All right, now.' I hold a hand in front of Dion. 'Let's just keep it steady.'

Through the gap between the pillar and the bulldozer, I

see the ute door crack open, and three figures emerge: Lily, Pat, Rodney.

Pat brings a hand to Rodney's shoulder, ushering him to his uncle. Then they approach us. Lily's wearing the same wide set of sunglasses she had at the hockey, and is tucked into a shepherd's jacket much too warm for the month. She looks small; smaller than I remember, anyway. Pat too, his shoulders are hunched, his head bowed almost in penance as he follows his wife. It's an embarrassment, the distance they have to cover while we stand watching. I don't know where to look; there should be escape hatches for moments like this.

'You'll have something for us, then.' Pat speaks through the gap, his voice like a collapsing bridge. 'That's the only explanation I could imagine for this, Lorraine.'

Up to now, he's been looking past me, his eyes held to some unspecified patch of day just over my shoulder. Now they find mine, and I can see the sharp and terrible shape of the disbelief inside him, a grey gnawing thing buried in his chest, feasting on him.

'I'm sorry, Pat.' Words are so easy. 'You can't imagine how...'

'That's it then, isn't it?' From deep inside her jacket, Lily throws the words at me. 'That's your key suspect gone, right? For the girl?' A sob slices through her voice. At her side, Pat lifts a hand to her shoulder and for once she lets it stay there. 'Our boy. Our Stu.'

When she shakes her head, moisture slides out over her

cheeks. Pat holds her even tighter; it looks like she's trembling under him.

'That's not it, Lily.' I let her hear me. 'That's not why we're here.'

'No?' Pat runs a hand under his nose, sniffing. 'How else do you explain it, then? Why else would that animal Tuck Mowbrie do this, eh? Unless he thought our boy was the one who...'

'He's accounted for,' says Dion. When I turn to him, he clams up.

'Who, Tuck?' Lily frowns. 'How do you know?'

'We're looking into anybody who could've been involved.' I'm aiming for something approaching neutrality, but I can tell that's not how it's being received. 'That's why we've come out here. We need to know everything there is to know about what Stu was up to last night.' I look to Lily, trying to find her eyeline under the glasses. 'What you spoke about on the phone, and where he was going.'

'We've been through this already!' Pat's rough voice sets my back on my feet. 'We've already given it all to Rick Ambrose, you useless cow!'

'Easy, love.' Lily squeezes him tighter. 'You heard what happened. They're only...'

'No, no.' Pat throws her off and she stumbles. Behind them Harry stirs into action, moving ahead with Rodney at his side. He looks ready to put a round in his brother-in-law, no matter who else is around to see it.

'We're done. You understand?' Pat strides forward to the

gap between the bulldozer and the gateway pillar, the thick metal treads obscuring his lower half. 'Come on.'

Lily pauses, staring across the gap to us. I'm close enough that I can see her eyes boiling with fury behind the glasses. 'The only time you get to say anything to me or my family is when you've got Tuck Mowbrie sewn up, all right?'

'Lily.' I move closer, but the gulf between us has never been wider.

'Tuck Mowbrie, charged and held.' She turns to go. 'Anything else, call our lawyer.'

Harry moves up to her side with Rodney behind him; her brother sets a hand to her back, speaking low. Then she sees Rodney sobbing, and she opens his arms for him, pressing him tight to her middle, as though she means to keep him there forever.

It won't do, I want to tell her. They grow, and they do things all on their own and you have to let them. You have to.

'Lily.' I call out. 'Who else knew about Stu finding the phone?'

'Just leave it, Lorraine.' Dion grabs me, but I brush him off. Through the gap, Lily has stopped in place. She turns, just enough for me to see the shades in her expression: confusion and rage, and beneath it all, the moving parts of some larger machine.

'What phone?' She swallows hard.

'The girl's phone. Jessica Mowbrie's.' I watch them all. Rodney is frowning through his tears. 'Did anyone else know about him being the one to find it?'

Besides half of Rickett's Circle, I should add. The sunlight thrown over me like an invisible net, over Hika in his Speedos across the fence, the day wrapping us tighter, binding us. I still can't say what he heard, or what he might've passed on to anyone. I can't say much of anything, really, not yet.

'I...we...' Lily's words come fast and muddy, like she's eating eggs right off the skillet. 'We weren't exactly broadcasting it, Lorraine.'

'But Mum.' Rodney pulls at her jacket; he's speaking so quietly I have to watch his lips to hear him. 'You were the one who...'

'If you've got problems keeping details under wraps in the station, then it's hardly our problem, is it?' Lily pulls her boy tighter to her side, hands set proprietarily over his shoulders. 'Now,' she sniffs, 'I imagine you've got plenty of work to do. And we've got a service to plan.'

They move away slowly, until they're far away enough to speak to each other without being overheard. Then their ute pulls quietly away, leaving only Harry watching us from inside his truck. He looks as though he plans to stay there all night.

'Well,' Dion sighs. 'I'd say that's that, then.'

I watch the ute disappear under the cover of trees. The remnants of a family driving slowly home. I know what that feels like. Not this exactly, but close enough. The sense of someone missing, of a ragged hole torn through everything, recasting the world in those strange shades of absence, the precise outline of the one gone. It never leaves you, that feeling. Especially when you're worried some of it is down to you. What you've done, or failed to do.

We turn and walk towards the patrol car. My feet scuff over the dry grass, the small sounds carrying me away from this place. All the while my mind is humming, turning over words and expressions, tracing meaning like veins of minerals snaking beneath the soil.

IT'S DARK BY the time Dion drops me home.

'You sure you don't want a lift to the stables?'

'Nah, nah.' I kick the car door open, eager for solid ground. 'I need the walk, mate. Especially after a drive like that.'

'Righto.' He looks at me through the open door, framed in a slice of light from the dash. There it is again: that lost-boy expression. Does he tell Amo about everything he comes across, I wonder? It'd do him some good, being able to bring someone else inside the tent. Someone he trusts, besides the biscuit lady at work.

'I'll see where forensics got to with the report and that.' He nods to himself. 'For Stu.'

I pat at my pocket. 'Give me a bell if anything comes of it. For now, we can use those boot prints, and the tyre marks. People have been nabbed on less than that.'

Dion snorts. 'Not by us, they haven't.'

'First time for everything, mate.' I let the door fall closed. Then, halfway to my place, I turn back and motion for him to crack the window. 'Any more bullshit from Sally Christiansen, you just send her my way.'

'I can handle a Landsdowne mum, Lorraine.' With a tight smile, Dion pulls away into the road, his red taillights receding into the dark. There's the twitch of a curtain next door, but this won't be enough of a story to travel; everyone already knows what I'm working on.

Inside, then. Some jellymeat for Tilly, a few extra tummy rubs for missing our couch time, and a roast spud and cheddar sandwich with a bit of that spicy chutney from Patel's. The rosé bottle gives me pause, swishing in invitation inside the fridge door, but now's not the time: it takes a clear mind to sift all the raw sediment in the hopper that is my brain. Instead, I pour a whole pot of coffee into the thermos, black and hot and damn near vibrating with caffeine. Then I'm out the door, walking to Bum-Bum. It's only when I'm at the footpath again that I notice the lawn's been cut. Bradley must've come by after school. 'You lovely thing.' I mutter into the night.

My feet carry me ahead over the cracked pavement, careful to avoid any eager tufts of grass. I'm a lot steadier with the new hip, but I could still go down hard in the wrong spot. There's not a soul around. All the usual evening traffic has ebbed away, leaving only me and a couple of local kererū fussing about in the trees past the bus stop. My hand reaches for the sandwich in my pocket, and I chew as I walk, letting the afternoon wash over me.

Pat Kelson. Lily Kelson.

Stu Kelson.

A long sigh leaves my chest, making me look up into the growing dark. The way Lily's voice broke as she spoke through that gap in the gateway.

That's it then, isn't it? Those hard eyes, wet and staring, carrying more weight than a person should. *That's your key suspect gone, right? For the girl?*

How strange grief can be. Turning her boy into those cold, distant words; reducing him to something practical, something to be sorted and classed. A suspect, a story. Someone kept at arm's length, not so close to the heart, as impossible as that might sound. And meanwhile, she can keep Rodney inside her hands, safe.

The similarities in their faces, those two. The boyish bounce in their cheeks, more obvious in Rodney's chubby little loaves. The way their noses both tapered into clefts in their top lips, giving them an unguarded resting expression. There's something of it in Jessica Mowbrie too, in a certain light. That sibling sense of exposure, of vulnerability. Or maybe it's only the hospital room that gives that impression.

All our little ones.

A boy strung against a tree, left to slip down into shadow. A girl found before she went too far down. And now, this whole town set against itself, like a palmful of broken glass being slowly clenched.

Jessie's got Bea with her, at least. That quick-fisted mother, ready to smash troublesome noses, and her uncle waiting with his hands ready. All Stu's got is a box and a few tired hymns. A handsome piece of stone to visit and a shiver across the back whenever they drive past.

Just like Debs. Just like Frank.

Behind me, I hear the scuff of a footstep. The night is still enough that it reaches my good ear. When I turn, a hooded figure, slim, takes a few paces and turns into a driveway. I don't catch his face—it's a boy, for sure—but I've seen enough in his movements to know he's not a neighbour. A little too self-conscious, the shoulders set back as though he knows someone's looking. I tuck my sandwich back into my pocket and keep walking, pretending I haven't seen anything.

Breathe, Lorraine.

At the next corner I pick up the pace as though I'm heading for the station and I look for a big enough car to cover me. There: a late model HiAce parked just past the dairy. I slip behind it, setting down my thermos and reaching for my keys in silence. I press them between my fingers, teeth forward and ready. My phone is in my pocket, but who would I call? The Chief is only held together with staples and twine and Dion doesn't always answer right away. I press my hands flat to the van doors, waiting to spring.

It doesn't take long for the kid to come into view. I hear his steps first, despite his attempts at stealth. He's looking sideways into all the driveways, his attention split. Then, right on time, the streetlights flicker on, their lemony yellow light slicing through the blue-grey twilight, and when he looks up, distracted, I'm on him.

'Don't!' As he turns, his eyes are huge and white. My spare hand grips his hoodie at the collar and my keys are ready. 'Please!'

'Jesus, Tāmati.' My grip relaxes and the keys slip out, jingling to the ground. 'Are you trying to put me in the bloody hospital too?'

His gaze drops to the ground. 'I'm…I'm sorry. I just…' The shock is turning into relief now. 'I had to see someone.' His expression crumples and he falls forward into me. I feel his shoulders heave under my hands.

'It's all right, kid.' I let him sob. Part of me wants to join him in it. 'It's all right.'

'Sorry.' He wipes his sleeve under his nose and reaches to the ground for my keys. 'Here.'

I tuck them back into my pocket and turn back to the van for the thermos. 'Come on then.' I nod us sideways. 'I've got a horse waiting.'

~

Bum-Bum snuffles into my palm, all eager snorts and lip-smacks, gobbling up the grain. He paused for a second at the unfamiliar company, but in the end his guts trumped his nerves.

'Bloody hell, fella.' As I scratch his neck, horsehair drifts away like dandelion spores. 'Anyone would think Roxy had been starving you.'

'Too much of that will give him the shits, you know.' Tāmati points to the grain bin, the streetlights from the road giving his face an impish aspect. 'How often does he get hay?'

'Mornings and nights.' I can feel myself squinting. 'I took you for a townie.'

He grins. I get the feeling it's his first in a while. 'Got an uncle up Taranaki ways, on my mum's side. He's into racehorses and that.' He moves closer and lifts a hand to Bum-Bum's neck, and the horse lets him keep it there. 'He's a nice boy, this one. Sometimes they get cranky in the old years, but he's chill.'

'He could give me a few pointers, maybe.'

'Yeah.' Tāmati eyes the pocket holding my keys.

The kid stays where he is, rubbing Bum-Bum across the shoulders and making him snort nice and low. The evening's warm, still, and we don't need to rush anything in this soft dark. When the boy turns to me, I see new tears across his cheeks. I fight the urge to reach out and gather him to me. He'll speak when he's ready.

'I wasn't, uh...' He falters, seemingly stuck between impulses. With a big breath, he rubs a hand across his cheek. 'I didn't tell you everything, before. At school, I mean.'

'Most people don't.' Steady, now. 'Not at first. It's okay.'

'No.' He shakes his head, his voice dropping away into a sob. 'It's not okay. You were...if I'd told you before, maybe he wouldn't have...ah, fuck. Fuck it.'

He drops his hands to his sides and turns away, his footsteps bristling over the dry grass. I stay where I am, and after a long moment by himself he comes back.

215

'Sorry.' He wipes at his eyes. 'I just…I don't know. I don't know how to get into it. Any of it.' He looks at me, then. Really looks. There's enough of a glow from the lights at the road that I can see what's in his expression. It reminds me of Sheena, after everything with Keith in the pines last year. A building coming down; a room emptied and swept.

'It's all right, Tama.' I let him see me. 'I know about you two.'

'Us two? What do you…' His voice trails away. 'Who told you?'

'Nobody, mate. Nobody told me.' I walk to him, leaving Bum-Bum to snort into my back. 'They didn't have to. Anyone could see it if they knew what to look for.' My arms go around him, and he lets me hold him. 'Just the way you watched him play was enough. The way he looked at you, too, knowing you were there.'

It all comes out, now. First, a small shaking, then bigger sobs, until he's nearly doubled over into me, shoulders hunched forward, arms loose at my middle. We stay that way for long enough that my collarbone starts to twinge, and I have to shift his head to a different spot.

'Dad keeps asking how I'm doing,' he whispers. 'Like Stu was just another mate.'

I rub his back, letting him cry. 'Just start at the start.' There's more still to come, more feeling to be let out of this boy, but time is tight. For Stu's sake, and for Jessie's, I have to press. 'The night of the party. Whatever you left out before, I need it now. All of it.'

He looks up at me through his fringe. 'It's just you, right? It won't be official or anything?' He looks to the road, then back to me. 'My mum said we'd need a lawyer and that, if I had to come in and give a statement.'

'Just me.' It's easy to say. A part of me might even believe it. 'Don't worry.'

For a moment, it looks like he might lose his nerve, but I hold onto him, a hand tight to each shoulder. Then he clears his throat and begins again.

'It was supposed to be a prank,' he sniffs. 'The thing with the bottle.'

'The GHB?' After a long pause, he nods. I keep my grip on him. 'Where'd you get it?'

'Not me.' He shakes his head. 'Heather. She said her cousin knew some people over in the Hutt. She reckons they'd done it before, at New Year's, in Coromandel or somewhere. The Mount, maybe.' He takes a long breath. 'I...we didn't mean for her to take that much.'

'Who? Michaela?'

'Neither of them,' he says. 'Look, it was...they weren't exactly stoked with it, you know? The whole debating club thing, and Stu hanging out with Jessie Mowbrie and that.' He pauses again. 'It would've been easier if it wasn't always the two of them, but Micks just kept coming along to everything Jessie did, all the time. Even when Stu tried to invite Jessie on her own, Micks always found out and came too.'

I let go of his shoulders. We're in the same water, now, both of us. 'What did she do, exactly? Why did she get offside with everyone?'

He shakes his head. 'It wasn't like it was just one thing. It was…it was like, no matter what Jess did, Micks had to get an extra run on the board somehow, by shitting on it, or whatever. Like the whole *Great Gatsby* thing.'

I feel myself grinning. 'She told me you guys were chatting about it on the drive.'

'We tried to, sure. But all Micks could do was say how lame the book was, and how boring. She had all these dense takes on the movie, and…anyway, she just kept going on and on. You could tell it was getting on Jessie's nerves, but she never said anything. I think it'd been getting on her nerves for quite a while, maybe.' He takes a long breath. 'I don't think Jessie ever really stood up to her. Not really.'

I think back to what Sheena said, about the two girls arguing in the street.

Nasty shit, Aunty.

'What then?' I keep his attention. 'Heather doses them up, and then someone at the party gives Jessie a hiding, eh?' His pupils jump with alarm. 'Then one of your mates gets scared and dumps her in the bush?'

'No! I…no, that's…look, I told you about them all drinking from the bottle and that, right?' His words come quickly, as though he's running out of air. 'We went outside, me and Stu. He'd been stressed about things with his mum and dad lately, and he needed to vent a bit. Heather, she…she mixed the stuff up with Baileys so Stu wouldn't have any.

Too sweet for him, even with the pump, you know?' A shard of wet feeling crosses his eyes. 'We went outside, just me and him, while the girls were all at the table together. Then Jessie came out, saying she wanted to show Stu something on her phone. She saw us.' He coughs. 'The two of us. Together, I mean. We weren't…we weren't doing anything, but still. It wasn't a big deal, though. It was like maybe she knew already or something.' A tear falls across his cheek, and I have to resist the urge to hug him again. 'They went to the spot in the trees where the Wi-Fi worked, so she could show him something. Something from an old Lange debate, she said.'

'The Oxford debate? David Lange?'

'Yeah, that's it.' He looks relieved. 'Anyway, they went into the trees, and I went back to the others.' He looks to the ground. 'That's it. That's all.'

'You did, eh?' I let the silence gather. 'Come on, mate. You've come this far.'

'She…' He looks to me again. 'Fuck it. She still had a thing for Stu, I think. So, I…I walked behind, after them. Just to see what she was up to.' His shoulders slump lower. 'Someone was riding a horse on the other side of the trees.'

'At night?' I think back to Lily's jerkin, and the horsehair clinging across the shoulders. 'You're sure it wasn't just a horse blasting around on its own, spooked by the lights or something? They can do that sometimes.'

He shakes his head. 'I could hear someone using a crop. Quite hard, it sounded like. Then the sound came closer to the fence, so I turned back. I thought Stu wouldn't want me hanging around anyway.'

I take in the information. 'What else?'

'The rest I told you already.' He wipes at his cheeks. 'Stu came inside after a while, and saw how messed up Micks was. He must've guessed Heather had something to do with it, because he made her drive her home. As a favour, I mean.'

I picture the crack of Bea's fist against Heather's nose. It shouldn't give me any satisfaction, but it does. 'And you?'

'Me?' He holds my eye, steadier than before. 'I stayed. I stayed with him.' There's the same glimmer in his expression. 'With Stu.'

It's all there, all of it. *I stayed with him.*

Behind us, Bum-Bum snorts, stamping his feet. 'It's getting on,' I say. 'How about I walk you to the main road, and we can call Dion? He'll drop you back to Langsford.'

Tāmati pulls out his keys, twirling them around his finger. 'I parked near yours.'

'Brave of you, with that car.'

He gives me another grin, less complicated than before, and we start the walk back to the main road. He seems lighter now, his movements less freighted, like a fresh shorn ewe, bare and jumping.

'What had they been arguing about, then?' I turn to him. 'Stu's mum and dad?'

'Hmm?'

I give him a second. 'You said he seemed a bit stressed. Needing to vent and all.'

220

'Oh, I dunno. Something about the farm, the succession planning or whatever.' His voice trails off. 'His mum always used to go on about how it would be Stu's to come into, later.' He sniffs. 'She could usually guess what Stu was thinking, most of the time. Not like Pat. Shit, she even guessed about things with us, I think. She kept squeezing my hand extra hard after she took us to see *Call Me by Your Name*.' A dazed smile comes over him. 'But she had a real blind spot about all that stuff with the farm and that. Not that it matters now.'

'No. I guess not.' I set a hand on Tāmati's arm, letting him know where I am. Ballast, another body nearby. That's all we need, sometimes. 'He never wanted it, eh?' I hold my voice low. 'The farm and all that?'

'Nah. It wasn't really his thing.' Tāmati wipes under his nose. 'He always helped out with the big things, the docking and the fencing and that. But I think he was hoping Rodney might be keen. He always talked about getting over to Aussie after Langsford. The States, even. I was helping him look at scholarships.'

I let him cry as we walk, trying not to look at him. All the while, the information turns over in my head. If Stu really was the last person seen with Jessie, there's a chance we've been looking at this all wrong. But here, now, that's not what's required of me.

'I know it's hard, mate.' We walk side by side, slowly. 'It'll stay hard for a while. I don't want to put you wrong. There will be nights ten, twenty years from now, you'll wake up in the night trying to tell him something.'

'Yeah?' He looks at me for a long moment, the moon trapped in his eye. 'I hope so.'

The streetlights bear us forward. One foot, then another.

'There's one last thing.' I take a breath, waiting until I have his attention. 'And this is important, now. Monday night, when you went out with Stu for his run. Something happened, didn't it?' I watch his movements. 'Something more than what you've told me?'

His gaze drops to the footpath again. Up ahead is the bridge. By the time we've reached it, he's decided he wants to speak. 'He was in a mood, about the bottle and that.' Here, he looks to me again, still cagey. 'You guys told him, didn't you? About the blood results for Jessie?' I nod. 'He kept pushing me on it, and pushing, until I told him about Heather and that. Then he was texting someone, but he…he wouldn't talk to me anymore, so I went back and waited outside the boarding house. But he…well, you know the rest.'

I do. I do know, but I need him to tell me.

'Who was he texting, Tāmati?' We come to the end of the bridge, leaving behind the low burble of the Ruamāhanga.

'I don't know.' He shakes his head. 'Honestly. But here, give me your phone.' I do as I'm told, unlocking it and handing it over. He types a six-digit code into my notes app. 'That's his passcode. For his phone, I mean.' He leaves a long pause. 'He didn't know I knew it.'

I stare at the screen, committing the numbers to memory, just in case I lose the bloody phone somewhere. Then it goes back into my pocket, and we keep walking.

Secrets and whispers. Half-heard utterances, and horses through the dark.

Whatever else this place has in store for us, we're together, me and this kid. He's what Bradley could be in a few years. I think about whether that would be a good thing, and it doesn't take me long to decide.

'Thanks, Tāmati.' I take his hand, and I squeeze. He looks at me again, wet eyes shining in the streetlights, a thumbnail of moon still floating in one of them. We walk together, lighter than before, no matter what else we still carry.

SOMEHOW I END up sleeping past my alarm. A good thing, too; it's just gone eight, and it's the closest I've felt to refreshed since the Borgs found Jessie. I'm buttering a piece of wholegrain and heating yesterday's coffee on the stovetop before I think to check my phone.

Don't freak out. It's from Moko. *Sheen is in the ward. Come when you can.*

I nearly take the front door off the hinges. It's only after a thistle stabs me in the toe near the road that I remember my shoes.

~

Moko's waiting outside the entrance when I get to the hospital, the stub of a roll-your-own hanging from his fingers, trying to blow the smoke away from the doors. It must be serious; he hasn't sparked up since Christmas.

'Bloody hell.' He drops the butt and scuffs it under his shoes, his gaze lingering on my forehead. 'You run the whole way or something?'

'Where is she?' It's like I've swallowed my tongue. 'Where's Sheena? What's...'

'It's all right, Aunty. Here, come on.' We step inside, and he guides me to a chair by the window, pulling it out for me.

'I'm not fucking sitting, Moko!' His pupils go wide. 'Where the hell...'

'Whoa, now.' He holds his palms up. 'She had a few pains in the night. And we're not too far off game day, so I thought... we thought it could be the big one, y'know? Contractions and that?' He gestures to the chair again, and this time I take it. 'It all passed around four or five, and it's been sweet since then. The midwife said it happens sometimes.'

'Is she...' My heart starts to slow down, and there's less of the washing machine feeling inside. 'Where is she?'

'Sleeping. The boyo's with her.' Moko smiles through a yawn. Past his shoulder, the bearded nurse from the other night picks up a phone at the desk, looking grave. His eyes meet mine across the lobby, and his mouth pulls tight. 'That kid's been bloody handy, you know,' Moko continues. 'Really pulling his weight. Anyway, they want her to rest up for today at least. And no more shifts at Seven Oaks. The midwife reckons she'll have to...'

'Lorraine. Did someone call you?' It's my mate the nurse,

out of breath himself, leaning down to my side. I didn't even see him cross the room.

'Me?' I squint up at him and get a face full of fluorescent lighting. All my wires are crossed and sparking. 'No, it's my niece, she's...fuck, it's not Rick, is it? The Chief?'

He stands. 'Come with me.'

Moko helps me out of the chair, frowning. 'Tell Sheen I'll come by later on,' I say.

'Righto.'

We're through the automatic doors before the nurse speaks again. Through a set of doors to the side, I see Rick's partner Lee walking past with a plastic container full of something green and leafy. A tiny part of me relaxes; he looks tired, but not panicked. It can't be about the Chief.

'She's come to.' The nurse whispers. 'The Mowbrie girl. Jessica.'

Everything inside my chest lurches to a stop. 'When?'

'Just now.' He shoves the next set of doors open. 'She's stable, they said. Enough to speak.' He wipes at his temple. 'We've left messages with the mother.'

'Jesus, she...how is she?' I pull my phone from my pocket, and it slips from my fingers, clattering to the floor. Dion. I need him here pronto. 'Fuck, sorry. I ran here, from my place. We'll have to...'

'It's okay. Take a breath.' We pause before the doors to the intensive ward, and he picks my phone up for me. 'They're just sorting out her fluids now.'

I wipe at my eyes, noticing how wet my cheeks are. I can't

say where all of this is coming from. It's like I'm trying to dodge multiple cars coming at me on the same road. He doesn't ask me if I'm ready, just pushes the doors open, and we walk into that white antiseptic channel. The smell is the same, all the chairs in their usual place, dutiful and waiting. Only now the rectangular pane of wired glass has something new to show me.

A girl.

She's sitting up in bed, eyes still half-lidded, her mouth cracking open just enough to receive a straw from the nurse at her bedside. Her hair is fanned out like tame fire against the pillows, more of it out of her collar than before. Then she turns her head, and she sees me. Jessie sees me.

~

'Just a few minutes,' the nurse whispers. 'The tubes have dried her throat out.'

'Lorraine?' Jessie speaks from the pillows, faint, but audible. She's rasping like an unoiled machine, but it's her. It's her voice. 'You're all wet.'

'Never mind that, girl.' I wipe under my eyes. I know we won't have long. 'God, it's good to see you like this, Jessie. Your mum's going to be bloody ecstatic, you know.'

Shifting against the bed, she pushes herself up, wincing as she moves. Every movement is costing her; I set my hands under her arms and help. There's still a thick bandage around one side of her head, and what looks like a small eggplant peering out from inside the gauze. She scans the window to the hallway.

227

'Where is she?'

'Your mum?' I cough. 'She went home to shower, girl. She...they've been here every day, her and Micks. Your uncle too.' I wait for her eyes to open again, then reach for her hand. Her skins feels hot, and somehow thinner across her fingers. In the hallway, another nurse comes past with a steel trolley. I pray for her to keep moving, and she does. 'Listen, Jess. I know it might be tough to talk about.' I squeeze her fingers just enough. 'But it's important. I need you to tell me what you remember. About the party, and everything before that.'

'The party?' One of her eyebrows dips below her bandage, pulling itself free from the tight ring of gauze. 'I...I don't...' She trails off, and her gaze slides to the ceiling.

'It's all right, girl.' I'm squeezing her too hard, I realise. 'Take your time.'

She takes a long breath, though it pains her. 'What happened?' Her lips stay parted, showing a row of neat teeth made furry by the oxygen mask. 'Was it an accident? Those gravel roads, and...'

'Someone found you in the bush, girl.' I speak as slowly as I can manage, expecting the door to fly open at any second to reveal an angry Mowbrie. 'Up near Atiwhakatū.'

'The bush?' She frowns, then closes her eyes. 'Who? Who found me?'

'Some trampers.' I lean closer. 'The party, Jessie. Stu's party.' I let the words reach her. 'What do you remember about it?' A long moment passes. But for the beeping machines, the room is silent. 'Maybe now's not the best time.'

When I go to stand, my hand slips from hers. Then her eyes fall open again. 'Tama,' she croaks. 'He was playing Frank Ocean in the car.' There's another long pause as she swallows. 'Not exactly Mick's favourite.'

'That's right, girl. That's right.' There are more tears on my cheeks now. I bend back down to her, letting them come. 'What else?'

In a halting voice, she gives me a lot of what I know already, one brief parcel of language at a time. The drive and the woolshed, the girls waiting for them, and Heather asking Michaela about Tuck's driving jobs. She mentions something about a broken chair, and a toilet that wouldn't flush, before she gets back to the bottle.

'It was something really sweet,' she says. 'Something Christmassy or something.'

'Bailey's.'

Her eyes brighten, just for a moment. 'That's it.' She leans back further against the pillows. 'Then I...we went outside, me and Stu, to, uh.' She frowns to herself, lost for a moment. 'I had something to show him, on my phone.'

There are voices in the hallway behind me, but I shut them out. 'Then what, Jessie?'

'There was a spot in the trees. He...he showed me how to stay in one place so the Wi-Fi worked. But it wasn't enough for the whole thing to play.' She coughs, a rattling sound descending inside her. I lean forward with the water cup, giving her the straw. A sour smell lifts into my nose, like a morning bedroom. 'Thanks. I really...I had to pee, I think.

Stu showed me a good spot, by where his mum and dad used to chop up meat for the dogs.' For a second, she smiles. 'The dog tucker, he called it. Then he went back to find Tama.'

She shuts her eyes again. It's a strain, of course it is. But I need her to push through. With my hand on her fingers, I urge her on, one ear still to the hallway. 'Go on, girl.'

'I must have been a little woozy, from the Bailey's and that, because I had to stop a few times in the trees. Then I found the block with the axe in it, and took a pee. That's...that's it, I think. I was peeing.'

'You're sure Stu went back?' My hand stays on her. 'Nobody else was there?'

She takes a sharp breath inward. I can see how it hurts her, all this talking. And yet, I need it. I need to let her hurt, just for a second.

'There was a sound.' Her eyes open wider. 'A sound behind me, like metal jangling. A chain, or something. Or keys, maybe.' I can hear doors opening somewhere over my shoulder. 'I don't know, Lorraine. I can't...I can't remember anything after that.'

'It's okay, Jessie.' A clearing in the trees. A chopping block, and the jangling of metal. I think of my phone in my pocket; I could've been recording this. 'You've done great. So great.'

She shifts her head to the side, wincing. It takes me a moment to realise her lips are moving. I have to risk another sour waft to hear her.

'...can tell you everything.'

'Who, girl?' I give her my good ear. 'Who can tell me everything?'

'Stu.' Her eyes open again, filled with light and colour. 'He'll know what happened.'

There's movement in the hallway, closer now. Before I can say anything, the door swings open hard, and the air fills with squeaking shoes. I feel Jessie flinch under my hand.

'Jess.' It's Bea, her face crumpling with relief. And beneath that, with disbelief. 'Oh, my love. My love.'

Jessie's arms go up as far as she can manage, waiting to receive her mum. I move back, making myself small, invisible. Even in Masterton, some things should stay private.

There's sobbing from both of them, and whispered words I can't make out. In the hallway, my bearded nurse mate watches through the glass, arms tucked across his scrubs, a warm and satisfied look on his face. Next to him, Michaela stares into the room, mouth open, arms locked at her sides. Her eyes meet mine, and I wave her into the room. She shuffles closer to me, staring with disbelief at her cousin.

'She's all right, Micks.' She leans into me, and I let her. Her arms are stiff, like laundry drying on a still day. 'It's okay. It's all okay.'

Michaela sniffs into my chest, still looking sideways at the bed. It's to be expected, a mood like this. Shock, and relief. There's a lot to take in. And anyway, after everything at the station I'm off her list of trusted friends. We stay where we are, as far out of the way as we can get in a room this small.

Then Bea lifts her head from Jessie. Her top lip is shiny and wet, but now's not the time to be precious.

'Come and see your cousin, girl.' Bea sniffs. 'Go on.'

With reluctant steps, Michaela crosses the space between them, setting her hand to the sheets. Her hair is loose and fuzzy. I can't see her face from where I stand, but I can imagine her expression from the angle of her body, and from her breathing.

Joy, and hesitation. The confusion of relief, the confusion of disappointment. I've been a sister. I know what it can be to have everyone's attention split down the middle like an icing bun, both halves somehow marred, the parts always coming out less than the sum. It's been her show alone, these last days. Now, they'll need to find their way back to things.

'Hey,' Jessie whispers. I can't hear Michaela say anything in response.

'Listen,' I cough. 'You need me to call Tuck?'

Bea wipes at her cheeks, her mouth pulling flat. 'He's on his way back from the coast already.' Her gaze lingers on mine for longer than I expect. There are such depths in her expression. A mum's relief at a nightmare over, and now new waters to navigate, new regrets to turn over in the silent hours.

'All right, then.' I clasp my hands at my front, watching the three of them. On the bed, Jessie leans back with her eyes closed; Michaela turns to me, giving me an in-between expression. 'We'll be back tonight, Bea. If she's well enough, we can take a proper statement.'

Bea clears her throat, looking sideways. 'A statement, eh?

You'll have your hands full, won't you? That Christiansen woman wanting a charge and all?'

'I think we've got that in hand for the moment.' I hold my eyes to hers, feeling a line strung tight between us. I can't say if she's thanking me or warning me off. Or both.

They're kettles on the boil, that lot.

From her perch against the pillows, Jessie's mouth is moving. 'Christiansen?' She coughs. 'You mean Stu's mate? What does Heather…'

'Hush, now.' Bea bends back to Jessie's side, setting her head next to her shoulder. Her daughter, her treasure. 'You just rest up.'

Outside the room, the hallway is empty. I catch a last glimpse of them as I go: three forms huddled together against the world outside, against anyone who might be looking.

Sirens through the warm dark. A flashing red light, and the breeze lifting against me. Then a lonely flashlight through the trees, showing the reaching hands of branches, the low clumps of watchful ferns, and no stars to be seen anywhere.

Lost, and found.

Back in the waiting room, I fall into an empty chair. My throat is full of dust; I look around for a familiar face, but even the usual nurse is gone. Moko and Sheena. Bradley. Christ, even Rick's in here somewhere, his head smashed to bits. Everything feels tilted, all angles pushed past their marks, all colours smeared together. I set a hand across my collarbone, feeling the little mended burr of me. Then I breathe, and I let myself come back from wherever I've been.

MOKO DRIVES ME, but not home.

'You're sure you're all right, Aunty?' He squints from the driver's seat. 'Reckon you could do with a cup of tea and a moe, eh? Leave the papers for some other bugger for once?'

'I'm sound, don't you worry.' I pat his arm, nearly convincing myself. Truth be told, I could do with him carrying me inside, but I'm not about to let that show. 'Do me a favour, though, would you?'

'Course.'

'Poke your head into Rick's room on the way back, all right? Just for a second.'

'The Chief? You trying to pop his head open again or something?' The ghost of a grin flickers over his mouth. 'All right. I'll give you a bell if he looks like he needs reinforcements.'

'Ta.' I shove open the door and lurch onto the footpath. 'And tell Sheena to remember what I said. No more shifts at Seven Oaks. Not until that baby is ready to wipe some arses of her own.'

'Auē.' He laughs from his belly. 'I'll tell her you said that.'

When he pulls away into the road my hands are shaking. The petrol station is right there, and a cup of volcanic coffee would damn near save me, but it'd be too much time in the light, exposed.

Dion's car is parked behind the station. I find him in the Chief's office, papers spread all over the desk.

'Bit presumptuous, eh?'

He grins. 'Light's much better in here. Not like that cave of yours.'

'Some days, a cave is the only safe place, mate.'

I lay myself down on the Chief's couch under the window, every atom of me feeling heavier than before. Then there's the gentle pressure of his hand on my shoulder.

'Take the day, Lorraine.' He speaks low and coaxing. 'Looks like she's going to be all right after all.'

'Yeah.' I set a hand over his. 'Not sure how her cousin feels about that, though.'

~

When I'm done telling him about my morning, Dion is still frowning, but in a different way. There's a cake half-risen in his eyes: a little more heat and patience and it'll be all the way done.

'She went out for a slash, she said?'

'Yes, Dion.' I take a long sip of strong sweet coffee. He's pulled one of the Chief's spare chairs up for me to use as a footrest, keeping me nearly horizontal. With the coffee in my system, I might nearly be able to stand again. 'You've seen a woolshed toilet, haven't you?'

'So, what then? We're back to the Stu theory, are we?' His frown deepens. 'I can't say I see it.'

'I can't either, honestly.' I nod sideways into the hallway. 'You saw how Stu was when they came in. He was so fired up about the idea of someone dosing Jessie, we could've fried an egg on him.'

'Who then, eh?' Dion crosses his arms behind his head, showing me dinner-plate sweat stains under his arms. 'The boyfriend, Tāmati? Or little Miss Muffet with the broken nose, the Christiansen girl?'

I'm not sure she'd be up to it. You saw how quickly Bea put her on her arse.' Above us, the Chief's ceiling fan spins slow and lazy. 'Plus, Heather was the one who dropped Michaela home. It would've been a hell of a drive to get from Tuck's place to Tārehu and out to the Tararuas in the window forensics gave us, right?'

He shrugs. 'Buggered if I know, Lorraine.'

I drain my coffee, tapping my fingers against the hollow mug. 'As far as Tāmati goes, he'd hardly drop by and fess up to knowing about the GHB if he'd tried to do Jessie in himself, would he?'

'S'pose not.' Dion scratches at his stubble. 'Honestly, I've not been at my sharpest these last few days.' He gives a long yawn. 'I fell asleep on the couch with our little ratbag at half three this morning watching Gordon Ramsay clips.'

We sit in silence. Outside, I hear the crash of a stock truck going past in the main road. Late summer lambs, probably; my nose fills with the phantom waft of lanolin baked by the sun. Then, in my pocket, my phone vibrates.

Sheena. *Home tonight they said. Need my bed. This one is punishing my arse.*

'Where's the phone, anyway?'

'Hmm?' I look up from the screen.

'Stu Kelson's phone.' Crossing his arms, Dion nods into the hallway. 'We had it bagged in the car, didn't we?'

'Rick gave it to Pat, I think.' There's something moving in my gut, the quick gnaw of a hunch solidifying. I can see where Dion's going; I should've got to the same place long ago. 'Fuck it. Grab your keys.'

THIS TIME THERE'S nobody parked at the Tārehu gates, though the bulldozer still blocks the cattlestop, a hulking yellow fist of stubborn metal. Dion pulls to a stop at the gravel verge opposite as the sun comes down over the scrub-covered hills and into our eyes.

'You messaged the Chief, right?'

'Lee,' I nod. 'Last time I saw Rick, he wasn't exactly in shape for reading texts. His head's still a split boot.'

Dion slips on his sunglasses and nods past the gateway to the gravel road snaking up through the trees. 'It's what, a couple of kilometres to the farmhouse?'

'Less to the woolshed.' I clamber out of the seat, swinging my legs to the ground.

'And you're, uh...you're up for the walk, then?'

The grass at the verge crackles under my feet, brittle with

the summer. 'I made it up to Atiwhakatū in the middle of the bloody night, didn't I?'

'All right, fair play. I was just asking.' He slips his hat off and tucks it inside the car. Then I hear him fiddling with the gun safe in the boot.

'What are you playing at?' I move to his side. 'You saw Harry Brooke last time.'

'Exactly my point. We should come ready.' Dion pulls out the rifle, slinging it to his shoulder. A shiver runs through me like it always does.

Metal and wood. A muffled crack, and the shot screaming past me like a hot bee.

'It's bad enough we're coming up without calling, mate.' I nod to the rifle. 'If they see you with that, things could get hairy. Uniform or no.'

He stands where he is, eyes narrowed. I can damn near read his mind: Martinborough, the Prendergast place, Justin. In anyone else's account, it'd be a reason to bring the whole bloody munitions room with us.

But I know better. 'It wouldn't have helped, Dion.'

I look to the ground. Dust and sun. A man's legs flailing out, his shoes scraping desperate tracks in the gravel as his life leaked away. 'Not the way things panned out. Trust me. You're the one with rank, here. But I need you to trust me.'

In a while, I feel his hand on my shoulder. 'Only if you're sure.'

'I'm sure.' I wipe my eyes and nod across the road. 'Come on. Not much light left.'

~

Right away, my shirt's sticking to me. It isn't long before I'm wet all the way across the shoulders and droplets of sweat are running down into my neck. Dion stays a few steps ahead, looking back to me every few minutes. It's only a mild incline, but I'm sounding more and more like my pony with each step, grunting and grumbling.

'The bottle.' I point to Dion's bag.

'Again? We're not even...'

'Give me the cunting thing.'

He looks like he's grabbed a hot stove but he does as he's told. I drain the last of the water and hand the bottle back.

'That's all of it.' Dion shakes the empty metal canister. 'So now we'll be staring down Harry Brooke with no rifle and a bad case of the drys, eh?'

'He'll be back on his own block by now,' I wheeze. 'Blockade or not, he's got his own mobs to run.'

'That's a hunch, Lorraine. Just a bloody hunch.'

Despite his grumbling we keep up a steady pace. Soon enough, the tree cover stops, and the sunlight comes over us. There's a flat stretch of road leading to the stockyards, and beyond that, the low green box of the Tārehu woolshed, its windows winking at us. Around us, the air glows with the last of the sunlight. Soon, these hills will turn from gold to grey, and the air will thicken to silvery blue, giving way to stars. There's no cloud out here, and nothing to get in their way.

Nowhere to hide, either.

'Stick to the fence,' I say. 'And don't bloody crouch down like that. We're not in the wrong here, mate. If they see us, they see us.'

'Righto.' Dion gives me a chastened expression, every bit the schoolboy. Over the fence I see three horses standing under the pines. Good-looking animals, tall and lean, kept strong with work. They'd be a good size for Lily; the biggest one might even seat Pat.

'That'll be it, right?' Dion points as we come past the wool-shed. Somebody's left the sliding door open at the wool dock; they'll have starlings in the rafters before long. 'The woolshed where Stu had his party?'

There's still enough light that he can see my expression. 'No, they've got two woolsheds, one for shearing, one for drinking Bailey's.'

Dion clicks his tongue. 'Don't get hōhā, Lorraine. I was just...'

'Yes, Dion. That's the woolshed.'

We move across the gravelled track leading to the shed, alongside a fence running down to some windbreak trees. They're Macrocarpas, mostly, with a few old leaning pines. Everything seems smaller than I remember, even the trees. Old Bill Kelson must've cut them back and replanted at some point. He's always been a clever one; he'll have known how to avoid anything coming down in the wind.

'That's about where Stu found Jessie's phone, I reckon.' I nod to the fence opposite the woolshed's front door. 'Or where he said he did, anyway.'

'Jessie said she had it in the trees, didn't she?' Dion frowns. 'By the chopping block?'

'That's right.' I breathe out long and slow, trying to calm my nerves. Everything is quiet around us. 'Come on, then. She'd have gone this way, towards the house.'

Dion follows just behind me, his footsteps dragging through the loose gravel on the track. I start to shush him, then I think: probably best to be obvious.

'Through there?' Dion nods into the trees.

'Yep.' When I squint, I can make out the yellow smudges of a porch light through the trunks. 'Can't be far now.'

We come to a steel gate. I click it open, making sure Dion closes it behind us. Then, in my good ear: hoofbeats like distant drums.

Someone was riding a horse on the other side of the trees.

'They won't jump the fence, will they?' Dion frowns.

'Not a big horse guy, eh?' I can't help but grin. 'Nah, mate. They're just checking us out, don't worry.'

He doesn't look convinced. 'I had an aunty on my dad's side growing up,' he points to his cheek, 'paralysed on one side. Walked too close to a Clydesdale and took a hoof to the back of the head.' He shakes his head. 'You lot are bloody mad to get up on those things at all.'

Ahead of us there's a clearing, and a few old wooden kennels up on short stilts. From the smell, the Kelsons haven't kept dogs here in years. In the middle of the space a round wooden block sits like a strange altar, an old meat axe sticking out of the surface. It's rusted all over; hasn't been used in an age.

'What do you reckon, eh? Good place for a girl to pop a squat?' Dion crouches down next to the block, the pine needles shifting under his feet. For a second he looks like he's going to start sniffing the soil.

'Every day is an education with you, mate.' I shake my head. 'It's as good a spot as any. A little exposed, but it would've been pitch black anyway.'

'Except for that porch light.' Dion nods ahead through the trees. 'The house isn't far off at all.'

I bend down, staring through the fading light at the earth around the chopping block, and I think back to what Jessie told me.

If Stu peeled off and left her like she said, she would've been feeling her way ahead in the dark. I try to picture how these trees would've looked to her, and how the air might've felt. Was there a footstep? The scrape of a boot against the soft cover of pine needles? A voice, or a breath of air, before the jingling sound? Before that grey void stretched across her memory, wrapping her tight?

'Lorraine.'

I turn, and I see Dion nodding sideways. Someone's standing at the edge of the clearing, next to one of the old kennels. The brother, Rodney. His long hair hanging beside his face, his features blank and impassive, watching us.

'Mum keeps the dogs behind the workshop now.' He sounds just like Stu, but softer. 'Our Huntaway, Stag, kept chewing through the mesh whenever Sock was in heat.'

'A Huntaway will do that.' I smile as calmly as I can. 'We

243

had a dog roam all the way to the coast once, just to get to a bitch.'

He watches me long enough for his guard to come down. There's something lost in his expression; earth after a bushfire, scorched and empty. Jesus, these last few days. At thirteen, it probably feels like his entire universe has been snuffed out. He shifts his weight to his other foot, and I see the length of something propped against the kennel. He reaches for it.

A rifle.

'Stay still! Don't you bloody…'

'Wait, wait.' I hold a hand up for Dion. 'It's all right. You remember us, don't you?'

'Yeah.' Startled, Rodney watches us, his hand still on the barrel. 'I was just…' He gestures to the rifle. 'Uncle Harry said to take a walk around and make sure everything was okay.' His gaze moves between us, then come to rest on me. 'After what happened, I mean.'

'I see.' I smile as wide as I can. 'Well, it's only us here, so you can keep that bolt nice and open, all right?' I walk towards him, steady and slow. 'You never want to trust the safety on its own, believe me.'

'That's what my uncle says.' Rodney lifts the rifle strap to his shoulder. It's much too big for him; he's doing his best not to look ridiculous but not quite succeeding. Despite the situation, I'm fighting off a giggle. He stands still, watching me with a serious expression. 'You were the ones who found him.'

His words come slowly but clearly. There's a resolve in him. Here is a boy used to being underestimated, to being swept to the corners. But we're here, now, and we're listening.

'That's right.' I look him in the eyes, and he doesn't look away. He lifts the rifle strap, settling the weight of the wood in a better spot. He seems to be making his mind up about something, but I can't say what it is. 'That was us, Rodney.'

'We're so sorry, kid.' Dion moves forward, nearly past me, but I lift a hand to keep him where he is. With a quick glance, I look through the trees, making sure it's just us.

'Remember yesterday, when we were talking to your mum at the road?' I keep my voice low and hushed.

'Yeah.' He looks to Dion, then back to me. 'I think so.'

'We were talking about your brother finding his friend's phone. The girl, Jessie. You remember? About how he'd seen it by the fence and brought it in for us?' When I pause, he looks sideways through the trees. 'You started saying something to your mum, but she didn't let you finish.'

He's still holding my gaze, but there's something different in his expression now, a new shade of complication. He goes to speak; he stops himself.

'She's in the kitchen.' He nods over his shoulder, shifting hair out of his eyes. 'She'll want you to talk to her, I think.'

His hands grip the leather strap with shaking fingers. A boy, carrying something much too big for him. He lifts the rifle and resettles it again, looking for a more comfortable place.

IT'S ONLY A short walk to the farmhouse, but the daylight has drained away even further; we have to follow Rodney as he picks his way through the trunks.

Then we're there, and it's something else to add to the smaller-than-I-remember list. When we were younger, the second storey of the Kelson farmhouse always seemed to loom over me and Debs like a giant wall of wood and windows, the metal roof glimmering so tall in the sun. Now it just looks like any other farmhouse: the wooden steps and the boot bin, the low metal hook bolted into the bottom step to help with muddy gumboots.

This was what it was all for. Bill Kelson and Arthur Brooke.

Rodney's hardly at the second step before Lily appears in the doorway, her expression quickening from disbelief to anger.

'You...' She looks to Rodney, then back to us. 'I told you

to leave off, didn't I? If you want to bother someone you can call Horiana. God knows she...'

'It's all right, Lily.' I look up the stairs to her, trying for a placating smile. 'We have some new information, and Horiana wasn't answering her office phone.'

I feel Dion staring at the side of my head. Leave it, mate. Just leave it.

'New information?' Her lips draw tight. 'About Stu?'

I move up the steps, until I'm next to Rodney. 'It's best if we all sit down.' From here, I can see how red her eyes are, how puffy her cheeks. Her pupils are still hard and black, though: the dense unshakeable core of her intact. I stare into the house. 'Pat too.'

She looks to Dion, her mouth twitching. With a quick sigh, she turns. 'Come on, then.' She gestures to Rodney. 'And put that thing back in the shed.'

The boy draws himself up straighter. 'Uncle Harry said I should keep it handy. Just in case anyone comes.'

'I don't care what he said. I can't be the only one keeping you two boys out of...' She falters, and the sharp edge under her words drops away. I can feel the breath go out of the kid. Then she gathers herself and moves closer to Rodney. 'Just put it in the shed, love.'

Rodney turns, redder in the cheeks than before, and steps back into his gumboots, walking around the edge of the verandah to a small workshop shed. Through the open door, I see saddles and riding gear, and a small stack of pea straw. When I turn back, Lily has disappeared; her steps are so light.

Dion looks to me, confused, and I nod for him to follow.

Inside, there's the comfortable smell of wood lacquer and a spirit of flowers from a dish of potpourri on a chest in the hallway. I've never been inside this house before; the closest me and Debs ever came was watching Dad drop off the Christmas cake from the gravel out front, and seeing little Pat—Pee-Wee then—grabbing Bill's shins as he exchanged gruff words of thanks and told dad to give our mum his thanks, before walking our best cake tin back inside with him.

Gifts, and thefts.

Then I hear the sound of rushing water. Through a doorway, Lily is at the kitchen sink, filling a kettle. The window beyond her shows us a gorgeous square of land: the paddock with the three horses grazing in the last minutes of the day, everything shot through with brilliant gold by the sunlight sluicing across the peaks from the west. I've always wondered what it must look like from in here, that paddock, and now I know. It looks like first prize. At the very farthest edge, there's a thick tuft of green bush: there must be a few rimu in there, still, and some white pine, the kahikatea. It's the corner of our old block. Dad used to take us there every year for a nip of port and some lamb sandwiches on Mum's birthday, and we'd look out on the Kelson place from the other side: the wide flat expanse of buttery summer grass so far away it might as well have been another country.

'I can see why Bill would miss this place.'

Lily turns to me, frowning. 'Bill?' She thumps the jug

down on its base and clicks it on to boil. 'What about him?'

Past the log burner and through the doorway, I hear footsteps. Pat emerges from the shadows, red-faced himself, and wiping a finger under his eye. 'Lorraine?' His eyebrows push together as he looks to Dion, then back to me. In his spare hand there's an old tea-towel; I hear the crinkle of ice settling inside a plastic bag. 'Did you walk from the road?'

'Not many other options, are there mate?' Dion crosses his arms.

'It was a good chance to remind myself of the place.' I keep my gaze on Pat, tracking his expression. 'Did you sprain something?'

'Hmm?' He looks at the ice pack. 'Oh, no. Just an old shearing thing, gives me grief sometimes.' He flexes his hand slowly and gestures to the table.

'I think we've got still got some Afghans somewhere,' says Lily. 'Right love?'

Pat gazes between me and Dion, his expression shifting. 'You've got something, then? About Stu?'

A new silence fills the space between us. Pat holds his eyes to mine, ignoring Lily. I point Dion to the chairs, taking one for myself; usually it'd be bad form without an invitation, but we're in different territory here. Pat settles himself down next to me, staring in expectation. The bag of ice crinkles on the table, already half-melted.

'It's Jessie Mowbrie.' I speak slowly, looking from Pat to Lily. 'She's come to.'

'She has?' Pat leans forward, making his chair squeak. 'Oh

Jesus, that's bloody fantastic news. We...is she, uh...how's she doing?'

At the bench, Lily doesn't move but I can see the information hit her. 'You told me it was about our boy.' Her words are tight and flat. She points to the table, to a short stack of papers. Photos of Stuart: a Langsford class photo, and one of him on a quad bike, grinning to split his face. 'You said it was about Stu.'

'We've been planning the service,' Pat mutters. 'It's...oh, bloody hell Lorraine, that's...she's pulled through. Jessie's pulled through.' He leans back against the chair and exhales. 'Her mum must be so relieved.'

Behind him, Lily's expression curdles.

'A few temporary speech things, they said.' Dion sets his elbows on the table, looking to me. 'Fracture's healing up nicely, though.' He jerks a thumb to the spot behind his ear.

'Look, that's good news. Really.' Lily pulls her arms tighter across her chest until her body is a coiled spring. 'But we're planning a service for our boy. You can't just come in here without any warning.'

'What's happened, Dad?' Rodney stands in the doorway, wide-eyed.

'She's going to be all right, Roddo.' Pat lifts a hand to his cheeks again. 'Jessie is. The girl, from Stu's party.' He pulls out the chair next to his. 'Here, come and sit down, mate. You've been on your feet all day, eh?'

'No, no.' Behind Lily, the jug clicks off, wreathing her in steam. 'There are still some photos we need, okay? Here.' She steps away from the bench, her arms held out to her son's shoulders. Her cheeks are pale, and her fingers grab him tighter than necessary. 'The ones from Castlepoint that time. The crab photo. You know the one.' She points the boy upstairs. He frowns, but complies. 'It's in the office, I think. Bottom drawer.'

'He's okay, Lil.' Pat speaks softly. 'He's interested, that's all.'

'He can help fetch the photos, Patrick.' Lily turns back to the table, arms crossed. Behind me, I hear Rodney's footsteps move up the stairs. 'God knows there's enough to do.'

When she sits down, I see it in her. She's used to burying it, but it's there, tucked down inside the bluster, inside her sharp movements and stern words.

Fear. And uncertainty; the lack of a sure footing.

'I spoke to her.' I watch Lily's face. 'To Jessie, at the hospital, after she came to.'

I hear the creak as Pat leans forward. 'What'd she say? Did she remember anything?'

'The tea.' Lily breaks away from me. 'I forgot all about it.'

She busies herself at the cupboards, opening and closing everything as though she's scaring off magpies. The teapot gets a real hiding in its journey from the top of the bread bin; I'm amazed it doesn't shatter on the benchtop.

'A few things.' I nod, looking to Pat. He's watching me as though there's never been a more important utterance. 'It seems she was drugged, too. Same as her cousin.'

'Drugged?' Lily frowns, shaking her head. 'No, no. That's… it's like we said. Like our boy said.' She points a finger to the table. 'They aren't into that stuff, Stu's lot. They'd never...'

'We've been through this.' Pat shakes his head, spittle forming at the edges of his mouth. 'Horiana's spoken with Rick Ambrose. There's no way we could know those two didn't take something before they came out here.' He huffs. 'It's everywhere on that side of town.'

'We've had a statement from someone at the party.' I watch Pat's expression. 'They set them up for it. Both of them, Jessica and Michaela.'

A red stain climbs up Pat's neck. 'It was that Tāmati, wasn't it? From Stu's class?'

'Who bloody cares who did what, Patrick?' Lily tosses the words at him. 'We're about to put our boy in the ground, and all you want to do is point the finger at his best mate!'

She slams a fist against the benchtop, and everyone jumps. It's loud enough to set the dogs barking outside. Pat looks to her in confusion, casting around for something to say. He stands and goes to her side, setting a hand carefully across her shoulder, as if she might scorch him. She bristles, but allows it to rest there. It's the first time I've seen physical contact between them, I realise.

'Listen.' I lean forward and lower my voice. 'There's something I need to ask you both, about the night of the party.'

Lily wipes at her eyes, watching me. She lifts a hand and sets it against Pat's, a gesture I'd call loving if I didn't know any better.

'Haven't we done enough bloody talking?' Pat shakes his head.

'It's okay, love.' Lily leans away from him. 'What is it, Lorraine?'

I gesture sideways through the doorway and up the stairs, and they seem to understand. We all lean forward to keep our voices to a whisper. 'We've heard Stu was a bit upset that night. A bit out of sorts.' Pat and Lily both frown; one of the expressions even looks halfway genuine. 'Have you two been having any difficulties, lately?'

'Difficulties?' Pat's frown deepens. He nods to the tabletop, to the photos of Stu. 'What, besides the obvious?'

'Before that.' I keep my voice even. 'Family stuff, farm stuff. Anything else you can think of.' Steady, now. 'Is there anything Stu might've overheard?'

A heavy silence hangs across the table. I can feel Dion shifting in his chair. Above us, there's the patter of Rodney's steps, and small creaks as the timbers settle in the roof, cooling as the sun recedes.

'Of course, we've had some tough times.' Pat sniffs, rubbing across Lily's shoulders. 'You've seen the lamb price, haven't you? And with the rates the way they are...Christ, if it's not the state of the OCR it's all that bollocks with Three Waters, and...'

'Excuse me.' Lily stands and pushes her chair sharply back so that Pat has to dart out of the way. 'The dogs need feeding.'

The three of us watch as she leaves, her footsteps slow and deliberate. Her cheeks look washed out, pale and trembling. And yet I can see it clear as day: she's damn near busting at the veins. Her footsteps move steadily outside and down the steps of the verandah, pausing for her boots. She doesn't bother closing the front door behind her.

'Sorry. She's…well, you can imagine how it's been.' Pat moves to follow her. 'Let me see if I can…'

'No.' I shake my head. 'Whatever she needs to do, let her do it.' I sigh, and Pat gives the same sigh back to me, his mouth pulled tight in apology. 'I'm fair parched, though.'

'Hmm?' He turns towards the teapot on the bench. 'Right, right. We're not exactly winning prizes for hospitality today, are we?' With a gruff chuckle, he fetches the mugs from the bench. They're beautiful, these mugs. Hand-worked, probably from Martinborough.

'There's still time to fix it, you know.' He gives me a confused look, and I let him sit with it just long enough to squirm. 'Those Afghans Lily mentioned.'

'Bloody hell, Lorraine.' Dion grins.

At the bench, Pat leans forward in laughter, making a parcel of his tall body. It's the first time I've heard him laugh, truly laugh. I can't help but think back to him as a boy. Little Pee-Wee, sitting on the front of Bill's quad bike, his dad's hat drooping over his eyes, his face full of expressions too big for his features.

'Your old man was a funny bugger too, you know.' Pat clucks his tongue. 'Old Mickey Henry. I suppose it runs, eh?'

'S'pose so. Lots of things do.' I nod into the hallway, letting him see me smile. No idea, this one. As it is with the victors. Jesus, if Dad only knew where I was, who I was talking to. He'd pop out of the grave just in time for his heart to go again. 'Bathroom's down there, is it?'

'Left at the end.' Pat pours the tea and sets a mug in front of Dion. I hear him clang the biscuit tin on the table as I step out of the room. Soon, Dion's got him prattling on about the grass cover lately, and whether Wairarapa Bush have much of a shot at the cup this year.

Good man.

I move on quiet feet; it's easier these days, with the new hip and all. Out the front door and across the verandah, then down into the open air all turned to grey. Soon, it'll be too dark to see. I know I don't have long.

THE DOGS HAVE stopped barking. It's a sure sign of where Lily is, and where I won't be.

A short stretch of gravel runs alongside the roses to the woolshed where Rodney left his rifle. Around the far edge of the house, I see the larger metal shape of the workshop, its rolling door rusted permanently open, and a pale light washing through from inside. I pause at the bottom of the verandah steps, scanning the silvery space in front of me. There are magpies flitting in the tops of the trees above the old kennels, calling the end of the day. I pat at my pocket; my phone has a decent enough light for me to take a look at the clearing around the chopping block, but I have a strong feeling we've seen all there is to see there. And anyway, whoever it is we're looking for, they would've had plenty of time to clear away anything useful, either on the night or later.

I take a few steps across the gravel, moving softly. There's too much information to sift: Pat's expressions, Lily's, even Rodney's. I can feel the scratching in my hands, the hot itch of some scrambled understanding slipping into the world, nearly graspable but not quite. Something will seem obvious later, I know it.

I feel the prickly chill of eyes on me. I spin around in the gravel, my heart swelling, but it's only the kid, Rodney, his soft shape held in a floating square of yellow light on the second storey, watching me. It's too far for me to see his expression.

'You poor thing,' I whisper. 'You poor, poor thing.'

When I lift a hand, he does the same, moving sideways to the task Lily has set. The dutiful younger brother. There will be a lot on him, this boy, now and in the coming years. He's a half-filled cup, and Pat and Lily have too much water to go around. It was the same with Mum and Dad after Debs went. She was older, sure, but it felt the same. Maybe it always does: the survivors blinking in the sunlight, trying to carry on.

'All right, now.' I take a long breath and turn back to the expanse of gravel, listening for anyone coming. I can think of Debs any old time. 'Here we are.'

To my side, over the fence and through the trees, there's the sound of stamping feet. A horse: something's caught her attention. Tāmati talked about hearing hoofbeats through the trees. It would've been a night just like this one: clear and still, the heat of the day dimmed to a merciful chill. How would the woolshed have looked from this side of the trees? Would there have been light through the branches, or the distant pulse of music from the party? Could someone watching— listening—have heard those kids outside, carrying on about Gatsby and David Lange?

A little poke around, then. And when Lily's back at the table, we can get into the specifics. The riding, for example. We can find out just who was outside that night, and what they might have seen. Maybe it'll jog a few more bits of information loose, or at least let me see the edges of whatever else this lot are hiding.

My feet carry me across the gravel, my old trainers keeping my steps silent. I keep my good ear to the workshop, but there's no sign of anyone: no Lily, no Harry. From the paddock at the far end of the trees comes the low bleat of a lamb calling.

Here I am. Here I am.

Around the side of the woodshed, an iron awning covers some old machinery. In the dark I make out the shape of a wood splitter; the low rusted plates of a set of discs stacked sideways. Bill Kelson wouldn't be too happy to see good gear lying unused; looks like it's a few years since Lily or Pat reseeded anything. Then, in the low shadows, a piece of the dark breaks off and moves sideways. My hand flies to my chest and I reach for something heavy but it's only a dog, a skinny heading pup, stepping on liquid feet to my side. He gives me a good long sniff.

'Hey, fella.' I can't see him too well, but I can feel the wet end of his snout press into my palm. A few deep breaths and my heart slackens. Then a low snort, and he's off, darting around the side of the woodshed.

It'd be easier, having Rick for this. With his steady bald dome around, I wouldn't be filling my undies at every sniffing pup; I wouldn't be staring at the rafters with my blood stoppered, watching for the fat shining eyes of possums. Instead, he's stapled up, still traipsing around in the mist of pills. Hopefully Lee won't be letting him get too used to them; I can't be file lady and acting Chief for much longer.

Back around to the driveway between woodshed and house, there's a big hunk of shadow where the Kelsons' ute sits. Through the open window of the kitchen, a burst of laughter comes from Dion, a second before Pat joins in. A few more minutes and they'll be wondering where I've got to. A quick poke inside the woodshed, then I'll rejoin them. I move through the doorway, and the smell of horse sweat fills my nose. Best not to risk the light switch; I dig my phone out and click the torch on, seeing Lily's saddle hung over a beam at the far edge of the shed, and the pea-straw to the side. My heel brushes against the butt of the rifle where Rodney left it, the bolt open and safe.

He listens, that boy.

The phone light shows me a bench with some leathermaking gear. There's a set of bridles and bits hanging on the wall next to a window dotted with borer. The gun safe is in the corner, closed but unlocked, the padlock hanging open with its key poking out the bottom in a stubby silver finger. A no-no, but not the biggest no-no I've seen. Not in Masterton, anyway. I move to the saddle, and my hands run over the leather worn with so many hours outside. This is no pony club saddle; it's seen time out under the sun and rain. Under the stars too, probably. Dad always loved seeing gear like this: the buckles buffed to a sheen from so much contact, the straps soft with use. You could read time in a saddle like this, he said. You could feel the days living under your knees.

The boots, too; they always had their own story to tell, for Dad. I crouch down and shine the light across the tidy row of riding boots, spotless and oiled. There's dust in my nose, but it definitely isn't the footwear. Lily takes good care of her things, and from the looks of it none of this stuff would spend enough time stored to get dusty.

My fingers run across the pairs, all the way down to a set of boots at the end. I lean forward and shine the light over them. They're an odd style, these ones, with the toes tapering into a sharp cleft. With careful fingers, I lift one of them, feeling its heft, its weight. There's a bracket of silver around the heel, with a stubby circle of spinning steel at the end: a spur.

I stay there, crouched, my breath trapped inside me, all my thoughts pinned in place. When I let the boot fall to the floor, the spur makes a jangling sound, and there are spiders across my neck, inside the collar of my shirt.

I lift the boot to do it again, wanting to be sure, when I hear a metal snick behind me, crisp through the silence. I don't need to turn around to know what it is.

I stand, letting the boot drop to the floor. The lightbulb

flares to life above me, making me squint. Blocking the doorway, the rifle tight to her shoulder, is Lily. Her spare arm is still on the light switch. I stand where I am, my shirt soaked against my back. The yellow light shines inside her eyes, making black stones of her pupils. She stares at me for a long time. I could tell myself she's making her mind up, but I know that's a lie.

The rifle bolt is closed, now. She's decided already.

'Come on, then.' Her spare hand goes back to the stock, holding it steady. Not that it'd need to be all that steady at this distance. 'Away we go.'

She nods outside, into the dark. The open doorway makes an inky black border around her. There's a new flatness in her voice, a sense of finality, of conclusion. A corner turned.

'There's still time, Lily.' My fingers grip my phone tighter, sweaty against the metal. When I speak, my words are quiet and choked. 'You can still put that down.' Mustering every piece of resolve I can find, I take a step towards her, looking past her shoulder to the farmhouse. It's close enough that they might hear me. 'We can just...'

'No.' She comes forward, faster, cutting me off. Her finger is on the trigger, calm and ready. She nods again, over her shoulder and into the trees. I stare into her face, looking for a foothold, something firm enough to grab. We've all lost something, I want to say. There are person-shaped holes in all of us. She only stares back, her expression as flat and still as a frozen lake. 'No, Lorraine. There's no time left for anything else.'

SHE REACHES OUT and gestures for my phone with her spare hand. There's nothing else for it. She's blocked me in, and by the time I might reach any of the mallets on the bench, she'll have used the rifle. She's handy with it, too; you don't need to look close to see that. I hand over the phone, still searching for something in her face; finding only the same blank distance.

Dion. Dion and Pat. They could still hear me. Jesus, Rodney even.

Anyone to distract her, to make her pause.

'Listen, now.' I whisper, holding my hands up as I move around her, slowly, to the door. 'You've had a shock, Lily. Everything with Stu.' She doesn't flinch to hear his name this time. 'I know you don't mean this.'

'Enough.' She moves on quick and sure feet, around the discarded boot, and reaches for the light switch again. The room falls away into darkness, and I feel the barrel press against my shoulder, the quick kiss of metal cold through my shirt. 'Let's go.'

Outside, the darkness holds us. The moon is up there somewhere, shrouded and blind. I step over the gravel, scuffing my feet just enough to make a sound, a mark, but not so much that she'll catch on. I wait for a voice through the dark, for the porch light to flare on, but there's nothing. My ears are strained from anticipation; it's all I can do to keep my thoughts from splitting my head open.

'The axe,' I whisper. 'The dog tucker axe. That was it, wasn't it?' I picture the shape of the butt, just right for the fracture behind Jessie's ear. 'What happened, Lily?'

'It doesn't matter.' She lets me feel the barrel again. 'Not now.'

The trees where they found her. The wet hollow, the blanket of leaves.

The trees where we found him. The rope pulled tight against his wrists.

A girl. A boy.

'It does, Lily. It does matter.' I slow down, turning to make her face me. There's enough phantom light spilling from the windows for her to see my expression. Whatever she might hold in her hands, I've got a weapon too. Information.

'If it was an accident, something you didn't mean, then all of this could…'

'If they hear you, we're done.' She hisses, jabbing the barrel into me again, hard against the ragged mend in my collarbone. 'I mean it. Go.'

I can make out only the faintest outline of her, one shadow among many. It's fitting, really: this last week, I've seen only shadows in her, and here, now, she's swallowed by them. I stare back at her, waiting for her to see me. To see what she's doing.

'Then what, eh?' I raise my voice just enough. 'You'll leave me where you left Jessie?' Past her outline, there's a new light. Someone's turned the hallway light on inside the farmhouse. 'Where we found your boy?'

'Don't you fucking dare.'

She's nearly on me when the porch light flickers on, throwing a half-circle of light across the verandah, down the steps and onto the gravel. We're standing just beyond it, still held in the black periphery of the tree branches reaching over us. Lily gives a start, pushing me roughly forward, her eyes wide and white. My feet catch under me, and I fall sideways into the gravel. It's my bad side, but I hardly feel it. There's a click as the front door opens.

'That you, Lil?' It's Pat. 'Did you finish up with the dogs? We were about to send out the search party.' There are footsteps against the wood, then a long pause. I can practically hear his thoughts shifting. 'Lily?'

She keeps her gaze on me, standing with the rifle still at her shoulder. I can't tell what Pat can see. Maybe something; maybe nothing. 'Go back inside.'

There are more footsteps as he comes to the edge of the verandah. All the while, the rifle barrel never wavers.

Then I hear the hard, ragged sound of surprise in Pat's breathing. 'What are you doing?'

My eyes go past Lily to him. Little Pee Wee, there on the same verandah. Still looking for his dad's shins to grab, to hold onto. Some larger safety, some solid point of reference. The porch light turns his hair alarm bell red.

Wrong question, Pee Wee. You're not far off, though.

'Lorraine?' This time, it's Dion's voice. Immediately my chest goes slack, all the trapped air leaving me. I might be on my arse staring into a barrel, but I'm that much closer to safe, now. 'Jesus, Pat, she's got the...'

'Quiet. Everyone.'

We stay where we are, our four bodies arranged in this improbable tableau, the black sky stretched over us, watching. Lily's still staring a hole into me, the rifle tight to her shoulder, her hands resolute at the stock. Then her eyes flicker sideways to Pat. The porchlight shows me how wet they are. With gritted teeth, she shakes her head and looks back to me. Pat takes a step forward, frowning out into the dark. Whatever he's seeing, it's clear he understands even less.

'What have you done, love?'

That's it, Pee Wee. A big slice of Christmas cake for you.

Lily doesn't seem to have heard him, heard the resignation in his voice. The dread, and the certainty. There are more footsteps, then the crunch of gravel.

'Stop,' Lily calls over her shoulder. 'Just stop, Patrick.'

Under the porch light, Dion goes to move forward, but I hold a hand up to keep him where he is. There are plenty of bones in this stockpot as it is, mate. He pauses mid-step, the big-faced boy-man, ready to do whatever needs doing. What a lucky kid he's got, having a dad like this one. Take a bullet, stay up watching Gordon Ramsay. Whatever needs doing.

'Lil?' Pat calls out again, and this time, Lily lifts the rifle away from her shoulder, just enough. A long breath slides out through her teeth, like a tyre with a bung seal.

'Inside.' The second syllable hides a sob. You'd miss it if you weren't listening. 'We'll do it inside.'

~

She arranges us at the far end of the kitchen table: me and Dion sitting with our hands visible, and Pat behind us. She lets him stand, or at least she doesn't push for him to sit. He looks about as confused as we are, Pee Wee. More, maybe. The rifle stays in her hands, the barrel no longer pointed at me, but still handy. Dion's phone is in the middle of the table, next to mine. He wasn't given a lot of say in the matter.

'Sure you're all right?' Dion whispers sideways to me. I nod, keeping my gaze ahead.

On her.

At the far end of the kitchen, Lily leans through the doorway, casting a quick glance up the stairs. Her movements are sure, almost practised. I take the chance to catch Pat's eye, but he's miles away, frowning like his mast's been snapped. I've never seen him this pale. Jesus, I've never seen anyone this pale.

'Lil, we can't just...' He seems to catch himself, and looks briefly to us, bunched at the far end of the table like naughty students. 'It's a mistake, I'm sure.' With open hands, he moves around the edge of the table, reaching towards Lily. 'Whatever's happened, we can...'

'Stay there.'

She points the rifle to the seat next to mine. It isn't easy for her, but she says it. Pat laughs, a small, dry sound swallowed by the space between us. Then his expression changes.

'I mean it.' Lily swallows hard, and the muscles in her neck pull tight. 'Sit.'

He slumps into the seat like something poured. With an absent motion, his hands go to the tabletop, one set of fingers moving gingerly over the knuckles on his other hand. The bag of ice is on the bench, still; the old injury must have been giving him some real grief. I notice a patch of pink scar tissue running across the skin under his fingertips, and a neat line across the knuckle from index to middle finger, nearly to his wedding ring. Inside me, the slow scratch of information turns to a loud knock. All the elements of the room seem to be remaking themselves: hand, chair, rifle. I squeeze my eyes closed, and the darkness greets me with its fuzzy chaos of colour.

Oh, I'm not sure about that, love. The low crack of the caramel inside that hard and ragged mouth, like bones giving way. *It's in every lad's blood to tomcat from time to time, but he put himself in a mucky spot, you know. The baby and all.*

Old Bill Kelson, spittle lingering in the cleft of his lips, stuck in that cabbage-smelling box with the heating stuck on, a silver square of the world redrawn for him every day out the window. A confused dragon, sleeping under his treasure map.

'Brother and sister.' I hear myself whispering. My words sound like someone else. 'Stu and Jessie. Jesus Christ, Pat. She's your daughter.'

A shearer, yes. But not from the gang.

Lily, rouseying from the neighbouring farm.

You knew it was pushing it, that shit with the lawyers.

A girl, and a boy.

Lucky thing.

'Does she know?' I look to Pat, then to the far end of the table. 'Did Stu?'

Lily meets my gaze with a flat expression. Next to me, Pat starts to sob. 'It was…it…' He splutters, his voice running dry. It's hitting him, now. 'How could you do this?' His hands come to his face, and his fingers clothe his eyes. 'How could you leave her? Our girl, on her own, in those trees?'

'Our girl?' Lily grips the rifle tighter, anger flashing through her. 'Don't you fucking dare call her that, Patrick.' She shakes her head, fighting to keep her voice low. There are wires pulled tight inside every word. 'All the things you've made me live with, messing around with that rutting bitch. All the cheques we've sent, all the…'

'At least tell me the fucking truth, love.' Pat sits up straighter now, his shoulders drawn back, tight and square. Dion shifts in the seat next to me, making himself ready; I shake my head at him, and I think he sees me. At the end of Lily's arms, the rifle barrel wavers, its single dark eye pointed at our hands, at our arms. 'You owe me that much.'

'The truth, eh?' Slow and sure, Lily shakes her head. 'No,

I don't think so. I don't owe you a thing, mate. Not a thing.'

The quiet in the room splits open with the crash of a fist against the table. It's Pat; he moved so fast, it's like action followed sound.

'You left her!' His neck is blooming with red; the noise makes Lily jump, though she regains herself. Above our heads, there's a single footstep, then silence. I picture him up there, Rodney, the boy, crouching and listening, keeping as still as possible, mapping the contours of the row downstairs. He'll be deciding where to put himself, and how to stay out of the way.

Was it the same for Stu, I wonder? Was he trying to make himself invisible, these last weeks? These last months?

What did he know?

'It was an accident.' I've never heard Lily sound so small. 'It was an accident, Pat.'

'You accidentally drove an hour each way to the bush, eh?' He launches the words from his chair, every syllable its own grenade. 'Dragged her into those trees by mistake?'

'I...I couldn't just...look, look.' She shakes her head, a note of irritation creeping in. 'That afternoon at the lawyer's, Pat, Bea fucking Mowbrie pushing and pushing, and we still weren't getting anywhere, right?' She leans forward, letting the rifle barrel fall sideways for a moment. Her eyes flicker to me, then back to Pat. 'She said something to me. Quiet so you wouldn't hear. Something like soon enough everyone would know.' Lily wipes a hand across her cheek. 'Starting with the kids, she said.'

Pat's face folds into a deep cleft of confusion. 'She'd never… she'd never have said that, Lil.' He shakes his head. 'She only ever wanted to make sure Jessie had…'

'Just listen to yourself, for Christ's sake.' Lily looks drained and weary. 'We've had nearly twenty years of bullshit from that woman and you still can't see it. You can't see a thing. Not with her, and not with our boy.'

'What do you mean, not with our boy?'

A long pause hangs over the room. There's the sense of countless unspoken words laid out under us. It's all there, in their expressions: dozens of arguments. Hundreds, maybe thousands, hanging in the background like radiation. It takes me a second to realise Lily is still talking, her voice hushed to a whisper. I have to lean sideways to hear her.

'I didn't know she'd be here,' she says. 'There was…after everything at dinner, I went out for a ride, remember? On Charlie.' Charlie. Of course. Gear as good as Lily's would never touch the back of a pony with a name like Bum-Bum. 'I saw them, outside the shed. The girl, with our Stu.' Moisture runs from her eyes. 'They were laughing, Pat. They were standing so close together. I wondered if…I wondered if she'd done it, finally. That woman. If she'd…if she'd told Jessica, and if Stu knew, knew about everything with you and her, then he…' Her voice falters and falls away, her mouth hanging open, wet and still. 'I thought maybe it was time. Time for us to tell him.' She nods upstairs. 'To tell both of them.'

'Jesus, Lil.' Pat takes his face in his hands again, hiding himself away.

She stares across the space between them, defiant. 'You don't have to believe me, but that's it. That's all it was.' She sniffs, gathering herself. 'I left Charlie in the paddock and came through the trees, looking for them. It was dark, and… she was there, by the old kennels. I…it was just her, on her own.' Her head shakes from side to side, long and slow. 'She had just stood up, and was fiddling with her jeans. I must have given her a fright, because she…she spun around too quickly, and she fell sideways.' Her words sound flimsy and light. 'The axe was right there. Right next to her.'

The dog tucker axe. That lonely piece of rusted metal, waiting in the clearing. It's just the right height for a person to really gather speed as they came down. Especially a tall girl, like Jessie. A gift from her dad, that height. Or a curse, maybe.

'She fell, Pat.' There are more tears, now. She lets them come. 'That's all.'

'Let's say that's true.' Dion's deep voice slices through the space between us, an unexpected draught of cooler air. Lily turns to him, frowning. 'Why'd you dump her in the trees?' He glances sideways to me. Expecting me to interrupt, maybe. No, mate. This one's all yours. 'Why not just call an ambulance?'

Lily's top lip draws up in disbelief. 'What do you think people would've said, eh?' There's indignation in her now. We all know the rules of the town, its whispers and its stories. 'Bea fucking Mowbrie spends two decades pushing for her girl to be written into our trust, and then only hours after she threatens me to my face, Jessica takes a knock to the head with

271

a meataxe, right in front of me, in the middle of the night? With nobody else around?'

The trust. Tārehu. There it is.

This place. This fucking place.

'What then, Lily?' I hold her gaze. 'Just tell us what happened.'

She stays where she is, cheeks wet and puffy, the rifle still laid across her forearm like a half-finished thought. Her balance shifts, her feet wavering; it's the weight of things, the feeling of a burden lifting, half-gone but not quite. I nod to the chair in front of her, urging her into it. She leans down into it, setting the rifle on the table, still within reach.

'I picked her up.' She speaks even more quietly than before. 'She was so…and I, I…' We're all leaning forward, now. 'I picked her up and I got her in the truck. We…I just drove. I drove, and then…I don't know.'

'How could you just carry on, Lil?' Pat shakes his head in a daze. 'You were right next to me in bed, at this table. How could you do it?'

There's a flash of yellow inside Lily's eyes, something cornered. 'Don't act like this is nothing to do with you, Pat. All your bullshit with that woman, your phone calls and your waves from the truck whenever we drove past.' She draws herself up straighter in the chair. There's real bile coming out, now, black and thick and long buried. 'Even Stu thought it was odd, the way you kept going on about the girl getting a spot on the debating team. As though Stu was nothing to be proud of. As though…'

'Don't call her "the girl",' Pat whispers. I'm pretty sure only I can hear him. 'Don't.'

'...bloody meddling and sniping, trying for years to take this away from us, from our boys.' Lily's words are rocks set loose down a hillside. 'Everything they built. Your father and mine, everything they've sacrificed. You'd put it all to the knife. All of it, by messing around with that tart. Everything they...'

'Everything they stole.'

I let them hear me. In the next seat, I feel Dion turn; I can tell he's frowning a wedge into his forehead.

'What's that?' Lily's mouth hangs slightly open, enough for me to see her sharp, small teeth.

'Bill and Arthur. Your dad, and his.' I nod sideways to Pat; he only stares back at me, this gangly package of long limbs and thoughts too difficult to take shape. 'You talk about building, eh? About sacrifice?' I point to the window between us and the land, the square of framed blackness. 'Did you ever stop to think about who might be on the other side of the ledger?' I set my hands on the table, my fists clenched. 'Did you ever wonder who had to make room for you?'

'Lorraine, we...' Dion clears his throat, nodding to Lily's rifle. 'You're steering us a fair way off the main track, don't you reckon?'

'No.' I hold my eyes to Lily. 'No, I'd say this is pretty fucking relevant, Dion.' I lean forward. 'All of this bullshit, Lily. Your legacy. Your boy's dead, and his girl wasn't far off.' I jab a thumb in Pat's direction. 'And for what, eh? So you can

273

hold onto a few more hectares?' I could say I don't know where this is coming from, but I'd be lying. A person watches the light slip out of her dad's eyes day by day, his shoulders more hunched, his hands more twisted, until he's damn near leaning into the grave. 'Admit it.' Louder, now. So the whole house can hear. 'You whacked her with it, didn't you? She didn't fall.'

'I signed the papers.' Pat crosses his arms. It's the first time he's sounded as though he believes what he's saying. He's staring at Lily.

'What?'

Slowly, he stands, gathering himself until he's standing tall. Here, now, he looks at home in this place. 'I signed the papers.' There's a long pause. 'And so did Dad.' I can hear the dry rasp of Lily's breathing. 'She's a beneficiary, Lil. She's on the trust, with Roddo.' He pulls a long breath into his lungs. 'And with Stu.'

'You wouldn't.' Lily shakes her head, her fingers moving around the rifle stock. I look to Dion, urging him to stay in place. 'You'd never have…everything we've done, all the… you wouldn't do it.'

'I did, Lil.' Pat's lonely syllables hang in the air. 'Just last week. It's done.'

There's a moment of stillness before it happens. I see Lily's teeth first, the knives inside her lips. She moves in a quick screaming blur, her hands raising the rifle as she rounds the edge of the table. Pat stands and rushes forward; I see where Dion's eyes are going.

'No, Dion!'

In a quick snatch, Dion grabs him, pivoting sideways and throwing his body between them. Around the far end of the table, I reach Lily, grab the barrel and shove it towards the ceiling. Her eyes are boiling with rage. She throws an elbow out, hard, catching me in the gut as I reach her, and the air huffs from my mouth but my hand stays tight to the rifle, the black steel like a branch I'm clinging to. I fall into her, knocking her into the bench. Her face flashes with pain, and the rifle falls through her arms to the floor.

Sound first, then action.

The laws of the physical world reversed, just for us.

My ears register the crack of the shot. At first I think it's just the stock hitting the wooden boards, or the barrel against the cupboard doors, until I see Lily's face: the wide oval of her mouth, the stubborn jelly around her pupils stilled and disbelieving. I follow her gaze, every atom of me leaping against its neighbour.

Please.

Please, not Dion.

'What...'

Pat's hand goes to his belly, and his fingers come away slick. In the ceiling's yellow light, the blood looks too dark, as though there's shadow leaking out across his hand. Then he falls forward, his arms against the tabletop, and slumps to his side.

'The rifle, Lorraine!' Dion yells, kneeling down alongside him. I grab the stock, keeping it with me while he talks to

Pat, his voice as steady as he can manage. He turns to me, and I register words.

Phone. Ambulance.

Beside me, Lily can only stare, her face as pale and naked as a broken fern stem. At first I can't see what she's looking at. Then I look up. The boy, Rodney, stands in the doorway, watching us.

WE'RE SCREAMING DOWN the Tārehu station track, loose gravel popcorning against the bottom of the ute. Dion's barely keeping us on the road, but now's not the time to complain.

'Talk to him, now.' I lean across Pat's torso, giving Lily room to speak into his ear. 'We need to keep him steady until the ambulance.'

She hesitates, before she shifts across to him and lifts his head to her middle with shaking hands. Beside them, I keep Dion's belt loop tight around Pat's belly, trying to maintain the pressure. The tea towels from the kitchen drawer are already soaked through. A gut shot: even with a twenty-two I should've known to grab a few more.

'How's he doing?' Dion calls back through the space between the seats.

'Just drive, mate.' When I look up, I see Rodney staring

from the passenger seat, a tall edifice crumbling inside his eyes. Whenever Pat tries to speak, it's to him, not to Lily.

'Roddo,' he whispers. 'You need to...'

'It's all right, Pat.' I try to sound steady, like we're on level ground. Truth be told, I'm coming apart like a tomato under a bootheel. 'We're nearly at the road. Look.' The tree cover stops, letting the stars through.

Dion starts to slow down.

'What are you doing?'

'The bulldozer,' he mutters. 'It's parked across the...'

'Uncle Harry left the keys in the tracks,' says Rodney. 'Just there.'

Dion pulls to a stop, and the boy leaps out, surprisingly nimble. In the truck headlights, I see only the flap of loose clothing, and long hair shifting. There's a pause before the machine gurgles to life in a deep, gorgeous growl.

'Great stuff, kid!' Dion yells out the window. 'Move that fucker!'

On the seat next to me, Pat spasms, going rigid for a long moment; the muscles in his neck pull tight and sharp. He's breathing too fast, and my hands are hot and slippery with him.

'Stay with us, mate.' I pull the belt tighter, checking it's still in the right spot. Everything is too wet to tell. 'Go on, Lily.'

'I...I don't...I don't know...' She stares at me over his head. Her mouth is moving, but there's no sound. 'What do I...'

'The crab photo,' I say. 'With Stu. Where was that, then? Riversdale?'

'Castlepoint,' Pat whispers. 'Christmas, remember?' His eyes are everywhere. 'He would've been four, our boy. And she'd just turned five.'

I catch Lily's eye. She's just sobbing, now, her face stained and puffy with disbelief. 'I never...I never...'

I try to get her to focus, but it's impossible. Outside, Rodney brings the bulldozer forward out of the way. He fiddles with the dash for a while, trying to kill the engine, his movements getting more and more frustrated, nearly frantic.

'Just leave it!' Dion calls out, and Rodney climbs inside the ute, carrying himself straighter than before. We pull ahead in a spray of gravel. It's twenty-five minutes to the hospital at Dion's pace; with any luck, the ambulance won't be far away.

'Roddo.' Pat holds up a long arm, his hand finding his son's. 'Didn't know you could drive the Cat, mate.'

The boy twists in his seat, blinking back at us. 'Uncle Harry showed me.'

'He did, eh?' It's too dark to see, but I can tell Pat is smiling. 'Proud of you, boy.'

'You've got plenty to be proud of, Pat.' I shift my hands across his belly, feeling for the wound; it's like trying to squeeze a side of beef into a pencil case. Outside, the landscape slides past in a long rush of dark. Fences and trees, cattle and magpies and lambs. It was familiar, once. 'And you'll have plenty more to be proud of, won't you?'

We come to a long straight, and Dion puts his foot down until the truck is eating the road, the engine screaming in our ears. Then, at the end of the stretch, new lights pierce the dark. Red and white, the spinning cones of the ambulance.

'Oh, thank Christ.' Dion flashes his high beams, getting ready to slow down. It's quiet, now, and Pat has stopped tensing up. The innermost part of me knows why.

'Dad?' Rodney sniffs, squeezing the hand in his.

'They're here, Pat.' I reach up and turn the cab light on. I'm not ready for the blood; my hands and forearms are soaked. 'They're here.'

I can pretend until I see his eyes. Then the easy softness in there tells me everything, the calm sheen undeniable. He looks like he's ticked everything off his list, and is getting ready to rest for the night. Before the world rolls over and gives him another day.

But this is it. This has been his day, and there won't be another.

'Pat.'

I shake him as hard as I can manage. My fingers go to his neck, pressing alongside his Adam's apple. There's no movement, only his warm skin and its stilled interior. For a moment, my gaze meets Lily's, and she lets me see the desolation inside her: that dusty, bare place, all love and hope and warmth swept off and away. She breaks away, looking to her son, and tries to touch him, bringing him closer. He stays where he is, staring at his dad.

Then the doors open, and new voices fill my ears.

I CAN HEAR the birds in the park from the station staffroom, busy with the morning. A clear sky, everything baked to stillness under the hard sun, these plains under the mountains like a golden plate held in the palm of some giant hand, town and streets and houses all arranged in their usual places. Dependable, steady. Despite everything.

And me. I'm held still, too. In my place.

I stare at the staffroom mug in front of me, its chipped mouth just as I expect it, stout and ready. A welcome thing, finding something as you expect it. You can't always say that about things, and definitely not about people.

Shuffling footsteps reach my good ear from the hallway. 'Whenever you're ready, Lorraine.' It's Rick, fresh from his bed; Lee dropped him off this morning with a handwritten sheet of instructions for me. A little blue pill every three hours—two, if things drag on at the funeral—and an orange one every four, for the swelling.

'Righto, Chief.' I drain the mug and stand, still a little tender in the belly from Lily Kelson's elbow. My bearded nurse mate gave me a look over at the hospital, after they'd made the calls about Pat. Some light bruising, apparently. Nothing for it but rest. 'Here I come.'

We're moving good and slow, today. I suppose we've earnt it. It's been all through the papers these last few days, so there's been no need to set the story straight in the neighbourhood. *Accidental shooting.* That's what Jamie at the *Times Age* has gone with. As for the rest of Lily's story, that's proven a little harder to summarise in a headline alone.

'Thought I had it for a second there, but no.' In his office, Rick leans back in his chair, tossing his best tie onto his desktop. 'Bloody fingers are like sausages these days.'

I nod. 'Lee told me to keep an eye on that.'

'Ah, yes.' Rick grins. It almost looks halfway normal, even with one side of his head like a misshapen bun, his cheek swollen all the way to the staples. His hat will be out of the question, I'd say. 'My trusty nursemaid.'

I pick up the tie and pull it around my own neck, making the old loop I used to make for Frank. It's dark in here; the Chief's got the blinds drawn, same as when Pat and Lily first came in. Fortunately, my fingers remember.

'They'd understand, you know.' A loop, then pull the knot tight. Trap the little bugger. That's how Dad used to teach us. Trap the little bugger, girls. 'If you stayed home, I mean.

You're only barely off the ward, Rick.'

I gesture for him to lean back, and I try to slip the tie over his head. The swelling must be worse than I thought; I have to let a little more through the knot and try again. This time, I make it over the staples, moving gently.

'Stuff that.' He shakes his head. 'A constable and a file clerk bring in Lily Kelson all wrapped up and ready to confess, and I can't even make it through her boy's funeral?'

'It's not just Stu's, remember.' I pull the tie into the right spot and fold his collar gently down. 'It's Pat's, too.'

Rick's fingers go to the knot, checking it for himself. 'You don't need to remind me, Lorraine. Graham's been on the phone every bloody half an hour, wanting to make sure Wellington were sending enough extra hands.' He gives me a satisfied nod. 'We're going to have a hard time getting them all into the sodding chapel. Lily's Arohata detail alone is going to take up a whole row.'

I picture her, there in one of those wooden pews the colour of good shoes, listening as the chaplain speaks over the boxes holding her boy, holding her husband. A moment like that, sitting with the end result of all she's done. Sitting with herself. I saw plenty of that feeling in her on that terrible drive back from Tārehu, and in the station after the hospital.

A reckoning.

'I'm sure we'll manage it somehow.'

The Chief watches me from his chair, his eyes calm and steady. He's the one still looking like he's been under a tractor, but right now it seems I'm the one with sympathy coming my way.

'Have a rest, Lo.' He nods to his couch. 'We've got time.'

I hear Dion pull up outside, the sharp rattle of his muffler echoing through the carpark. I'd love to lie down. Really, I would. But these last few days there's been a tape loop in my head: Harry Brooke, pale beneath his beard, shoving open the door in the hospital ward and clasping Rodney to him. Then the shark stare Lily gave me in that woodshed, the yellow flare of the lightbulb showing me nothing behind her eyes. And beneath everything else, a louder and more vivid image, its colours etched clearer than anything else: Hika in his deck-chair with a jug for the afternoon, those brave Hawaiian Speedos tighter than ever, listening in on my phone call to Dion, getting ready to ferry whatever I'd said onto his cousins, onto his nieces. All that stuff about Stu finding Jessie's phone, about Stu being the suspect.

A girl, found.

A boy, lost.

And I think it was me. Intentional or not, maybe I lost him.

'Lorraine?' Rick is frowning, but only one of his eyebrows can get in on the action. 'What is it?'

'I...' I rub a finger under my nose, smelling the nectarine waft of the Chief's fabric softener. 'I don't know if I should...'

'You've scrubbed up well, then.' Dion leans against the doorway, nodding at my blouse, at my best shoes. He's in his dress uniform too, though without any of the Chief's lopsidedness. Then, seeing us, his face clouds over. 'I can always come back if you need.'

'It's all right, mate.' The Chief stands slowly, hands flat against the desk. 'We're all set.'

He shuffles his way to me; I stay where I am and let him come. I can tell myself it's to let him feel useful, being able to comfort me; I can tell myself I don't need it.

Then his big hands come to my shoulders, and I let myself lean against him. We stay like that for a while. Everything in the room is still.

'Just try not to snivel on my good jacket, eh?'

I lean back and give his arm a slap, just hard enough. 'You sod.' When I turn around, Dion has a glass of water for me; I didn't even hear him leave the room. 'Thanks.' I wipe at my cheeks, and we move into the hallway, letting the Chief fossick around for his shoes. 'How's that boy of yours been doing?'

'Box of fluffy ducks.' He yawns through a grin. 'Even let us sleep until half five.'

'Generous.' I drain the glass and hand it back.

'You sure you're feeling up to this, Lo?'

I look into his face, but it's not him I'm seeing. It's Pat.

Little Pee Wee, the tide gone all the way out of him. Those eyes, open and staring across the backseat of the ute, and my hands warm with his leaking insides. The night outside split open by red flashing lights just like the night they found Jessie. The night they found his girl.

'I'll be fine.' I nod sideways into the Chief's office. 'Him, though.'

Dion grins and leans closer. 'It'll be a while before I'll catch any more shit about my spelling, I'd say.'

'Wouldn't bet on that.' Rick breathes out through clenched teeth, pulling on his shoes.

'Hang on, the laces.' Dion moves through the doorway, but I grab his arm. There's so much I need to say; I can hardly feel my tongue.

'Listen. The phone. Stu Kelson's phone.' I keep my voice low. 'Do you remember seeing it, that night?'

'What, in the house?' Dion frowns, his forehead crinkling. 'Don't think so. I wasn't exactly looking for it, though. Not once everything…well, you know.' He cocks his head. 'Why?'

'Tāmati said Stu was texting someone that night. When they were out running.' I listen to the Chief puffing with his shoes, swearing under his breath. 'I want to know who.'

'It can wait, can't it?' Dion moves to Rick's desk, bending down to help him. 'Let's just get through the service, Lorraine. The forensics guys said they'd be bringing everything from the house into the station this afternoon anyway.'

'From the house?' Rick calls out. 'Whose house?'

'Don't worry, Chief. Here.' Dion ties Rick's shoes with quick, sure hands, doing his best not to look him in the eye. It's quite the recalibration for these two, and both men seem pretty keen for it to be over. 'Steady?'

'Steady enough.'

Dion stands and gives me a conspiratorial eyebrow wiggle; it's all I can do not to chuckle. Then the Chief stands, slowly, and lifts a hand with a suspicious amount of ceremony.

'Hang on.' He coughs. 'Before we head out there, I…I should say, ah, all things considered, it's been…well, it's been a prick of a time, lately.'

'It's all right, Chief.' Dion makes room for him to move through the doorway. 'We only…'

'No, listen.' Rick gathers himself. 'Even after I took a knock, you two kept hammering away at it. And now look, eh? Just look where we are.'

Indeed, Rick. Just look.

A boy about to go in the ground, alongside his dad. And when it's all over, we'll bus his mum back to her remand cell.

'Thanks, Rick.' I nod, glancing to Dion. 'Really.'

Dion coughs. 'Yeah, thanks.'

The Chief taps at his desktop, putting a cap on things. 'Enough of all that, then. Let's get to it.'

I duck downstairs to grab my phone, making sure I've got enough tissues in my handbag. It's weird enough carrying the bloody handbag at all; I haven't had much use for it since typing college. Then, I see some missed calls on my phone. It's Moko; he's texted too.

Kick off, aunty. No false alarms this time.

I'm back at the top of the stairs before I know what I'm doing, my heart in my mouth, all colours rushing together. Today, of all days.

Every moment has its inverse.

'You'll need to make an extra stop on the way, mate.'

Dion gives me another terrier head tilt. I must be smiling.

I'M SITTING NEXT to Sheena's bed in the maternity ward, watching her sleep. It's still dark outside, and will be for a while yet. The windows show me the inky predawn, the hushed space filled with its own special sense of promise. We're all lying still, here in this room: my niece under the blankets, her cheeks slack with the job she's done, and me with my feet up on one of the plastic chairs, a grey woollen blanket covering me. And, tucked tight against my chest, her face somehow serene and furious at the same time, is our girl.

Baby Keith.

They had a hard time with that, the nurses. Her name and all. My mate from the front desk even took me aside for a word, but Sheena was adamant. Moko too. So Keith she is.

'There we are, my girl.' I whisper into her wee head, my fingers brushing over the cover of dark hair across her crown, smelling her. I'd forgotten this feeling; it's been so long since Bradley was born, and even then things were different, the feeling in the room a little more tense between Sheena and the nurses. But here, now, it's perfect.

For the first time since I can remember, everything feels right.

Keith yawns in her sleep, settling herself back against my chest, her fingers stretching and grasping, miraculous and strange. She feels like something I shouldn't be seeing, this beautiful and impossible girl. And yet I'm here, holding her. The nurses said it'd be a while before Sheena's epidural wore off; I'll have another hour of Keith to myself, I hope.

On the bedside table, my phone chirps.

How's our girl? It's Moko. *Toast and Milo for me and the boy. Then we'll come in.*

Take your time. I type slowly. *She's sleeping like a champ.*

Through the crack in the window, I hear the muted rattle of the day's first milk tanker. Coming back from the conversion blocks down past the river, probably. A shiny silver vessel ferrying that rich bounty through the dark. It's this little girl; she's got me feeling sentimental about bloody milk tankers. My phone vibrates again. Dion this time.

Getting on ok? There's a bouncing bubble. *How's your niece?*

All good thx. I lean down to Keith's forehead, smelling her. I shouldn't ask him, really; I don't want to puncture this cocoon I've made for myself. And yet, I can't help it. *How about the service?*

There's a long delay, followed by more bouncing. *Can I call?*

I tap the phone icon and tuck the metal square under my ear. Dion answers before it rings. 'Morning.' He sounds sleepy.

'I have to whisper.' I hold a palm gently over Keith's ear. 'I've got company.'

'Ah.' I hear footsteps, then a door squeaking closed and a jug being switched on. 'All good otherwise?'

'Yep, yep.' Her eye twitches, and I move my mouth away. 'Come on then. Out with it.'

He exhales long and slow, gathering himself. 'Jesus, Lorraine. I don't know where to begin.' Then, in his taut, weary voice, he fills me in.

I can picture the whole thing: the two hearses pulling up to the chapel, parking on the grass, and chaplain Graham waiting to lead everyone inside. Dion didn't mention it, but I can picture the man's nostrils flaring at the wheels on the grass. It almost makes me grin; not quite.

The team from Arohata had set up their own row for Lily, right up front. They even let her sit next to Harry and Rodney, the three of them hemmed in on either side by the officers. They were in there already when everyone else arrived, says Dion, to limit the risks of anything kicking off. The chaplain led a smaller group of Langsford boys inside, mostly Stu's hockey mates, and a handful of girls from Aquinas. Heather Christiansen was there with her nose all bandaged up, he said, and still with a pear-shaped bruise under one eye. Tāmati was there too, putting on a brave face, though Dion could tell he was only just holding himself together.

The service was already underway, Dion tells me, when

they came in. He and Ambrose were in their spots near the front of the chapel, tucked to the side in case the Chief needed to duck out. They had the chapel doors open to let everyone outside hear the proceedings, and not long after Graham started the reading, a rising wave of murmurs swept through the rows. It was Bea and Jessie Mowbrie, with Tuck behind them, coming up the aisle and looking for a seat. There weren't three seats together anywhere, so Bea found a spot for Jessie near the front, and she and Tuck stood at the back, Bea folded under her brother's arm.

'Christ alive,' I whisper into the phone, careful not to shake my head too hard.

'Yep,' says Dion. 'You can imagine it, right?'

Soon people were on their feet, hissing for the Mowbries to get out. Bea looked ready to bolt, apparently, and seemed to be pleading with Tuck to go, but he stayed firm with her. Then Lily started pointing back at them and carrying on, but before she could say too much, Harry sat her back down. It was the strangest thing, Dion says. He noticed Rodney speaking into his uncle's ear, and after a few moments Harry asked the Arohata officers to make room on their bench for Jessie.

'She was obviously overwhelmed,' says Dion, 'the poor thing.'

Jesus, who wouldn't be? But she did it. She joined them, face streaked with tears, still moving with slow and deliberate steps. Rodney made room for her, apparently: as far away from Lily as they could manage in a single cramped row. Once she'd found a spot, Bea and Tuck retreated to the back of the chapel.

Good lad, Rodney. Something bright may yet come out of this mess, I suppose.

The cemetery was where things really got out of hand, Dion explains. The whole crowd could see everything without having to get it all second-hand through the chapel doors. They got Pat in the ground without any outbursts, apparently, but once they started lowering Stu, Lily went for it, screaming at Tuck, and ordering the Chief to arrest him. Then Jessie fell over and there was a rush of people trying to move her out of the way.

'Dehydration, the paramedics reckoned,' Dion tuts. 'The papers got it all. It'll be on the news tonight, I'd say.'

'Imagine it.' Baby Keith stirs against me, then settles with a low snort. 'Jessie having to sit in the same row as that woman.' I shake my head.

'It was bloody rough,' says Dion. 'Rough as guts.'

'Always eloquent, mate.' In the bed, Sheena rolls over. An eye cracks open, before she rolls back again. 'What about Michaela?'

'Michaela?' I can hear Dion frowning. 'Can't remember seeing her. She might've been in the back somewhere, maybe.' There's the sound of a knife on toast. 'I could ask around?'

'Nah, nah.' I let my thoughts drift. 'But pick me up on your way to the station, all right?'

'Yeah?' Dion takes a bite. The toast wants butter, from the sound of things. Maybe it's part of his rugby-season prep. 'You sure? I reckon Rick would be fine with you taking the day, Lorraine. The week, maybe.'

I picture Lily standing next to those two dark gouges in the earth, waiting to receive two wooden boxes. It was a boiling hot day yesterday; at the very least, the world should've given her some rain to hide in, some cloud to shield her. Whatever she's done, she deserved that.

'I'm sure.'

Dion rings off, and I slide the phone back onto the table. Keith sticks her fingers in her mouth, sucking them.

'Take the day, Aunty.' Sheena's words are slurred with fatigue. 'Go on. Those buggers can wait.'

In my arm's, Keith's eyes come open, their dark centres like shining stones. She opens her mouth, and a sharp cry jumps out of her. In bed, Sheena opens her arms. I watch while they nurse.

'You lot will be just fine without me.' I brush a strand of hair from my niece's face. 'Moko's on his way in, anyway.'

'Ow.' Sheena lifts the baby and sets her back against her breast. 'She's a hungry girl, this one. Just like her mum.' She nods to my phone on the table. 'Tell the big guy to get a bag of mince and cheeses from Kuripuni.'

'Righto.' I do as I'm told, my fingers tapping away. In the hallway, I can hear the quiet clatter of the nurses starting their morning rounds. Outside, there's light creeping over the lawns, sweeping away the dark. 'How are you feeling, girl? Besides wanting a kai, I mean.'

'Bloody sore.' A tired grin comes over her. 'But here she is. Just look at her.' We sit, and I set a hand to her shoulder.

Here she is.

'What was that I could hear?' Sheena yawns. 'About the Mowbries and that?'

I stand slowly, sending cracks through my joints. 'I'll tell you later.'

THE FORENSICS GUYS have cleared a space downstairs at the station, in the corner next to the copier where the carpet still hangs together, and as far away from my spider friend as possible. They've bagged and itemised everything from the Kelson place: about a dozen boxes in all, plus the rifle upstairs in the munitions room. Dion can deal with that; he knows I don't care for that room in the slightest. And anyway, the rifle itself won't exactly be crucial evidence given that there was an officer was in the room at the time.

And a records clerk, not that I'll make a whole lot of difference.

'Did they scrub the floor or something?' Dion wrinkles his nose as he shifts the boxes around. 'I can smell Ajax.'

'Dunno where they would've found any.' A chuckle escapes me. 'Must've bought their own.'

'Very posh.'

I nod along, but we both know how useful it's been having that lot to look things over in the farmhouse, taking photos of what I'd just as soon forget. The floorboards under the table, the golden wood streaked with black where Pat fell. The discarded rifle by the wood basket where Lily dropped it, its barrel pointed at the hearth. And, hardest of all for reasons I can't quite grasp, the woodshed where her best saddle hangs, its deep brown leather shining like a secret still kept.

Images and impulses; scraps and rags of memory. It's always like this. The way the yellow light flooded the room, showing me her face. The way the rifle barrel held me in place, a tiny circle of patient shadow coiled and waiting.

What would she have done if Pat hadn't stepped out onto the verandah just then?

'Here, let me grab that.' Dion must have noticed my hands shaking. He takes the topmost box. 'You all right, Lorraine?'

If they hear you, we're done.

'Stu's phone.' I sniff, wiping at my nose. 'I'm not seeing it anywhere.'

In a moment of mercy, he looks elsewhere. 'It'll be here somewhere.' He moves his hands carefully through an open box. 'It has to be.'

I prop my hands against my desk, waiting for the shakes to dissipate.

Keith. It helps to think of her, the baby, our screaming parcel of rude new life, reaching and grasping. She doesn't know yet what we can do to each other.

'Shit, look at this.' Dion holds up a sheaf of papers inside a bag, smoothing out the tag to read it. 'From a filing cabinet in Pat's office, it says.'

'Yeah?' I take them out of his hands and squint through the plastic cover. It's a signed amendment to the deed for the Tārehu trust, adding one Jessica Rose Mowbrie as a beneficiary alongside Stu and Rodney. I lift it higher into the light, letting the pages fall open inside the bag. Pat and Bill signed it on the Sunday after the hockey game: the same day they'd all come into the station with Horiana Paul to give a statement. Shit, it was Horiana herself who took care of the paperwork. It takes me a moment to put it together.

Pat. He would've wanted to keep it out of the usual loop of Brooke lawyers.

'He did it.' I feel my head shaking. 'He actually did it.'

'Fuck me dead.' Dion whistles through his teeth. 'She'll get half now, right? Jessie? Now it's only the two of them?'

Rodney and Jessie, thrust together. The boy making room in the pew. 'I suppose so.'

'Lucky for some.'

I set the papers back in the box, safe and sound. Sure, Lily might do her best to challenge the situation. She might even have a few threads to pull, what with Bill Kelson's brain going to lamington in his hot little box. Lord knows she'll have enough time on her hands, even with her own trial to worry about.

I picture them sitting together in the chapel. A new brother. A new sister.

A father, lost before he could be found. Before the poor girl even had the chance to know him. Maybe Rodney will tell her. Maybe she can build a picture that way.

'Here,' says Dion. 'That's Stu's, right?' He holds up a bag with a phone inside, the screen scratched but intact. I remember it from the roadside.

'Looks like it, yep.' I try switching it on inside the bag, but the battery's dead. 'You've got a Samsung, right?'

'Hang on a sec.' He bounces up the stairs, reappearing with the charger in just a few seconds. 'We should check with Rick first, right? Before we…'

I crack the seal just enough to slide the cable inside, clicking it into place.

'Never mind then,' Dion huffs.

'He's resting at home, mate.' I hold the bag carefully. 'We can fill him in once we've got something.'

'You're the one always farting on about the evidence guidelines.'

A charging symbol appears, and it takes another minute for it to light up. Then I slide my phone from my pocket and find the code Tāmati gave me. With my breath trapped in my chest, I type it in. Right away, the home screen appears: Stu posing with his hockey mates, with Tāmati visible from the eyes up, his arm held at just the right angle to get everyone in frame. Stu's perched behind the row, tall and smiling. I can't help but see Jessica in him now.

'Texts are that button there,' Dion jabs a finger at the bag.

'All right,' I move my thumb over the screen. 'Keep your hair on.'

There's a list of contacts: Dad, Tama, Mum. At the top of the most recent messages, there's one from Wee Bro.

Rodney.

If you've gone somewhere just tell me. It's from the night he disappeared. The night we found him. *I won't tell mum.*

It's like someone's driven a truck across my chest. I fold forward into myself.

'Lorraine?' I feel Dion's hand on my shoulder.

'I'm okay.'

It's horrible, what we're doing. And yet we owe it to him. To both of them, really. Stu and Pat.

There are older messages from Rodney, from the day after the party.

Mum still not talking to dad, he writes. *There's not even any porridge.*

It'll be okay, Roddo. There's a single X. *They just get like that sometimes.*

No more of this; it should be theirs alone.

I click out of the exchange, looking for something from the night he left the boarding house to go running. There: eight-fifteen. An exchange with someone listed as M.

I feel everything shudder to a halt. Michaela.

Need to talk, writes Stu. *Cops said Jessie took something. Showed up in her blood.*

Defs felt different from the other times, M replies. *I was real out of it. Jess too.*

There's a gap of about twenty minutes. Tāmati; it must be when he and Stu were arguing. Then Stu picks up the exchange again.

Going for a run. Get outside for a bit.

I could come now, M says. *Meet you somewhere in mum's car.*

Stu replies after just a minute. *She won't mind?*

She won't know. Still at hospital.

K. There's another gap here. *Turnoff in fifteen.*

Wait for me.

I feel the floor shifting under me again. Nothing feels stable.

'Jesus.' Dion shakes his head. 'Michaela?'

When I close my eyes, I see her face as she'd opened the door that night. The tremble in her expression, all colour dropped out of her. And in the hallway behind her, Bea, fresh from the shower, her skin red and raw from the scrubbing. The air had felt different: prickly and charged, a storm moving inside those walls.

A boy.

A boy stands at the side of the road, waiting, his face thrown into illumination by the headlights from a passing truck. A familiar car pulls up. In just hours, we'll find him. Before the sun comes up; before the birds start to stir in the trees above him, around him.

Someone is driving that car. Someone he knows.

'We have to get her in,' says Dion. 'We have to get the whole bloody lot of them in.' He sinks into my chair, making it squeak with his weight. His hand slaps to his temple. 'Fuck,

Lorraine. What if she was right? What if Lily was right about Tuck? He could easily have...'

'We don't know.' There's sand in my throat. 'We don't know anything yet.'

I set down the evidence bag and lean against the copier, letting my eyes lose their focus. A phone dropped in the gravel at the road's edge; a rope pulled tight into the boy's wrists where we found him. And between those two images, a murky grey space getting smaller with every new detail.

A car, and a road. Footprints, and marks in the soil.

He was lean, this boy, but tall. Whoever took him had to be capable of carrying him, at least for a while.

A rope, and a car. A road.

I see the wall again, now. I stand straighter, coming back to myself.

'There's something we need first.' I look to Dion, letting him see my expression. He's here with me, a bright light blinking through the fog, pointing the way through this strange mist. These are my neighbours; my people. I need him with me to help me find the edges. 'Before we bring anyone in.'

'What?' He waits for me to speak. 'What is it?'

I reach for the evidence bag and tuck the phone back inside its box, clicking the side button to lock the screen. Whatever else is in there, it can stay hidden.

'The joyride camera,' I say. 'The timber plant.'

Dion frowns through the dusty basement light. Then he understands.

DION CALLS AHEAD from the road, his phone pressed to his ear as he takes us through the town centre, past the Farmlands and the queue of cars and the KFC, through the roundabout and alongside the new softball pitch.

'He's away?' Dion turns to me with a dubious expression, his spare hand gripping the steering wheel as if to choke it. 'Well who's…hang on, hang on. I know it's nearly changeover, mate. But it's urgent.'

There's a long moment while Dion listens. Whoever's on the line, they've got plenty to say. Or maybe they're just taking a while to get to the point.

'Yep, yep. Look, I…' A cluck of the tongue. 'Fine, fine. That's all we need anyway. Yep. Righto.' He ends the call, exhaling loudly. 'Christ, you'd think I was asking the guy for a kidney.'

'He'll help us out?'

Dion nods. Truthfully, I'm not even sure I want to see what's on the tape. 'Said he doesn't know much about the cameras, but he'll see what he can do.'

We take the last corner past the machinery yards. I hold a hand up for Dion to cut the speed. 'The bloody plant's not going anywhere.' Soon, I see the smoke tower in the distance. We come over the bridge, and he indicates for the turn.

'You don't really think Michaela could've done this herself, right?' Dion squints sideways. There's a truck hurtling towards us in the other lane; I'm pretty sure he sees it. 'I mean, her dad, sure. But her?'

The truck flies past, making the patrol car rock.

'I wouldn't say I'm the expert in what people are capable of.' I think of Pat and Lily in the Chief's office that first day, the way the light striped across their faces. 'Not after this last week.'

At the gate to the timber plant, we pull in and give our names to a silver speaker inside a cracked orange box. It sounds like the guy Dion just had on the phone. After a terse exchange, the gate creaks slowly open.

'That's where they put it up, look.' Dion points to a hemisphere of plastic stuck like a limpet to the gate pillar. 'Mostly it's aimed at the fence, there. Where those little shits got in last time.' He takes a pause. 'But you're right, Lorraine. It could give us the road, too.'

'That's if this joker can even get us the footage.' I nod into the plant carpark. 'Where'd he say the usual guy has gone?'

'Up north, for the AGM.'

We pull in, and Dion parks in the manager's spot, right next to the entrance. Behind us, there are forklifts crossing the yard, ferrying pallets and boxes in all directions. There's something calming about all this activity; no matter what else is happening in this town, these guys will be shuttling back and forth, mouths pulled grim and tight, waiting for smoko. I get a face full of pungent grey steam and my eyes start to run.

'Give it a minute,' says Dion. 'You'll come right.'

Behind the glass doors, a short round guy in a yellow-striped shirt under orange hi-vis watches us. He looks like marmalade toast.

'I've got ten minutes.' There's a dab of something on his top lip, just under the nostril. Hummus, I think. I hope. 'There's trucks coming at half three, and I've got a stack of dockets you wouldn't read about.'

'Listen mate, we're looking into a bloody...'

'That's fine.' I put myself between them and give Dion the kind of glance I usually use on Bradley and his mates. 'We won't keep you long.'

The guy frowns at me, and for a second it looks like I'll have to rattle off my credentials before he seems to think better of it and us into a small open-plan office. The nearest wall holds a framed picture of a tall pile of sawn logs. Just in case anyone forgets what business they're in.

'Bash hooked it up to his computer,' Hummus says.

'Bash?'

'Bashir,' mutters Dion. 'The manager.'

'I think he scribbled his password down somewhere here…' His stubby fingers pluck a note off the side of the monitor and type the credentials in, muttering. When the desktop appears, he starts clicking on different icons, still swearing under his breath.

'It was a tennis brand or something,' says Dion.

'A what?' The guy gives him an angry-stoat expression.

'The camera.' Dion points to the screen. 'He was telling me about setting it up.'

'Wilson Systems.' I nod to a camera-lens icon in the corner. 'Is that it?'

Hummus clicks a few more times, and we're looking at a thick grid of files; there must be more than sixty. 'Thing's got multiple views,' he says. 'Fence, driveway, yard.' A few desks over, a phone rings, setting off a new round of muttered swearing. He stands, holding up a hand to keep us where we are, then stomps over to take the call.

'Those look like the files for Monday.' Dion leans forward, reaching for the mouse. 'Do you reckon there's any way we could…'

'Wait.' I grab his arm, looking sideways. The guy doesn't seem to have seen him, thankfully. 'Just let him think he's doing us a favour, all right?'

Dion huffs, but stays where he is. The guy's droning on and on, making the poor sod on the other end of the line repeat everything at least twice. All the while, the window full of icons sits mute and still, waiting for us. Fence, driveway, yard. Surely one of those will have captured something useful.

Surely.

Eventually, the guy finishes the call and snaps the phone back into its cradle, scribbling something down before he gets up. 'Look, I can't stay yarning to you two all day.' When he comes closer, I see fresh droplets of moisture on his temple. 'There's trucks on the way, and...'

'The dockets, yep.' I smile as broadly as I can. 'You've been such an incredible help, mate.' I nod, and Dion does the same. 'I can tell you right now, Chief Ambrose is going to be chuffed to hear it. Now,' I nod to the screen, 'I reckon we can just take a look on our own and let you get back to it. Sounds like you've got a lot on.'

'Oh, no, no, I couldn't, uh...Bash wouldn't...'

'We can fill him in later on, once we've wrapped everything up, okay?' I gesture to Dion. 'We've got his details. We'll let him know how helpful you've been.'

The guy looks between us, still unsure. His tongue creeps out of his mouth, sweeping over the dab of hummus. He doesn't seem surprised to find it there. With a huff, he looks to his watch.

'Twenty minutes.' He points to the computer. 'Log off when you're done. Head office is huge on security these days. We've all done the training.'

My eyes go to the note on the desk, which says *bashpassword*. 'Got it. Thanks.'

With a last grumble, he moves across the office and disappears from view. I cluck my tongue at Dion. 'Too much stick, not enough carrot, mate.'

'The guy's got a bloody attitude problem, Lorraine.'

I lean down into the seat and click to open the files. The fence isn't much help: all we get is a view of the wire mesh leading down into the ditch at the back of the plant, and a sliver of roadside covered in long grass. Ditto for the yard. But the driveway could be promising: the camera gives us a clear view of the road just past the turnoff. Even better, there's a lamppost just across from the entrance.

'There,' says Dion. 'Try Monday, six to midnight.'

I open the file, and the footage starts playing. My hands are damp.

The camera is set to take stills every three seconds. We speed up the footage, watching as cars and trucks move past in a jerky little dance. The light changes as the time stamp gets closer to eight, then nine, the logging trucks and hi-vis workers pulling in and out of the plant gradually giving way to the lifestyle block types, their utes and SUVs shining and spotless. It's clear enough that I can tell the make and model of the vehicles, but the licence plates are pretty much impossible. Unless a car pulls directly into the plant, there's no chance.

'Hang on,' Dion points to the time display. 'Slow it all the way down.'

The counter reads 9:38 in the evening. We let the footage play out in real time, waiting with hushed breath. I keep expecting Hummus to explode back into the room, demanding to know what we're still doing here.

'Bugger it, Lorraine.' Dion sighs. 'There's no way we could...'

'Wait.' My heart is in a vice. 'Look.'

On screen, a late-model station wagon is moving past the plant. We see its front half, the windows nothing more than a series of blank silver squares. Then, in the next frame, the boot. I feel myself scowling. Masterton's pretty big on station wagons, and Bea's is about as anonymous as they get: a silver Mitsubishi with plenty of tread in the tyres. Half the mums in Landsdowne have the same car.

'Wait,' says Dion. 'Is it parked?'

I squint and lean forward. He's right; the back of the station wagon is frozen in place. Whoever's driving must have pulled over. Then, a flurry of movement: a single frame holds a figure, tall and thin. A teenager, darting around the back of the car and away, legs stretched out, arms tucked tight into himself.

'It's him.' I can only just hear myself. 'It's Stu Kelson.'

In the next frame, the car is gone. Whoever is driving must have been chasing him. We cycle through the footage, but there's nothing else.

'The fence, Lorraine.' Dion speaks with quiet finality, every word a closing door. 'Try the fence view. Nine thirty-eight.'

It takes me a while to find the right file, my fingers are so unsteady. Then we come to the same spot, seeing the long view of the fence, and the clutch of longer grass from the road verge in the corner. Right on time, we see Stu's tall fuzzy figure stumble to the edge of the road. One of the frames shows him looking back over his shoulder, his arm held up to protect himself, blocking whoever's coming. His face is just a smear of pixels, but even so, I can see his eyes, open and pleading. Then the front of the station wagon enters the frame, the car pulling up into the tall grass at the roadside. There's a second figure, running. Stu tumbles over, and both figures turn into a single grey shape, thrashing and moving, until one subdues the other.

'Lorraine.'

'I know.' My mouth is filled with dust. 'I know, Dion.'

My hand goes to the mouse, and I click stop. It's enough.

I MAKE DION drive as slow as we can get away with. We're matter between states right now; one thing becoming another. There's nothing coming over the radio, nothing to distract us from our destination.

At the first roundabout, Dion lifts a hand to a dusty ute heading south. It's Roxy, and she returns the wave, her eyes snagging on mine through the space between the vehicles. It must be written on me, this feeling, even through car windows.

'She's, uh…' Dion clears his throat. 'She's been taking good care of your pony, my aunty?' He looks sideways. 'Giving him plenty of feed and that?'

I can only stare through the windscreen, the late summer sun flaring bright in my eyes.

'Lorraine?'

I feel Dion looking at me. There's nothing to say, and thankfully, he seems to know it. Instead, he just drives, taking us through those empty, sunbaked streets, the bright blue day stretching out over trees and houses, over listing caravans sandwiched into the corners of driveways, over trees drooping apologetically in the heat.

'We should radio the Chief, at least,' says Dion.

A magpie rises up from a nearby fence, lifting against the sky like leftover punctuation. It must be hot out there, but inside my chest there's only ice.

'Later.' I nod ahead for him to make the turn. 'It can wait.'

~

Like always, there's room to park outside Sheena's. Dion pulls over, cutting the engine, and it ticks as it cools, the small sound reaching my ears as if from a great distance. When he slips off his sunnies and sets them on the dash, I lay my hand over his. 'No, mate.'

'Huh?' He frowns. 'But what if...'

'The uniform.' I point to his chest. 'It'll be too much. Just let me go in.'

He stays where he is, wearing his thinking face. 'Listen, Aunty. Everything at Tārehu, Lily and...shit, you've done enough, all right?' He sets a hand to my arm, gentle and knowing. 'It's time to share the load, don't you think?'

I push the door open and the sound of the street fills my ears: lawnmowers and birdsong and the ever-present clatter of trucks in the distance. On another day it would be reassuring, this daily wash of noise. Now it's just a reminder of what I'm about to shatter.

'This isn't your place, Dion.' I heave myself outside, letting him see my expression, and shut the door.

'No, fuck that.' I'm hardly at the footpath before he's behind me. 'This isn't a debate.'

'Mate, you…'

'If it was up to you, you'd have gone up to the Kelsons' place alone. And then where would we be, eh?' His eyes are wet with feeling. 'I'll stand outside. Just in case.'

I hold his gaze. This man. This boy.

'Okay.'

Our feet carry us across the pavement, past the edge of Sheena's garden. Her house is empty and quiet, still. That'll change with wee Keith, but I can't think of her now.

It's only a few houses down to Bea's place. Not far to walk, but I take my time getting there. The concrete path takes us down the side of Bea's place to the verandah. Tuck's parked his truck out back, and he's got a couple of sawhorses set up side by side. There's a long piece of timber laid out across them. A weatherboard, looks like; I noticed one that needed patching the night I came by after Langsford. The lounge window is open all the way, letting me hear voices, low and relaxed. There's the easy clinking of a teaspoon against a mug, and a cutlery drawer sliding closed.

'Here.' I hold a hand to Dion's forearm, squeezing him. 'Stay here.'

I climb the stairs to the front door and pause there, a fist hovering in place ready to knock. I'm in a pocket of shade, here on the verandah, sun held at bay and out of my eyes.

I could stay here. Just a few minutes, in this in-between place.

Then there's movement behind the door. Someone walking down the hall must have heard me. There are footsteps and then the door swings slowly open.

'Lorraine?' I see Tuck's eyes first, squinting slightly, then opening all the way once he sees Dion behind me. He's got his Bintang singlet on and his stubbies are dappled with a fine mist of sawdust. 'What's going on?'

Just past his shoulder, the photo of him at the beach with the girls, all wet hair and smiling eyes—and something else in the image now. A secret held far away from Jessie, far away from Michaela. The weight of something too big to share.

'Need a word.' I nod down the hall, my voice held low. 'Inside would be best.'

He hesitates for a second, a hand scratching at his chin. I can see the impulses shifting in him: first, he looks to the kitchen, then past my shoulder to Dion and back to me. A quickening of panic. And, beneath everything, a sentiment altogether more pure.

Relief. I saw it in Lily, too, that night in her kitchen.

The relief of a secret on its way out into the open. The sense of stale air meeting daylight.

'All right.' He shifts his beanie up against his forehead, settling it down in its usual spot just above his brow. 'She's in here.'

Moving slowly, he gestures through the doorway, leaving room for me to go first. Part of me hesitates to let those hard fists and quick arms out of sight, but his expression seems far away from anything rash. For now, anyway. The door closes, and I can't see Dion anymore.

'Trev?' Bea calls out. 'Who's that?'

I move through the doorway into the kitchen, pausing at the end of the table. She sees me, Bea, and her mouth stays slightly open, the briefest frown travelling over her face. There's a mug in her hands, and steam curling up over her fingers. Past her, a television is on and the girls are curled up on the couch: Michaela at one end, upright, and Jessie's familiar feet dangling off the other end. Michaela has turned to look at me, I realise. In the shadow, I can't quite see her eyes.

'This about the service, is it?' Bea sets the mug down and moves towards me, her hands on her hips. 'We had every right to be there. They can't bloody well...'

'Sit down, Bea.' I hold my voice firm.

It was quiet before I spoke. Now it's a tomb. Bea looks to Tuck, then over her shoulder to the girls. Her fingers go to her neck, making white indentations in the blotch of red at her collarbone. When I look to Tuck, he gives her a tight nod.

'It's all right, Bea.' He moves past me and pulls out a chair, waiting for me to sit. 'It's only Lorraine.'

'Only Lorraine?' Bea turns for a moment, looking out the window to the driveway. To open space, to escape. When I sit, she does the same, moving slowly. Her hands stay clenched at her sides, the tendons in her arms taut. The fist she threw into Heather Christiansen's nose; the handpiece that cut open Pat's knuckles nearly twenty years back. It's easier to see it all, now. What she could do.

'Dad?' Michaela pauses the movie, calling out in a hesitant voice.

'It's okay, love.' Tuck stays looking at me. He knows; he must know. And yet, like all of us, there are things he has to say. 'It's okay.'

'The night we found Stu.' I look between them. In this light, their eyes are identical: twin pockets of low-burning flame. 'Tell me again where you were.'

'We've been through this, Lorraine.' Tuck clears his throat, crossing his arms. 'Didn't your boss call Derek Lau already?'

'Not you.' My heart is a netted fish. 'Her.'

'Me?' Bea shakes her head. 'You saw me yourself, Lorraine. In the hallway.' Her arm lifts, her fingers pointing to the spot. There's a tremor under her words. The red splotch at her neck, the way the towel had clung so tightly around her scrubbed skin. 'Don't you remember?'

I hold her gaze. 'Before that.'

'Mum, what's...' From the lounge, I hear Jessie's voice. 'What's going on?'

'Nothing, girl.' Bea turns with a quick smile, then looks to Tuck, imploring. He doesn't give her anything. 'You just lie down, now.'

'This is it, Bea.' I set my hands on the table, loose and ready, and bring myself forward, speaking low enough that the girls won't hear. 'I can't promise it'll be so easy, later.'

315

Bea stays watching me, expressionless. She's silent for so long I start to wonder if she's actually heard me. Then from the lounge comes the soft padding of socks over thick carpet. Jessie leans against the doorframe, her face still puffy on one side, the daylight in the kitchen making her squint. She lifts a hand above her eyes, and Michaela steps beside her, a hand to her cousin's shoulder.

'You ask our girl, here.' Bea points to Michaela. 'Ask her. We came straight home from the hospital. Didn't we, Micks?'

Oh, you snake. You horrid, horrid thing.

I don't need to look at Michaela; I can feel her lost expression from where I sit. And anyway, no matter what happens, I'll still need to see her in the neighbourhood. The only way I can keep my head on straight is if I don't have to think about what she knew.

Wait for me.

'There's footage, Bea.' I watch as panic kindles in her. In the chair next to me, Tuck lets out a long breath, rubbing at his eyes. 'There's footage from outside the timber plant.'

'The timber plant?' Jessie looks to her mum. 'What's she talking about?'

Bea stares at me across the table, fists clenched. An entire spectrum of feeling cascades through her expression: the lighter shades of disbelief and the tremble of rage, of indignation. Then a calmer colour shows itself. Something like acceptance, like grace.

'They don't have to be here, Lorraine.' Her voice falters and drops away. 'They shouldn't be here.'

'No.' Tuck looks down at the tabletop, speaking from his chest. 'Enough, now. We've all had enough.' When he looks to her again, there are tears across his cheeks. 'It's okay, girls. It's going to be okay.' There's a long pause, before he points to Bea. 'You owe it to them.'

She holds his gaze. We stay like that for what feels like an age: the girls leaning against the doorframe, the three of us around the table. I hear the descending whine as a load of washing finishes and I wonder who's going to hang it out. Then she speaks.

'I...it was meant to give them a scare, that's all. That's all it was, girls.' She brings a shaking hand under her noise, sniffing. 'Send a message to the whole bloody lot of them. To Patrick especially.'

'What do you mean, Patrick especially?' I lean forward against the table. I know I'm pressing her harder than I need to, but I can't help it.

'I knew, all right? I knew they had something to do with what happened to our girl.' Bea spits out every word like a hot ember. 'And they did, didn't they? They fuckin' well did.'

'What, then? You give their boy a hiding, and that's that?' My hands are shaking. 'If you only wanted to scare them, then what was the plan once they'd brought him back home, eh?' I look to Jessica. 'It would've brought everything into the open, wouldn't it?'

Bea sets one hand in the other, pressing a thumb into her palm. 'I thought it was time.' She speaks quietly, but clearly. 'Time for all of it to come out.'

Next to me, Tuck stares to the ceiling, blinking through wet eyes. Beyond him, I see Jessie move forward, her feet wavering beneath her.

'You?' Her mouth is moving, but I can't hear her. 'You did that? To Stu?'

Bea shakes her head, making tears spill across her cheeks. 'It was just a scare, love. The pump and everything, I never... he knew. He knew it was only a scare.'

'He did, did he?' I think back to the footage, to the fear in his movements, the animal panic as he fled across the road, cowering in the grass. 'And when you left him there with the rope cutting into his wrists, did he know then?'

Slowly, Bea reaches out to take Jessica's hand. The girl stays where she is.

'How did you even know where to find him?' Jessie sniffs. 'Didn't he...didn't he go missing outside Langsford or something?'

Tuck meets my eye. In the doorway, Michaela steps forward to speak.

'I'd heard about him running at night.' Bea speaks quickly, squeezing Jessie's hand tighter. She doesn't look at Michaela. 'I knew if I waited long enough he'd show up.'

'He'd never have gotten in the car.' Jessie turns to her cousin. 'Not unless...' Her voice falls away.

Exactly.

The mill footage was far too grainy to see inside the car; all we could make out was Bea climbing out and lunging across the road to get to Stu. But I can't help thinking of the

318

expression in Michaela's face that night: the in-between look of someone not quite believing what just happened.

'Here, Jess.' Tuck stands, sliding his chair back and reaching his arms around her. As he moves, he looks to me. His expression holds an offering: that for this, this for that. I'll be gaining a kid, his eyes are saying. At least let me keep my own. 'Why don't we just sit, eh?'

Jessie stays standing. A stiff breeze at the right angle through the window could carry her off, and yet she stands. Her eyes go to Michaela.

'I'm sorry, love.' Bea wipes at her cheeks. 'I never meant for any of this.'

Tuck moves closer to Jessie, until her head rests at his shoulder. Behind them, Michaela just stares at the floor. There's something fraying between the cousins, some long-serving tether giving way. Tuck just whispers to Jessie, letting her know he's there.

'This footage, then.' Bea looks to me. 'Who else has seen it?'

'Fucking hell, Bea!' Tuck hisses. 'There's a bloody cop right outside the door! You think it's all just going to go on like before, eh? Like you haven't fucked it all?'

'I...' Jessie whispers. 'I don't feel well, Uncle.' She tries to lift a hand to her face, but falters. 'I need to lie down.'

'Here, let me.' Bea stands and goes to her, but Jessie holds up her hand, keeping her where she is.

'I've got her,' Tucks nods. 'Come on, girl. I've got you.'

He lifts Jessie into his arms, picking her up as though she

weighs nothing at all. They move into the hallway, leaving Michaela behind. Then, with a look from Bea, she leaves too, her eyes stuck to the floor.

Just the two of us. My hand goes reflexively to my phone. I feel weary, all of a sudden, all the weight of the last week bearing down on me. When Bea stands, one hand unsteady against the back of her chair, all I can do is watch. Then a long sob escapes her, and when she looks to me again, she seems emptied.

'You believe me, don't you?' A hand comes to her neck, playing idly at her clavicle. She swallows hard in her throat. 'You can't know what it is, to have to hide like this. To have to pretend, for so long. Old Bill, and Pat himself, they...'

'It doesn't matter.' When I look at her, I see someone much smaller. This house, this furniture. She's made it, all of it. This nest; this trap. I point over my shoulder to the door. 'Come on, then.'

She stays where she is, watching me. Then she moves past me, slowly, to her shoes. When she opens the door, the daylight makes her flinch.

DION OPENS THE backdoor of the cruiser, keeping his eyes to himself. He's learning, that one. Some things don't need to be seen; not by everyone, anyway.

Bea moves down the footpath a few steps in front of me. At the open door she hesitates for a second, eyes darting. Exits and escape routes, low fences and cars parked with the keys tucked inside the wheel arches. Then I move beside her, and she gets the picture.

'Come on, now.' I hold an arm up to guide her. Rubbing a hand across her cheeks, she slides into the backseat, and Dion gently pushes the door closed.

'Did you get it?' He whispers and leans closer. There's something final in his expression.

'Tell Rick to meet us at the station.'

He nods. There's sweat beading at his temples; he tucks his

forehead into the inside of his elbow, leaving a dark patch of moisture. This is weighing on him too: finding that boy, there in the dark, alone; and his own boy so young, so small. He turns to walk to the driver's door, and I grab his hand.

'It's all right, Dion.' Some things are so easy to say. 'It's done.'

He squeezes me back, wiping a palm across his cheeks.

'Rick's on his way.' Dion nods to me and sparks the ignition. With a quick look to Bea in the backseat, he pulls into the road. I hear a sniff behind us, but otherwise it's quiet.

In a driveway just past the corner, a woman about my age is splitting wood, stacking it against the far end to dry. It's warm now, but she'll need it soon enough; we all will. I'll be using that stack of Patty's letters to get things started. Maybe I'll even open one of them.

Coming towards us, Moko's new Commodore is creeping slowly up the street. I can make out Bradley in the backseat, leaning forward into the gap between Sheena and Moko, talking and gesturing. My niece is tucked low in the passenger's seat, baby Keith's blanketed shape pressed tight to her chest. She sees our car, frowning automatically, before she recognises me and smiles.

'Not sure what the Plunket ladies will have to say about that.' Dion clucks his tongue. 'No baby seat and all.'

My gaze goes to the rear-view mirror, and I find Bea staring back. 'Heard Sheena had a little girl,' she says.

'Keith, they're calling her.' For the first time, it doesn't sound strange to say.

Outside, the sunlight breaks down through the tree branches, falling on us in pieces. I think of the room waiting for us: the scratched table and the walls holding us in. The microphone with its red light staring, waiting for these nights and afternoons and mornings to be spoken aloud, turned into ink and paper and weekend editorials and chatter and low whispers at bedtime.

More pages for my files. More of this town turned into mute information.

'You tell her.' Bea sniffs, and her voice breaks off. When she speaks again, her words are cracked and wet. 'You tell her to look after that little one.' I don't turn around to look at her; I can give her that much. 'You tell her to hold her tight.'

Dion slows for the turn, waiting for an opening in the traffic. He could always pop the lights, but there's no rush. Not anymore. I keep my eyes to the window.

'I will, Bea.'

A boy, lost. A girl, found.

'I'll tell her.'

In the opposite lane, a truck slows down to make room, flashing its lights for us to pull in. We make the turn, and we drive on.

ACKNOWLEDGMENTS

This book was written over the course of fifty-seven egg & cheddar breakfast buns (multiple sittings) at Comets Café et Disques, 38 Rue Léon Frot, 75011, Paris. A huge thanks to Liz Owen, Patrick Whatman, Steven Thomas, George Titheridge and Emma Scott for early notes on all things Dyson, ginger ale, sausages and mate. Thanks to Michael Heyward, Mandy Brett and the entire Text team for your support, care and vision, and for knowing when a book is the right book. Thanks to Jade Chandler and the Baskerville team, and to Caitlin Landuyt, for giving Lorraine her travelling papers. Thanks to Sarah Lutyens and David Forrer for putting books in the right hands. Thanks to Craig Sisterson, the one-man Department of Aotearoa Crime Fiction, for your tireless advocacy and support. Thanks to Clémence Michallon for braving the NYC rain, and for tolerating the *Sopranos* chat. Thanks to

William Brandt for braving the Wellington rain, and for such warm encouragement. Thanks to Fiona Sussman, James Oswald, Shelley Burr, Gigi Fenster, Emma Styles, Mark Wightman, Natalie Marlow, Alex Gray and many others for the kind words on *Paper Cage*. Thanks to Te Puni Kaituhi O Aotearoa for getting behind emerging writers. Thanks to Sarah Vallance, Harry Baragwanath, Andrew Vallance, and all whānau members past and present, for tolerating the years between visits. Thanks to Sri Utari and Ali Wahyudhi for helping in every way imaginable. Thanks to Mary Baragwanath and Pamela Warner for every single book. To Pomme, stop barking. To Alma and Noah, thank you for letting Papa leave the house. To Dianny, thank you for our babies, and for keeping the lights on.

ABOUT THE AUTHOR

Tom Baragwanath is a writer originally from New Zealand, currently living in Paris. His debut novel *Paper Cage* won the 2021 Michael Gifkins prize and was shortlisted for the Ngaio Marsh and Ned Kelly awards.

RAISING READERS
Books Build Bright Futures

Dear Reader,

We'd love your attention for one more page to tell you about the crisis in children's reading, and what we can all do.

Studies have shown that reading for fun is the **single biggest predictor of a child's future life chances** – more than family circumstance, parents' educational background or income. It improves academic results, mental health, wealth, communication skills, ambition and happiness.[1]

The number of children reading for fun is in rapid decline. Young people have a lot of competition for their time. In 2024, 1 in 10 children and young people in the UK aged 5 to 18 did not own a single book at home.[2]

Hachette works extensively with schools, libraries and literacy charities, but here are some ways we can all raise more readers:

- Reading to children for just 10 minutes a day makes a difference
- Don't give up if children aren't regular readers – there will be books for them!
- Visit bookshops and libraries to get recommendations
- Encourage them to listen to audiobooks
- Support school libraries
- Give books as gifts

There's a lot more information about how to encourage children to read on our website: **www.RaisingReaders.co.uk**

Thank you for reading.

[1] OECD, '21st-Century Readers: Developing Literacy Skills in a Digital World', 2021, https://www.oecd.org/en/publications/21st-century-readers_a83d84cb-en.html

[2] National Literacy Trust, 'Book Ownership in 2024', November 2024, https://literacytrust.org.uk/research-services/research-reports/book-ownership-in-2024